GRAVE SECRETS

A MANHUNTERS NOVEL

SKYE JORDAN

Enjoy!
Skye Jordan

1

Ian Heller worked the flimsy lock on the back door and slipped into the duplex in less than twenty seconds.

Where was the challenge in that?

He silently resettled the latch on the door and paused in a laundry room the size of a closet, anticipating the unexpected. Hell, he was hoping for it. A pet they hadn't known about, a surprise visit from a friend... Who was to say that the sheriff himself wasn't sitting in the living room waiting for his ex?

But no. There would be no excitement tonight. No hand-to-hand combat. Not even a damn reason to draw his weapon. And for the hundredth time, he second-guessed his decision to give this supposedly elite, civilian special-ops team a try.

Then again, he didn't exactly have offers coming at him from every direction.

"I'm in."

"Copy that." Sam Slaughter was the Manhunters' expert hacker and, tonight, Ian's lookout. "Quickstep it, dude. I'm freezing my balls off out here."

"In and out," he assured Sam. This would be so easy, Ian couldn't even legitimately call it a job.

Wind battered trees against the rotted siding and rattled the single-paned windows. The space was warm compared to the nasty Montana weather, but his breath still billowed in the air.

He moved into the doorway leading to the kitchen. The room was immaculate—nothing but a toaster on the counters and an empty sink. Two wooden chairs were pushed under a tiny table. An ancient desktop computer and keyboard took up most of the tabletop. The short drapes on the windows had been gathered back in perfect mirror images of each other. On the stove's handle, a single kitchen towel had been folded into a precise rectangle and hung directly in the center of the bar. Three pictures on the fridge—all of the kid, Jamison—were lined up in precise order. A whiff of pine and lemon lingered in the air.

He was pretty sure if he opened the cabinets, he'd find canned goods lined up in alphabetical order.

Ian's sixth sense vibrated along the back of his neck. "Someone's OCD."

"You must be talking about yourself," Sam's voice sounded in Ian's ear. "Because I've never known a woman who's OCD about anything but shoes, hair, and makeup."

Shoes. Ian glanced down at his boots and pulled a rag from his back pocket to wipe the soles. He flipped on his LED headlamp, pulled off his gloves, and dragged a listening device the size of a pushpin from his pocket.

"Remember," Sam said. "Kitchen, living room, bedrooms. Once those are in place, you can look for the ledger."

Ian rolled his eyes. "Dude. Give me a break. I may have been out of the game awhile, but I'm no grunt."

"Just sayin'," Sam said, conciliatory.

Hiking his ass to the kitchen counter, Ian swiveled to his back. He tilted his head, angling the light toward a crevice in the corner where the cabinets met to wedge the bug into the shadows.

"What the...?" Sam said. "They're back. Heller, you've got incoming."

"What happened to the grocery store?" he asked, incredulous.

"Fastest fucking store run in history," Sam agreed.

"Milk, bread, and eggs." Everly's voice joined the group. She'd been surveilling the mother-son pair while Ian took charge of tactical assault. As if this could be called a tactical assault. "I cut in front of them in line to buy a pack of gum. I took forever to find my wallet and my money. She freakin' offered to buy the damn thing for me. And they still made it back here in fifteen minutes."

Ian shut off his headlamp, rolled off the counter, and moved into the living room, headed toward the hallway. Something caught his eye before he cleared the kitchen. He stopped and scanned the table again. A small black box was hidden behind the monitor. Ian recognized the company logo, and his curiosity was piqued.

"Her detail's in tow," Everly said. "One of the deputies has been following her as long as I have."

"Consistent with the intel," Sam said.

"She's got a VPN router by her computer." Ian cut across the living room, ducking into a hallway. Maybe he'd have some fun tonight after all.

"That's *not* consistent with intel," Sam said. "Why the hell would a single mother and waitress in a backward Montana town need to scramble her IP addresses?"

"A better question," Everly said, "is how did a woman with a five-year-old get through the grocery store in ten minutes flat?"

"She's clearly supernatural." This from Sam.

"Clearly," Ian agreed.

The front door opened, the living room light turned on, and Ian's heart kicked. It wasn't like a woman and a kid posed physical risk, but blowing his cover and exposing the op—his first with the team—before it even began would be disastrous, not to mention embarrassing as hell. His self-esteem didn't need any extra dings right now.

"Mom," the boy said, "can I bring Deputy Corwin cookies?"

"It's late, honey, and a storm's coming." Savannah moved around the kitchen, putting groceries away. "Time for a bath and bed."

"He's got to be hungry. He's been out there since I got home from school. He can have the Oreos from my lunch for tomorrow."

"Fine," Savannah sighed. "Then straight into the bath."

The front door opened, closed, and silence filled the house once again.

"Bail out the back, dude," Sam told him.

No way. This was just getting fun. "I only need two more minutes."

In the boy's bedroom, Ian attached a listening device to the back of the mirror, then moved through the short hallway toward the mother's room, pausing to reach for the smoke detector on the ceiling. Positioned at the opening to the living room, the device was in the perfect location to give Ian a view of almost every corner of the tiny house.

"What in the hell are they doing?" Everly asked over the earbud, now staged outside somewhere.

"Delivering cookies to the cop," Ian muttered. "I can't believe we're surveilling the fuckin' cookie fairy."

"Don't start," Everly warned.

Ian pulled the cover from the smoke alarm. Only, it wasn't a smoke alarm. "What the fuck?"

"What?" both Everly and Sam asked at the same time.

Ian squinted to get a better look at what he couldn't quite believe he was seeing. "Someone else has eyes on her."

"No shit," Sam said. "I'm watching her tail eat Oreos while I turn into an ice cube. They're heading toward you, bro. Hit the back door."

"Watching her from the *inside*," Ian clarified as he slipped into the mother's room. With groceries to put away and a kid to get to bed, her own room would be the last place she'd visit tonight.

"There's a CCTV unit hidden in the smoke detector. Looks like a GSM device."

Ian ducked into the shadows of the hallway just as mother and son came through the front door. When Savannah and Jamison returned to the kitchen, Ian slipped into the larger of the two bedrooms.

"Perfect," Everly said, her voice edged in sarcasm. "Whoever put it there just recorded you breaking in."

"Not necessarily," Sam said. "It could be activated by movement, but it could also be a dial-in. One that doesn't record unless the person who put it there dials in to turn it on. That would save battery life. If they aren't watching right now, they'll miss him. The fact that someone else has eyes on her only confirms we should too."

"Provably the ex, trying to get dirt for the divorce," Ian murmured.

"Can we play To the Moon and Back tonight?" Jamison's bubbly voice came toward Ian, and he pressed his back against the wall as the Bishops made their way into the boy's room.

"It's too cold, baby," she told him.

"But we've never done it with Deputy Corwin outside."

The scrape of dresser drawers came from Jamison's room, but in Savannah's room, the soft scent of roses and spice filled Ian's head. Savannah's scent. The one she left floating on the air when he'd been in the café for breakfast that morning. The one that kept him focused on her cute little body too long.

Unlike her son's room, which had been decorated in a baseball theme, her room was stripped down. No pictures. No head or footboard on the full-size bed. One nightstand and one dresser-mirror combo that looked as old as the house.

"You comin' out anytime soon," Sam asked Ian, "or are you just going to crawl under the bed and sleep there?"

"Don't be a creeper," Everly told Sam.

The kid continued to ask a million questions without ever

waiting for an answer. "Don't deputies go home? Don't their families miss them? Why does Dad send them here?"

"You'll have to ask him for a change, buddy," she said, her voice weary. "I don't know what to tell you anymore."

"Please, Mom? Can we play? I promise to be faster than ever, and I'll take a bath and go right to bed, no bedtime story."

"Promises, promises," she murmured, then sighed and caved. "Fine. I guess we should."

The boy whooped, and his footsteps pounded through the house as he ran into the front room.

"What's happening?" Sam asked.

"Bugs in place," Ian said even as he pulled another one from his pocket and applied it to the back of the alarm clock by Savannah's bed. Unlike the single unit in the hallway placed by an unknown entity, these bugs would get a clear signal in every room. "Waiting for an exit."

When the boy returned to his room, the light went out, drenching the house in darkness again, along with a sudden silence. Ian eased to the open doorway, listening for their conversation, but he couldn't make out the hushed words. Then creaking underfoot in the hallway sent Ian back into the shadows of the bedroom.

"Going dark," he told the team to let them know he couldn't talk as he stepped into the closet. The space was empty but for three sundresses, one pair of sandals, and one pair of tennis shoes, everything lined up in an oddly precise manner. The woman would shine in basic training.

She crossed the room and paused at the window. The moonlight illuminated a radio in her hand. "Wait for my signal."

"Roger that," the boy's voice returned.

Anticipation tingled along Ian's spine. What in the hell was this?

Savannah tucked her radio beneath her chin, snapped the front of her parka, then pulled her hair into a short ponytail. She stood in front of the window on the far side of her bed, head bent as if she were deep in prayer. She was eerily still, and Ian swore a thread of desperation joined the electricity in the air.

Finally, she pressed her free hand to the window sash and her thumb to the lock. She used the other to speak into the radio. "*Pumpernickel!*"

The whisper held such urgency, such raspy seriousness, Ian had to reassess what he'd heard. But Jamison's laugh trickled in from the other room, confirming his mother had said something completely absurd.

"This is serious," she murmured.

His laughter cut off abruptly.

Another moment. Another word. "*Go!*"

Ian tensed, expecting a flurry of movement, but the kid didn't laugh. The mother didn't move.

"That was good," she praised the boy. "I thought you'd jump at that."

"Nope," he returned with pride in his voice.

"Batman."

A snicker came from the kid, but ended almost before it began. Followed by the mother's now-obvious attempt to catch her son in a false start. "Now." "Daffodil." "Peanut Butter."

Ian rolled his eyes.

"What's taking so long?" Sam wanted to know.

Ian ignored him.

"Eagle." "Run." Savannah continued, all followed by nothing. Then she said, "To the moon and back."

"I love you," the boy answered.

Savannah pushed against the window lock and lifted the sash with one hand. She dropped the radio into her pocket with the other. Then she was out the window head-first in a tuck and roll that happened so fast, Ian almost missed it. Somewhere else in the house, a thump touched his ears—the kid opening his own window.

Ian rushed to the opening in time to watch mother and son race off into the darkness of a thickly wooded greenbelt stretching behind the house. He stared at the footprints in the snow reflected in moonlight with his heart hammering and his mind spinning.

What the fuck? It was three degrees outside and eight o'clock at night. The kid had school in the morning, and Savannah worked the early shift at the local café.

"Did they just *bail*?" Sam sounded as shocked as Ian felt.

"Yeah." He exhaled and settled. "They're playing some kind of twisted game."

"Are you sure she didn't make you?" Sam asked.

Annoyance flared. "Are you fucking kidding me?"

"No offense, dude," Sam added. "Chill."

"I don't think they're playing a twisted game," Everly said. "I think they're practicing their escape."

"If Bishop is listening in," Ian wondered aloud, "why isn't he monitoring both sides of the house? Why have just one guy out front?"

"Maybe because it's so fucking cold out here," Sam offered, "they know she couldn't get far without the car, and the car's out front. If the car's home, she's home."

"And you can't see both the front and the back from one vantage point," Everly said. "He's already messing with his staff by having someone dedicated to watching her. He can't afford to have two guys watching her. Come out, Heller. We're done here."

"I'll meet you at the mining office in ten," Ian told them.

"Roger that," his teammates said in unison.

But instead of heading straight to his truck and the second of three tactical installment sites of the night including Lyle Bishop's office at Bishop Mining and Hank Bishop's office at the sheriff's department, Ian followed in the Bishops' footsteps, careful to put his feet right where Savannah had placed hers so he didn't leave a third trail.

He'd walked over a quarter of a mile before he heard their voices in the night. Ian leapt over the pristine snow to land behind the thick trunk of a pine tree.

"That's three times in a row," the boy told his mom as they made their way back to the house. "You're not letting me win, are you?"

"Never. You're getting really fast."

"I'm doing the tuck and roll you taught me. It doesn't even hurt in the snow."

"Right?" she said, her voice happy. "It's fun too."

"So fun," her son agreed. But his voice turned nervous when he asked, "Does Dad think the bad guys who killed Mason will hurt us too?"

"Who told you Mason was killed by bad guys?"

"Dad."

"Your dad shouldn't say those things. Is that why you wanted to play To the Moon and Back?"

"Sort of."

"Look, sweetie." Savannah stopped and crouched, closing her gloved hands around his arms. "What happened to Mason was terrible and sad. But it doesn't have anything to do with us. There's nothing to be afraid of. Your dad is just...he's just...overprotective."

The boy nodded, and the two started toward their house again.

Ian waited until the *chunk* of the front door closing echoed in the night, and their bedroom windows closed with a *snap-snap*.

He trekked through knee-deep snow on his way to the truck, where he'd parked on a side street. He turned on the heat full blast, then knocked his feet against the running board to shake off the snow clinging to his pant legs.

Once he was thawing out in the truck, Ian replaced his team's earbud with the one listening in on Savannah's duplex, and pulled onto the street. The sound of running water and the boy's laughter filled his ear but did nothing to quell the sense of unease curling in his stomach.

This certainly wasn't one of the high-risk, clandestine black-ops missions he'd performed for Uncle Sam, but it might not turn out to be as boring as he'd anticipated either.

There was some dark shit going on here.

2

S avannah Bishop stepped between the empty tables in the café to scan Main Street, her stomach coiled with tension. At nine a.m. in Hazard, Montana, all the young men in town were at work in the mines. A few retired guys chatted near the front of the restaurant, bundled for the ten-degree weather. Thunder growled in the distance, promising another rare bout of thundersnow. And there was still no sign of the person Savannah needed most.

"This nasty weather's been causing trouble for days." Misty, Savannah's coworker and only friend, cleared a table nearby. "She may have gotten hung up in the pass."

Savannah cut a look at Misty. "Like Mason got hung up in that mine?"

The cops were holding all the information surrounding Mason's death close to their bulletproof vests, leaving everyone in town to speculate. The way Mason could be here one day and gone the next—*dead* the next—reminded Savannah how brief and tenuous life could be. Reminded her how badly she needed to get out of this town and away from Hank. The finalization of their divorce brought both relief and fear. She honestly didn't know what Hank was capable of anymore, and she wasn't sure what to expect from him when those papers came through.

Misty's gaze joined Savannah's out the window. The café's morning rush had passed, and they slowed to catch their breath for the lunch crowd.

"The first thing I thought when I heard about Mason..."— Misty met Savannah's gaze—"was why couldn't it have been Hank?"

Surprise cut across Savannah's ribs. "Misty. He's still Jamison's father."

"He hasn't been a father to Jamison in years." Misty squeezed Savannah's shoulder, and turned away. "She'll be here."

"She should have been here an hour ago, and she's not answering her phone." Her stomach coiled with tension. If something happened to Audrey because of her involvement in Savannah's divorce, she'd never forgive herself. "I told her to come Saturday so Derrick could ride with her."

Savannah had been working with Audrey for two years on this divorce. The only attorney with enough guts to take Hank on, Audrey had bravely defied Hank's attempts to keep her out of town.

After several threatening confrontations with deputies at the county line, Audrey believed Hank was listening in on her conversations with Savannah. Now they communicated on disposable cells Hank didn't know about. Audrey also started bringing her boyfriend with her on the three-hour treks. As the city attorney in Missoula, Derrick held influence in realms outside Hank's circle of power in Hazard County. Seemed the element of surprise, and the threat of witnesses and a lawsuit, was the only way Audrey could get past the county line.

"Girls." A customer's friendly voice broke into Savannah's thoughts. "Can I get more coffee?"

"Of course, hon," Misty said, then told Savannah, "You know

how sketchy cell service is. Hold it together. You're close, honey. Really close."

She was close. But instead of feeling excitement or even relief, an overwhelming sense of dread hung over her, as gray as the storm clouds filling the sky. The last four years felt like an interminable hell. Jamison was the only thing that kept her going. Jamison gave her the will to face and fight the tyrant Hank had become, despite her fear.

The bell over the door signaled a new customer. Savannah stuffed her stress and turned away from the window with a forced smile. "Good morning, take any seat you'd—" Her gaze focused on the guest, and her stomach turned to rock: Lyle Bishop, her soon-to-be ex-father-in-law. She exhaled and shored up her walls. "Lyle. I'll have Misty bring you coffee."

"No need," he said, setting his parka on a wall hook before leaning on the counter. "Won't be here long. Just stopping by to pick up Jamison."

Savannah frowned. "Jamison's in school."

"Not anymore. He's feeling puny. Hank's picking him up, and I'm taking him back to my house for the day. What are you feeding that boy to give him so many stomachaches?"

Savannah would have to have another talk with Tammy, the school secretary. The school knew to call her first, but Tammy had a crush on Hank and jumped at any reason to call him. "That's a question for Hank. He's the one who never feeds Jamison a home-cooked meal."

"Can't hardly expect the man to be a chef when he's working around the clock to keep his community safe with no woman at home to keep things running smooth. No, Savannah, that blame belongs to you, breaking up your family. Too damn bad it's Jamison who suffers."

Fury exploded in Savannah's bloodstream. And, yeah, a hell of a lot of irrational guilt as well. She took one step toward Lyle before Misty cut her off, sliding a cup of coffee in front of him and saving the man from Savannah's impotent rage.

"Karen just finished a batch of cinnamon rolls," Misty told Lyle, drawing his attention. "Would you like to take a couple with you?"

Savannah turned for the kitchen and blew past the café's owner, who was busy baking. She moved down a hallway leading to the employee bathroom, where she ran the water while she fisted her hands and clenched her teeth.

Almost over. Almost over. It's almost over.

She splashed her face and kept her eyes closed as she imagined the sweet little bungalow she'd been eyeing in Missoula, almost two hundred miles away. Just far enough to get out from under Hank's scrutiny, but close enough to allow twice-monthly weekend visits for Jamison.

She and her son would finally have the opportunity to make real friends. She could take him to a therapist without worrying about bias and brainwashing. They would be free to go to the grocery store or a movie without a deputy watching their every move.

But how she and Jamison would travel that bridge terrified her. And that stoked her fury. A fury she held on to with both hands. Without anger, she'd slide into fear. And fear paralyzed.

Savannah cooled her temper with another splash of water, dried off, and returned to the counter. Lyle had moved to a table where he read the paper with a cup of coffee and a cinnamon roll.

Savannah cut a look at Misty, who shrugged and muttered, "I thought caffeine and sugar might soften him up a little."

As if the man could hear their conversation, Lyle glanced up. His gaze burned into Savannah with bald, bitter resentment. The man had always hated her. He'd covered well enough for the first year she and Hank had been married. Then Jamison came along, and Lyle had become an overbearing presence in their lives, dictating and demanding. He had infiltrated her life, her marriage, and her family with manipulative, hateful tendrils that had ultimately ripped them apart. And Hank had not only let his father invade their family, he'd adopted Lyle's controlling nature and turned into a man Savannah had never known. A man she never would have married.

Even after years of being separated from Hank, Savannah still felt jumpy facing off with either one of them. They were truly mirror images of each other. Which was exactly why she picked up the coffeepot and wandered to his table.

"Relax and enjoy your paper," Savannah told him as she topped off his coffee. "You don't have to worry about taking Jamison today. My shift ends soon. I'll take him home with me when Hank drops him off."

"Arrangements have already been made—"

"I wish Hank had called me before he thought to burden you. We know how busy you are."

"It's Hank's day."

The days Jamison should have been with his father had stopped mattering to Hank the day Savannah walked out of the house. But she wasn't about to start a fight she couldn't win. "A boy needs his mom when he's sick. But thanks for pitching in."

"It's not your decision to make." He was talking to her back, but that didn't keep him from attempting to assert his dominance. Like father, like son.

By the time she'd reached the coffeemaker, her façade had melted and she was trembling—with fear, with frustration, and, yes, as much as it shamed her to admit it, with hate.

Savannah refilled the coffee grounds to give her hands something to do. To give herself a moment to collect her emotions.

Misty came up beside her, and Savannah's irritation broke through. "Not my decision to make?" she rasped, trying to keep her voice down. "I've only been making every decision about Jamison from the moment he was born."

"Take the counter until he's gone," Misty said.

Savannah agreed. She was one incident away from snapping, and that would only hurt her situation.

She refilled coffee for customers, catching up on as much of their lives as they would share with her. Hank had spent years slowly alienating the population of Hazard from Savannah with lies and subtle threats.

When the café's door opened again, the sweet tinkle of the bell tightened all her muscles. Savannah steeled herself to face Hank. But when she turned, Savannah found... The new guy.

She'd served him yesterday but hadn't gotten his name. In truth, he intimidated her a little. He was a rugged wall of muscle and confidence with a stern expression and intense eyes. He didn't smile. Didn't say much. And seemed to see everything all at once. He wasn't exactly menacing, but he wasn't friendly either. And she was—admittedly—averse to men with an edge.

"I'm regretting my decision to give you the counter," Misty said, stepping up to the coffeemaker and filling a fresh mug. "Tall, Dark, and Mouthwatering just came in."

"Shh," Savannah whispered over her shoulder, but she couldn't argue with Misty's assessment. Edge or no edge, the man was attractive.

He glanced around the café as he shrugged out of his parka and hung it on a peg beside Lyle's. Savannah allowed her gaze to slide down his body—just once. Just a two-second glance. She was light years away from entertaining the idea of having a man in her life. And even if she were ready, this man wasn't her type. She needed someone light and positive, with a good sense of humor. The strong, silent type hid things and hurt people.

She offered him a clipped "Good morning."

"Mornin'." He turned and met her eyes, but only for a millisecond before his gaze dropped away. Something Savannah saw far too often.

The day she left Hank, he'd sworn no man would ever touch her again. He'd gone above and beyond to make sure every male of a certain age knew she was off-limits. His authority and reputation ensured men kept their distance and spread the word. She doubted any man in town between the ages of twenty and sixty could identify her eye color. She just hadn't expected it from such a newcomer.

Savannah wondered if he'd heard the rumors about her already or if she was just so messed up, she saw the behavior in everyone, real or not.

Oh, what it would be like to live in a town free of rumors and fear.

He wandered around the bend of the counter and took the last seat, facing the door. When she came his direction with the coffeepot, he picked up a menu without meeting her gaze.

He's heard. Figures.

"Two days in a row," she said. "No one passes through here this time of year. You must be stayin' around or visiting family."

Most hunters, fishermen, backpackers, and skiers stuck closer to Missoula or Whitefish. With Canada as Hazard's north border and the Blackfeet Reservation as the east, there was little reason to come to Hazard unless someone worked in the mine. Which was exactly the way Lyle Bishop liked it.

"Seen Mr. Baulder?" he asked without taking his eyes off the menu.

"Not yet." The mine's general manager was a daily regular, but Savannah was pretty sure his hands were full with the changes brought about by Mason's death. She pulled out her order pad and a pen. "Are you the replacement committee?"

"Replacement committee?"

She lifted her gaze to his and found his eyes deliberate and focused on hers. They were hazel, a little more brown than green. A burn zinged across her ribs. She spent the next few seconds trying to figure out if that sensation had been fear, excitement, or simply shock. One second, she was thinking, *How refreshing.* In the next, *He won't last here long.*

"Did you miss the news?" she said. "Everyone's been talking about it."

"News?"

"Mason..." Just saying his name scored her ribs with angst. "A miner was found dead in one of the tunnels."

"Oh, that. Yeah, I heard." The spark in his eyes went flat. "Too bad."

Too bad?

A man's death was *too bad*?

His reaction hit Savannah wrong. Everything about this place was wrong—the land, the people, her situation.

"I'm usually good with names," she said, "but I can't remember yours."

"I didn't give it."

"Maybe I saw it on your credit card."

"Always pay cash."

He wasn't warming up. And Savannah was getting really sick of the cold shoulder. "Have you ever heard of a thing called small-town hospitality?"

His gaze lifted again. "Heard of it."

"If you're going to be staying around, you might think about using some."

His eyes sparkled with a hint of humor. One Savannah didn't share. It was way too little, way too late for her. "What can I get you, Mr. Anonymous?"

He seemed to find her irritation amusing. When he looked at the menu again but didn't answer, Savannah's mind wandered back to her concern over Audrey and ratcheted her tension higher.

"Never mind." She plucked the menu from his hands. Her patience for life was shot. And what in the hell was he going to do —find another place to eat? Not around here. "Don't strain yourself with a big decision like that. I'll just get you what you had yesterday."

He sat back, his gaze speculative. "*I* don't even remember what I had yesterday."

The simplicity of his open and focused gaze gave her goose-flesh. It could also be the almost-grin crinkling the corners of his eyes. The way his golden-tipped brown hair fell wherever it wanted. The three days of stubble dirtying his jaw.

Didn't matter. Another day or two and he wouldn't be looking at her anymore. Certainly wouldn't be talking to her.

"Three eggs, over easy," she told him as she wrote it down. "Hash browns, crispy. Sourdough, buttered. Bacon, chewy. Orange juice, large."

"Good memory."

"It's the most you've ever said. Guess that makes it memorable."

One dark brow lifted. "Your attitude, on the other hand—"

"Sign at the door." She waved her pen that direction. "No unsolicited opinions. I've definitely had enough of those for one day." She slid his breakfast order under a metal clip and rolled the wheel toward the kitchen. "Order up."

Savannah kept her hands busy refilling sugar and condiments on the bar, but a familiar knot of self-disgust expanded in her gut. She hated the way the last few years had changed her. She'd lost her sense of humor. Her patience had worn as thin as the thread-bare carpet at the diner's front door. She had one friend—Misty, and one interest—Jamison.

By the time she'd returned to Mr. Anonymous's mug with the coffeepot, her worry over Audrey had gnawed a hole in her gut.

"Rough morning?" he asked.

A missing attorney, a perpetually lingering divorce from an abusive asshole, her controlling soon-to-be ex-father-in-law watching her from a few feet away, the son she lived for in the middle of this tug-of-war and coming home sick... Yeah, it had been a rough morning.

"Mason's death has everyone on edge," she told him.

He didn't respond, his gaze on the coffee filling his mug.

The bell above the door chimed. With her mind on Audrey, Mason, Lyle, and Hank, the sound jarred her from her thoughts, and her hand jerked. Coffee splashed over the rim of the cup, hitting Mr. Anonymous's hand.

"Oh no." She grabbed a rag from under the counter and covered his hand, sopping up the coffee on his skin. "I'm so sorry. Did I burn—"

His other hand covered hers. "I'm fine." He held her gaze with eyes that somehow reassured her. She felt the connection in the pit of her stomach, a warm, coming-to-life tingle. "My skin's as tough as leather."

"Hi, Mom." Jamison's voice pulled her gaze from his and jump-started her mind.

Hank was right behind their son, and his gaze was on the new guy's hand still covering Savannah's. Fear burned away the momentary pleasure.

"Hey, there." She pulled her hand from Mr. Anonymous while she patted his dry. "Be careful," she told her son as he climbed to a stool. "I spilled coffee." She flicked a look at Mr. Anonymous, painfully aware of Hank's laser focus. "I'm really sorry. Can I get you some ice?"

He barely shook his head. "I'm fine."

Savannah let her gaze linger another second. There was something new in his eyes, something that settled her. As if he were saying, *You're fine too. You've got this.*

She found herself offering a nod before focusing on Jamison. She reached toward her son to feel his forehead. "No fever. I hear you're not feeling too great today. What's going on?"

Jamison plopped down a piece of paper and a fistful of crayons, but he was definitely subdued. "Tummy ache."

Hank lifted his chin toward Lyle, who was chatting with other customers, then leaned on the counter, facing their son. But his gaze homed in on the new guy, clearly sizing him up.

"My dad said he'd take Jamison—" Hank started.

"No need." Savannah replaced the coffeepot. "I'll take him home. My shift's over soon."

Hank finally looked away from Mr. Anonymous, who diligently kept his eyes on his coffee. "Don't go babying him, now. It's just a stomachache."

His voice was light and congenial, the tone he always took when other people were around. She knew it as his I'll-show-patience-now-but-you'll-pay-for-it-later tone. One that still made nerves skitter up her spine.

She felt Mr. Anonymous's gaze on her, but she didn't meet his eyes. Any other man in town would have retreated to the farthest corner of the café by now.

Ignorance was bliss.

When she didn't pick a fight over how she cared for Jamison, Hank pushed a little further. "All right, then, you go ahead, take him home. I'll pick him up after work. Then we can all have dinner together—like a family."

Oh, hell no.

"I've got to get back to work." Her words were careful, deliberate, and measured. Just enough to push Hank back, but not enough to send him into a tirade—at least not with others watching.

The new guy glanced toward Jamison. "Whatcha drawing?"

Savannah recognized the gesture for what it was—an attempt to defuse tension. She also knew it would backfire.

"Picture," Jamison said without looking up.

"You like baseball?" he asked.

Jamison nodded.

"I'm a Giants fan," he said. "How 'bout you?"

Her son finally glanced up, his expression flat—something Savannah had dubbed the Hank effect. "I like the Rangers."

Hank held out a hand to the new guy, pushing his arm right in front of Jamison. He hit their son's hand and forced his crayon from its path. Jamison frowned up at Hank, but the narcissist didn't even notice.

"We haven't met," Hank said, turning on that good-old-boy grin. "Sheriff Bishop."

The new guy reached over Jamison's head, forcing Hank to lift his hand to shake. That one gesture sent Mr. Anonymous to the top of the heap in Savannah's eyes.

"Ian," he said, holding Hank's gaze as he gave a solid shake.

Ian—strong, straightforward, a little different. Kind of like the man himself.

When Ian tried to pull his hand back, Hank held fast, still grinning. "What brings you around?"

Dread coiled in her belly. Her fingers dug into the rag in her hand in anticipation of the confrontation just moments away.

Ian deliberately broke Hank's grip and cupped his hands around his coffee. "Work, I hope."

Hank crossed his arms and leaned on the counter with a chuckle and a condescending "Another drifter for the mine." When Ian didn't take the bait, Hank pushed. "Might want to rethink that. A man died in those tunnels a few days ago."

Savannah let out a deliberate, slow breath, grappling with the anxiety Hank always induced. Still fearful the wrong word, the wrong tone, the wrong look would let the devil out.

Ian didn't seem to notice. He reacted much the way he'd reacted to Savannah when she'd shared the news, with nothing but a nod. Jamison, on the other hand, darted a worried look at his father, then Savannah.

"Please don't talk about that around Jamison," she said.

Hank's gaze cut to her, anger flashing. Her gut jumped in

response. "Shielding him from reality isn't healthy, honey. We've talked about this."

Ian offered up another buffer, telling Hank, "Thanks for the heads-up."

"I'll take care of Jamison," Savannah nudged Hank, needing a reprieve from the angst. "You can go."

The cook slammed his palm against the bell behind Savannah, and the sound cut down her spine. She jumped and turned. "Jesus, I'm right here."

He muttered an apology as she grabbed the plate. Savannah collected her frayed nerves before sliding the food in front of Ian. "Here you go. Can I get you—"

"Where you from?" Hank interrupted.

Savannah ground her teeth.

"No, thanks," Ian answered Savannah first. "I've got everything I need." He set down his coffee, picked up his fork, and looked Hank directly in the eye. "Drifters are generally from all over."

His answer held just enough sarcasm, just enough challenge, to make Savannah tense again. Her nerves couldn't take any more trouble for one day.

"Let him eat," she told Hank. "Go. I'll have Jamison call you later."

That cold, sharp gaze of his cut into her again. "You know I like it when you get bossy, but let's keep that in the bedroom, sugar." Then he looked at Ian. "Seein' as you're new round here, you should know—"

"Hank." Savannah was sick of this manipulation. Sick of being controlled. Sick of hiding all the ugliness. Sick of the constant fear. "Don't—"

"Mom," Jamison looked up, his pretty blue eyes swimming with unease and instantly turning Savannah's heart to jelly. "Can I have toast?"

Diversion. Their son had taken a play from Ian's playbook.

Jamison's one question reminded Savannah of just what was at stake. Of just what she had to do to make their life right—stand up to Hank.

"Of course," she told her son. Before turning to order the toast, she met Hank's gaze deliberately. "Goodbye."

The muscle in Hank's jaw jumped. He turned his gaze on Ian. "I'll be seeing you around."

Ian remained focused on his breakfast. "Uh-huh."

Hank shot one more warning glance at Savannah before turning toward the dining room and taking a seat at Lyle's table.

Savannah asked the cook for an order of toast, relieved the confrontation with Hank was over.

At least for the moment.

3

N *o love lost there.*

Ian's mind churned with this new information. Nothing in a file could compare to the nuance gained by witnessing people and situations in person. And there was more than nuance here. One word on paper: divorce, didn't begin to encompass the very real conflict buzzing through the Bishop family.

He sipped his coffee and watched Savannah move behind the counter. She had a great little figure. Maybe five foot three, maybe a hundred and twenty pounds. Her sexy, compact curves made Ian restless.

But Savannah Bishop was out of bounds. *Way* out of bounds. Besides, she wasn't the kind of woman who just slept with a man and walked away the next day. No, Savannah Bishop was a forever kind of girl. And Ian was not a forever kind of guy, which was why he was still a bachelor at thirty-six.

"What color are the Giants?" the kid asked, turning his face up to Ian. He had his mother's sky-blue eyes and a painfully innocent face.

"Orange and black." Ian dug his fork into the egg on his plate.

The boy had drawn another stick player on the page and picked up his orange crayon to scribble over it.

"Are you going to be a miner?" Jamison asked without looking up from his drawing.

Ian resisted the urge to roll his eyes and picked up his coffee instead. For reasons he couldn't begin to comprehend, kids gravitated to him—in Afghanistan, Iraq, Syria, Albania, Turkey, every godforsaken Third World country where he dropped his gear. So much so, his team had dubbed him the Pied Piper.

The US was different. Kids didn't run free, didn't talk to strangers. But he still got too many stares, smiles, and wayward visits from children as they wandered away from their parents at the airport or the grocery store. They obviously hadn't gotten the memo that Ian didn't even particularly like kids. But over the years, he'd discovered how adults overlooked a child's ability to pick up on all sorts of information—from their father's secret weapons cache to their community's planned attack on local military forces.

"Don't know yet," Ian told him. "How 'bout you? Are you gonna be a miner when you grow up?"

The kid crinkled his nose in a derisive expression. "No."

"Right. Probably a sheriff like your dad, huh?"

Jamison cut a look at Ian. "Hell, no."

Ian chuckled, surprised and amused.

"*Jamison.*" Savannah's hushed voice held an edge. One that made Ian choke back his laughter and Jamison cringe.

"My fault." Ian stepped up to cushion the blow. "I'm not exactly the best influence."

"Jamison has his own mind, and his language degraded long before sitting at this counter next to you. He makes his own decisions. Don't you, Jamison?"

"Yes." He met Ian's gaze, then his mother's. "Sorry."

Savannah reached across the counter, ran her fingers through her son's hair. "I'm sorry you don't feel good."

The sweet moment was interrupted by the cook's "Toast" from the kitchen.

Savannah retrieved the plate and set it in front of Jamison. Once her son was buttering the bread, she settled her gaze on Ian, and a blip of awareness hiccupped through his system.

"I stopped apologizing for my ex a long time ago, but I'm sorry you had to get caught in the middle of that...thing..." Her gaze darted toward the sheriff's table, then back, with color staining her cheeks.

"Not a problem," Ian lied. It was a problem. Just the thought of the confrontation raised his protective hackles. He'd always hated bullies. That had come in handy in the military, where he'd been tasked with eliminating tyrants. Now... Now he didn't know much about anything. "Ex, huh? He's still wearing a wedding ring."

"Yes, *ex*," she said with finality and frustration. "I'm getting the final papers today. He doesn't have to believe it to make it real."

Ian nodded at Savannah's determination, amused. "Explains your attitude today."

She caught his sarcasm, and her face eased into a tired smile, followed by light laughter that reminded Ian of warm rain in the jungle. When the woman smiled, she fuckin' glowed from the inside out.

"Funny," she said. In the next instant, fatigue fell over her expression. "But true."

Then she returned to work, treating him with the same pleasant efficiency she offered all her customers.

He picked at his breakfast, absorbing the undercurrents of tension in the café. Savannah repeatedly checked her cell phone. The sheriff watched her like a lion with half a dozen thorns in his paw. And Lyle's frustration grew with his son's short attention span for their conversation.

"Why do you like the Giants?" Jamison asked.

"They're my home team. Why do you like the Rangers?"

Jamison shrugged.

Ian let it drop. He'd never understand the workings of a child's mind. And he didn't want to.

He was just settling into the silence when Jamison asked, "Are you scared of working in the mines?"

"Haven't been down there much." In fact, he'd only been in a mine once—to locate Mason's body.

There weren't a lot of firsts remaining in Ian's life. He'd been in caves and caverns all over the world. He'd rappelled down mountains, cliffs, and buildings. He'd scouted underwater cities of rock and coral and jumped out of aircraft at every altitude. *Damn* he missed that fucking job.

Trekking into that subzero tunnel hoping to find an injured undercover operative and finding a dead one instead had been Ian's first time in a working mine. And his first time leaving a man behind. A fact that gnawed at him.

He glanced at the kid. "How 'bout you?"

"A few times. Don't like 'em."

"I don't blame you." He took a bite of his bacon. "You're awfully talkative now that Dad's not hovering. In fact, you don't look very sick to me. You don't have a bellyache, do you?"

His crayon froze. Guilty blue eyes darted to Ian's face.

When he didn't respond, Ian nudged. "Having trouble at school?"

Jamison dropped his gaze and shook his head.

"Then why don't you want to be there?" Ian asked.

The boy cut a look at his father, at Ian, then returned his gaze to his paper.

"Oh," Ian drew out the word in an undertone. "It's Dad's night. But if you're sick—"

"Don't tell Mom," he whispered with a belated "please?"

"Don't have to, bud," Ian said with sympathy. He wouldn't want to be that prick's son either. "I'm pretty sure she already knows."

Jamison's shoulders sagged on an exhale as if the weight of the world had him pinned to the ground.

A son not wanting to hang with his cop father? The quintessential hero? The big fish in an itty-bitty pond? That spoke volumes.

"Gonna get grounded?" Ian asked.

"No."

"I'd have gotten grounded."

"Did you get grounded a lot?" Jamison asked.

Ian huffed a laugh. "A lot."

That made the kid smile. And damn if he didn't look just like his mother.

Ian pulled his cell from his back pocket to check the time, then called the mine's office to see if anyone had an ETA on Baulder. He got a recording and hung up without leaving a message. Didn't look like he was going to be interviewing for the mine today.

He texted his new boss, Roman. *Baulder's a no-show.*

All the men at the power table stood to leave. Ian meditated into his coffee as the sheriff said goodbye to his son and took another shot at Ian with "Don't get lost in those drifts, now."

Then Bishop called toward Savannah, who was taking an order from an elderly man at the bar. "Have him ready to go," he ordered. "I'll be home round seven."

Savannah never looked away from her customer. Never broke stride in her conversation. But Ian would bet it raked along her nerves the same way it raked along his.

Shake it off.

She was not his concern. His mission centered around uncovering a counterfeiter and a murderer. This time around, he'd have to leave the bully—and the bullied—to their own problems.

When the café door closed behind the men, Jamison looked at Ian. "Do you know what drifts are?"

"No. What are they?"

"The tunnels," Jamison told him. "Is that what happened to Mason? Did he get lost down there?"

No. Mason had been found—found out.

Ian didn't plan on answering, but Jamison stared, imploring a response with those frightened eyes. The kid was like a baby bird pushed out of the nest, and Ian just couldn't leave him there to flail.

"I don't know, buddy," he lied again. "How old are you?"

"Five and a half." Jamison returned his gaze to the paper but just rolled the crayon between his fingers.

Ian finished his coffee and pulled out his wallet to pay. Movement just outside the front doors caught his eye. A car that had been parked at the curb when he arrived slowly rolled forward. By the time he realized there was no driver, the sight of another car's front bumper came into view.

"What the...?" Ian murmured, trying to understand the bumper-car derby beyond the window. He stood, frowning as the second car stopped directly in front of the café's front glass doors —a Hazard County Sheriff's Department vehicle.

"Savannah?" The second waitress—a Misty Klein, according to the mission file—called toward the dining room, and her voice rang with we-have-a-problem tension.

Savannah looked at Misty and followed her friend's gaze out the doors. Her arms dropped to her sides. Her face crushed into a frown. Her jaw unhinged. "*What* in the...?"

Ian glanced back to the doors as a deputy stepped from the cruiser.

Savannah marched to the entrance, ripped a random jacket off the hooks from the many hanging there, threw it around her shoulders, and swung one front door open.

"Mom?" Jamison sat up straight.

She shot a stern glance over her shoulder. "Stay inside."

Then she stepped out and walked to the curb, one rigid finger swinging from her car to the cruiser to the deputy.

"Mom?" The boy turned on the stool, looking out the door.

Ian put a hand on his shoulder. "Your mom's got things under control."

But the boy vibrated with tension beneath Ian's hand. Jamison slipped off the stool and took a step toward the door. "*Mom.*"

Savannah didn't hear her son. She was ripping on the deputy. Her voice drifted through the glass, touching Ian's ears.

"Nothing any of you do would surprise me. The only thing that would surprise me is any of you thinking on your own instead of following Hank like you've got rings in your noses. I know exactly what you're doing and why, and it's not going to make a damn bit of difference..."

Savannah went on. And on. The deputy shut the driver's door and sauntered around the trunk toward the sidewalk with a smirk on his face. He was older, in his fifties, and smug as hell. When he reached Savannah, he rolled back on his booted heels, lifted his chin, and crossed his arms, sending the nothing-you-say-makes-a-damn-bit-of-difference message loud and clear.

"Since you know so much, Savannah, I'm sure you know that parking within fifteen feet of a fire hydrant violates title nine, section nine-dash-sixty-four-dash-one-hundred and seventy of the Hazard County code—"

"I *wasn't* parked within fifteen feet," she yelled, clearly losing her shit. "You *pushed* my car in front of it. I have a café full of witnesses—"

"Not one of which will come to your rescue."

Jamison slipped from beneath Ian's hand and started for the door. "*Mom.*"

Ian caught the boy's arm and crouched to Jamison's level. "Hey, buddy, they're just talkin'. Your mom's okay."

But her son clearly believed something very different.

Customers were watching out the windows, and the cop was right, not one person seemed the least bit interested in getting involved. Not even her friend, Misty, who drifted toward Jamison, clear apprehension on her face.

"If you stay here," Ian told Jamison, "I'll go check on things. Okay?"

Jamison offered a quick nod and scrambled back onto the stool.

Ian dropped a twenty on the bar beside his plate while Misty sidled up to Jamison and wrapped an arm around his shoulders. "It's okay, honey. Your mom knows how to handle those guys by now."

More nuance not in the file.

Ian moved to the door and reached for his jacket—but it was gone. He glanced around the floor, then out the front—and found Savannah wearing it.

"Now, Savannah..." The deputy hooked his thumbs in his duty belt. "Just calm down. Did you take your medication today?"

"I'm not *on* medication, and you know it."

"Maybe you ought to see Doc Brown about that. Maybe that would cut down on all these infractions you've been getting lately."

Ian pushed out the doors. The frozen air hit him like a brick. He drew a slow, tight lungful of ice as he paused behind Savannah.

"They're all goin' in your file," the deputy continued without bothering to glance at Ian. "Wouldn't look good to have all these random violations piling up. Might make you look...unstable."

"I hope you're not calling that"—Ian glanced at Savannah's ancient Subaru where it now sat dead center in front of an iced-over fire hydrant—"a violation, because I just watched you push that car thirty feet forward with the bumper of your cruiser."

All eyes turned on Ian, and silence thickened the air. Savannah made a quarter turn toward him, her expression clearly confused to have someone in her corner. "You...you shouldn't get involved in this. It's not—"

"This isn't any of your business." Corwin—according to his nameplate—pointed at the café. "Just head on back inside and finish your breakfast."

"I'm a witness to an abuse of power by law enforcement," Ian told him. "That makes it my business."

"Too many tickets and your car will be impounded, Savannah," Corwin continued, undeterred by Ian's presence. "Now how are you going to take care of a little boy without a car in this freezing weather?"

"That's not going to be a problem," Ian said, "because there's no reason for a ticket here."

Corwin flicked a look at Ian, dismissing him instantly. "Who's this, Savannah? You got yourself a boyfriend? Before your divorce is even final? While you've got a young boy at home lookin' to you as a role model? How is that going to look to a judge? You really don't think ahead much, do you?"

Ian opened his mouth to answer for her, when something bumped the back of his legs.

"Mom?" Jamison's worried voice touched Ian's ears before his gaze settled on the boy, half hiding behind him. His breath billowed in the air while his eyes, darkened by dilated pupils, darted around the group.

"Jamison," Misty called from the landing. "Come back in here. It's freezing."

"Honey," Savannah said, "Go back inside. I'll be right there."

"Why don't you *all* go in?" Corwin suggested.

Jamison's face crunched in a belligerent frown even as his hand fisted in Ian's jeans at the knee. "*No.* I'm not leaving my mom."

"Come on now, buddy, don't use that tone with a police officer," Corwin said. "I'm not the enemy. You brought me cookies just the other night, remember?"

"You weren't mean then."

"You weren't mean then, either." Jamison turned his head

away and pressed his face to Ian's jeaned thigh. Something pulled deep inside Ian. He needed to end this.

He pulled out his phone and stepped around Savannah and Corwin to snap photos of the cruiser's bumper against Savannah's. Of Corwin, his nameplate, and his badge number.

"What in the hell do you think you're doin'?" Corwin barked.

As he moved, Jamison moved, keeping Ian between himself and Corwin. The fact that the boy was afraid of a deputy who worked with his father, a man who, by all accounts, should have been a member of Jamison's second family, gnawed at Ian.

"Jamison, go back—" Savannah started, turning toward them.

"Put that away," Corwin ordered.

Ian stuffed it into his back pocket again. "It's gone, it's gone," he placated, lifting one hand in surrender and dropping the other to Jamison's head to reassure him. "But you should know I already grabbed a video of you pushing her car in front of the hydrant. As a concerned citizen, I feel it's my duty to enlighten the public to random acts of police harassment. I don't think you'd want this story reaching media outlets." He grimaced, sucking air through his teeth. "That wouldn't be good for you. Not good at all."

"You piece of—" Corwin made a swipe for Ian, but he was slow, and Ian easily stepped out of reach.

"Actually, I think you might be the one looking like..." He glanced at Jamison. "Well, you know. To the public. To your boss. Tell you what, let's all walk away and call it good. What do you say?"

Corwin glared at Ian. "I say you'd better watch your back, boy. You've just used up your one free pass as a new mucker." He made a slow turn on his heel, his gaze on Savannah over his shoulder. "Behave, girl. I'm watchin' you."

"Same, Don," Savannah shot back. "Same."

Corwin sneered as he dropped into the driver's seat. As soon as the cop retreated to his car, Jamison abandoned the safety of Ian's legs and ran to Savannah.

She dropped into a crouch in front of her son. "I told you to stay inside for a reason." She tugged on one of his earlobes. "Do I need to check your ears for wax?"

Jamison smiled and squirmed from her touch. "No."

She turned him by the shoulders and gave his butt a soft swat. "Inside, now."

The boy whisked by Ian and reentered the café. Corwin pulled his cruiser away from the curb, and Ian watched all the tension and fear drain out of Savannah. Her face perked up with color. Her shoulders lowered. Her posture softened. And she released a deep sigh.

Savannah crossed her arms and looked up at Ian, hesitant with her words. "Thank you. It was nice of you to intervene, but these guys don't play by the rules." She pulled her phone from the pocket of the half apron around her waist. Her screen lit up with a recording symbol. She tapped the stop button and smirked up at him. "You didn't get a video of them pushing my car, did you?"

"What makes you think that?"

"I didn't see your phone out at breakfast."

He grinned, shrugged.

The bell on the café's door tinkled again, and Jamison ran back out. He offered the picture he'd been drawing to Ian. "It's for you."

A pang hit him dead center in the chest. *Ah, shit.*

With a sigh, he accepted the picture, playing down his interest. "Well, thanks."

Then the kid was gone again, disappearing into the café with a new bounce in his step. Ian told Savannah, "He looks like he's feeling better."

She stared after the boy, eyes narrowed. "I was just thinking the same thing." She started toward the café. "Come back in. You've got to be freezing."

"I have to get going." He rolled the picture into a tube.

At the doors, she turned. "What about your jacket?"

He grinned. "You're wearing it."

A second of confusion clouded her eyes before she looked down. "Oh... Oh, jeez. I'm sorry." She shucked the parka as if it had lice. "I burned your hand *and* stole your jacket. I think *I* owe *you* a tip today."

"No problem." He took the parka. "You warmed it up for me."

She offered his jacket along with one of those sunshine-and-blue-skies smiles. "I hope your day gets better."

"Yours too."

"If I see Tim—Mr. Baulder—I'll let him know you were here."

"Thanks."

Ian shrugged into his jacket and started down the street. Smiling. He was smiling. And there was no reason in the world for him to be smiling. But Savannah's heat sank into his body. And her rose-petal scent lifted to his nose.

He was feeling lighter than he had in a long time when he spotted Everly standing at the corner, leaning against the building.

Ian slowed and glanced over his shoulder to make sure Savannah was gone before he stopped to talk. He and Everly hadn't been on the same Manhunters team while employed by the government, but like any special forces unit, they partnered with other teams for a large-scale mission. Their teams had worked together often enough for him to know he could trust her with his life.

"Did you find Rosen?" he asked. "Is he part of this mile-thick blue wall?"

"I found him. And, surprisingly, he's not, but he is squirrely."

Joe Rosen was the deputy with the Hazard County Sheriff's Department. According to the mission file, Rosen's disgruntled attitude over his boss made him the perfect source inside the department. He and Mason had become friends, hanging at a local bar after work. Now Rosen's friend, one who'd been pushing dark boundaries in town, was dead.

"Understandable," Ian said. "Is he willing to help us?"

She turned toward her Jeep, parked on the other side of the street and still running. "I'll tell you out of the cold. Get in."

Inside, Everly shivered, pulled off her gloves and put her hands in front of the vents. "I think I'm going to need a couple of weeks in Bora Bora to thaw out after this."

"That'll go over well with Roman," Ian said. "Who did you tell Rosen you were?"

"Investigator from the DOJ, following up on Mason's death." She reached across the console, opened the glove box, and pulled out a file folder. Then tapped into her phone, placed a call, and put it on speaker, looping Roman and Sam in on the conversation.

"Is Heller with you?" Roman answered.

"Here," Ian said. "Boss, can you have Sam double down on my background cover?"

"I'm here." Sam's voice came over the line. "Considering our military counterpart already scrubbed all their operators' files, you look like exactly what you're claiming to be, a retired army rat."

"I just met Bishop," Ian said, "and he's going to dig into it."

"I guarantee he won't find anything," Sam assured.

"Rosen confirmed Mason's assessment that the Bishops are dirty," Everly said, "though he doesn't have any hard evidence of that. Just his own observations."

"The slippery ones rarely leave a trail," Ian said. "And which Bishop?"

"Hank and Lyle. Rosen says Savannah's caught in an impossible situation."

"Impossible how?" Sam asked.

"No family or means to speak of," Everly said. "He paints her as a devoted mother stuck in this frozen town with a vengeful shit for an ex. An ex with all the power, money, and control in their relationship. Seems like most of this town is in the same situation. The Bishop mines touch everyone here—they either work for the mine, have a loved one who works for the mine, or depend on the employees of the mine for business. Rosen's wife grew up here, and they moved from Utah two years ago to take care of his sick mother-in-law. He hates it here. Hates Bishop, hates the culture of fear and manipulation inside the department, but they don't have the resources to move again. The medical bills are sucking them dry. And Rosen says if Bishop finds out he's talking, losing his job would be a best-case scenario."

"Murder being the worst?" Ian asked.

"Affirmative. He's sure Hank killed Mason, but he doesn't have any proof."

"If he killed Mason, Bishop must be in on the counterfeiting."

"Mason could have been involved with Savannah," Everly speculated. "Bishop's the kind of guy who wouldn't take that well."

Ian's mind bent that direction. "If they were involved, Savannah couldn't have been that invested. She's more scared than sad over the topic, and she's not showing any signs of grief, even home alone."

"Sam told me we haven't gotten anything good from the bugs." Everly offered the folder she'd pulled from the glove box to Ian. "Rosen gave me the autopsy report."

"Any forensic evidence?" he asked.

"The coroner classified it as an accident," Everly said, "so no in-depth forensics were done."

"Not exactly a surprise," Ian said, skimming a read of the autopsy. "Coroners in the backwoods are notoriously inexperienced."

"And this one undoubtedly falls under the Bishop power structure," Everly said.

Ian searched his mind for a crack in the Bishops' perfect wall. One they could chip away at until the barrier crumbled and all the dirty secrets spilled out. "Can we get Mason's body? Do another autopsy? Look for Hank's DNA?"

"Already on it," Roman said. "What does Rosen say about the passports?"

"He hasn't heard anything about passports, but that makes sense. Bishop wouldn't tell his men about the scheme. He wouldn't risk having a higher authority come into his territory."

Ian shook his head. "They've got every damn angle covered."

"I think Rosen and Savannah are the chinks in that chain," Everly said. "They're scared of him, they're strong, and they want out."

"We don't know where Savannah stands yet," Ian said. "There are custody issues to consider. As long as she's stuck here, she won't turn on her ex for the same reason no one else will."

"I disagree," Everly said. "She doesn't let the cops walk all over her. She's already practicing her escape. We've got to get our hooks into her before she disappears. Sooner rather than later. Rosen says Savannah's detail is twenty-four seven unless she's at work. They get her schedule every week and rotate the duty during her off hours through the deputies, though Rosen says Corwin's bad attitude has earned him more surveillance time than others. They actually fill out a report, chronicling Savannah's movements while they were on duty. According to Rosen, they embellish her activities as well, and everything goes into a file created for the sole purpose of gaining control over her. And get this," Everly added. "She can't cross the county line."

He cut a look at Everly. "What do you mean?"

"All deputies have strict orders to stop her at the county line and turn her around. By force if necessary."

"What the fuck?" he asked, more a revelation than a question. "Are we still in America?"

"Sounds like she's either got something on him that he wants to keep in-house," Roman said. "Or he's afraid she'll run with the kid."

"Or, of course," Everly added, "he's a psychopathic, controlling bastard who enjoys making his ex-wife's life miserable."

Ian thought back over his confrontation with Corwin. Of Savannah's and Jamison's reactions to Hank in the café. Imagined how trapped she would feel, knowing she couldn't get out, no matter how willing she was to deal with her financial limitations. And if she knew or suspected Hank killed Mason, she had to wonder if he would do the same to her.

"That's fucked up." Ian let his gaze blur over the snow-covered street ahead as his mind wound back around to the reason they were here.

"Did you find Baulder yet?" Roman asked.

Ian closed the folder. "No." He looked at Everly. "But it's a good time for Everly to hit the café and put in her application. Morning rush is over, and the owner's in the back, baking."

"Put that on hold," Roman said. "You two come to the office. Sam's pulled up some good intel. Let's put our heads together."

"Roger that," Everly said, then disconnected and glanced at Ian. "By the way, you were the perfect white knight for Savannah."

Ian huffed. "All I did was stop a public fight in front of her son."

"There were sparks between you two."

"Bullshit." He glared out the windshield. "I'm starting to think this whole idea—me working with this team—is bullshit."

"You think this is bad? Try security for a Silicon Valley high-rise or bodyguard duty to an entitled hip-hop mogul."

Ian groaned.

"Perspective, my friend. Perspective," Everly reminded him.

"This may not be like the blood-pumping missions we had over-seas, but there are other benefits, like higher pay and time to take a real vacation or cultivate a relationship. And not all our jobs are as tame as rooting out a shadowy counterfeit underground. We get our share of action. This is your first mission. Give it a chance."

"You must get some kind of kickback if I commit."

Everly's fist landed right in the middle of his gut.

Ian grunted a laugh. "I see your sense of humor's intact."

"Maybe I think you deserve a life with more in it than mind-numbing, meaningless days spent as a rent-a-cop. Savannah's cute. I'll admit, you both suck at flirting, but she was trying her rusty best."

Ian scowled at Everly. "Shut up."

"And the kid... You still have the touch, Piper."

"Don't even," Ian pushed the car door open. "I'll meet you at the office."

SAVANNAH'S HAND shook as she set down a teacup in front of Audrey. She slid into the seat across the booth and opened the wooden box filled with over a dozen different types of teas. "I wasn't sure what you'd be in the mood for today."

"Something with whiskey," Audrey clipped as she pulled an orange-spiced tea bag from the box. "Maybe I'll get a room for the night and hit Judd's Saloon later."

Judd's was a favorite hangout for the miners—right up there with Sugar Daddy's, a brothel in the middle of nowhere smack between Whitefish and Hazard. Savannah hated Judd's, but... "If Misty can watch Jamison tonight, drinks are on me."

The way Audrey's mouth tipped into a stiff smile made the nerves in Savannah's belly buzz. The other woman settled the tea bag into the water while she twirled a strand of her honey-brown hair around her finger. She was measuring her words, Savannah knew.

She glanced toward Jamison, sitting at a table in the corner. He was playing a game on Savannah's cell, completely absorbed, his tongue barely sticking out the side of his mouth. Love and fear mingled.

She refocused on Audrey. Her attorney had told her the deputies had met and detained her at the county line, as Savannah had feared. "How'd you get through?"

Audrey closed the lid on the metal teapot. "I installed a dash cam and told them that if they didn't let me through, the encounter would be all over the internet within an hour."

Savannah relived that morning's confrontation with the deputies and how Ian had also used video—or at least the threat of it—to limit their manipulation. "I think I need to wear a video camera around my neck twenty-four seven." She rested her head in her hand. "I hope those nerves in your eyes are just from the drive and those idiots at the county line."

"Only partially."

Dread swamped Savannah. Her stomach bottomed out. "Oh God. Please don't tell me there was another problem with the divorce." The weight of the possibility pushed her deeper into the booth's seat. "I can't take this anymore. I need him out of our lives. We need to get out of this town."

Audrey leaned forward and covered Savannah's hand on the table. "I have good news and bad news. I'm not going to ask which you want to hear first because you obviously need to hear the good." She pulled a manila envelope from her briefcase and laid it on the table with a smile. "Your divorce is final."

Your divorce is final.

Savannah's breath caught. She repeated the words in her head, inspecting Audrey's gaze for gravity, for confidence. When she found both, all Savannah's air rushed out. She melted with relief so deep, a sob ebbed from her chest.

"Oh my God..." She kept whispering the words while emotion spilled through her—elation, fear, relief, guilt, regret, excitement. Hope.

For the first time in years, she had hope.

Savannah lifted her head, smiling while tears blurred her vision. "*Really* final? It's done? No more wrenches in the system?"

"Not for the divorce. That's the good news. Brace yourself for the bad news."

She held her breath and went stone-still. But the look on Audrey's face gave the news away, and terror clawed at Savannah's gut. "No..."

Audrey winced and nodded as she pulled more papers from her briefcase. "He's suing for sole custody of Jamison."

"*No.*" Fear and fury raged in a flash fire. Jamison looked up from his game, but Savannah didn't have the strength to pretend or console him now. "No, no, *no.*" She curled her hands into fists to keep from slamming them on the table. "No, goddammit. He can't—" *Have him.* "He won't..." *Take care of him. Won't love him.* "No."

Audrey's hands covered Savannah's, and she dipped her head to meet Savannah's gaze. "Just because he wants it doesn't mean he'll get it."

Jagged emotions eddied through Savannah like the icy rapids of the Bitterroot River. She pulled from Audrey's touch with fear cutting at her insides. Pushing to her feet, she turned her back to Jamison, pressed her hands to the table, and forced her voice low.

"He and Lyle have every judge in this county in their pocket. His deputies have been padding 'my file' with false charges. Just this morning, they..." She shook her head and pressed her fingers to trembling lips. The power Hank and Lyle wielded in Hazard County overwhelmed her. "We both know if he wants it, he'll get it—no matter what." She closed her eyes and gripped the table with a whispered "Maybe it's time..."

Time to run. Time to hide. Time to disappear—to another state, another country...

"He's just fucking with you, Savannah. He can't take care of Jamison himself. This is just another attempt to torment you because he's a small, mean, cowardly excuse of a man."

She straightened and crossed her arms. Yes, he was messing with her. Yes, he was a small, mean, cowardly excuse of a man. But somehow, this felt like his last stand. Like he was telling her that if she didn't come back, he'd take Jamison—a final fuck-you to Savannah. And if he took Jamison, Hank certainly wouldn't need her for anything.

Mason's death popped into her head again.

She squeezed her arms, pushing the dark tendril back into the depths of her mind. "How can I move three hours away if I'm going to have to come back here for court hearings? With a new job? And Jamison's new school? And we both know how it would look to a judge—especially a judge here—if I moved Jamison three hours away from Hank now."

"I agree," Audrey said. "Considering the circumstances, I think you need to wait until custody is finalized before you move."

Savannah pressed her hand to her forehead. "This will never end."

"I've already filed a petition against the hearing," Audrey said, "citing the custody arrangements in the divorce papers. This will take time to clear up, but we *will* clear it up, Savannah."

She didn't believe anything at this point. All she knew right now was that even though she'd gotten the official divorce from Hank, he still had her in shackles. She would spend the next ten years paying off Audrey's bill, even at the ridiculously low rate the woman was charging. Hank, on the other hand, had his father's unlimited finances to keep Savannah in legal battles until Jamison turned eighteen.

This would *never* end.

With her hope extinguished, she felt lifeless.

"Thank you—for everything," She leaned in to hug Audrey. "I could never pay you enough for everything you've done for me and Jamison. Without you..." She teared up again, pulled away, and shook her head. "I'm sorry. I need a break. I need to get Jamison home. Can we talk later?"

"How 'bout if I bring dinner and wine around six?" Audrey offered.

Savannah smiled, but her cheeks pushed tears from her eyes. "That sounds perfect."

"Hey." Audrey grabbed her hand. "Don't lose hope, honey. I'll fight that bastard to my grave, if necessary."

Savannah laughed, thanked Audrey again, and bundled up Jamison in his parka. Even braced for the cold as she stepped outside, it still stole her breath for a long second. Seeing her car parked smack in front of the fire hydrant brought everything back in a heated rush—a symbol of years of manipulation, of struggle, of abuse. So much abuse.

After settling Jamison in the back seat, she rounded the driver's side, and the flutter of plastic caught her eye.

They'd left her a ticket tucked into a plastic sleeve and shoved under her wiper blade. Savannah jerked it out, crumpled it into a ball and shoved it into her pocket. "Fuckers."

She took a deep breath before she opened the driver's door. She needed to settle. To find even ground. Hell, find any ground. Jamison would pick up on her distress, and his anxiety would skyrocket. Living with his father would ruin Jamison. Absolutely demolish him. Savannah knew. It had almost destroyed her.

Savannah's heart felt frozen and heavy as she stared up at the mountains towering over the little town—very much the way Hank and Lyle loomed over her and Jamison. She could still remember being overwhelmed with the beauty here and awed by the town's history when she'd first come to visit. It was harder to remember being head over heels for both Hank and his family.

So many broken promises and crushed dreams. There was no part of that hopeful, dreamy girl left inside her now. Hank had killed that part of her a long time ago.

She exhaled heavily, and as her breath billowed in the air, thoughts of running returned. Because she'd never leave her son in the hands of men like Hank and Lyle.

Never.

4

Ian jogged up the stairs of the Manhunters' temporary headquarters, an industrial building just south of White-fish, forty minutes south of Hazard. Level one was leased by a drop-ship company. Roman Steele, Manhunters' founder and commander, had arranged a short-term lease of the second floor, which had been abandoned by a telemarketing company gone belly up.

He hit the top step, turned the corner, and paused. The perimeter of the space had been cordoned off with glass-walled offices, all surrounding a sea of cubicles. In one glance, Ian pinpointed Roman in an office on the right, standing at the printer and talking to the company admin, Camille. Across the space on the left, Everly sat at a conference table, chatting with Sam. And both were shoving something delectable into their mouths.

Ian's gaze darted to a telltale pink box adorning the conference table and huffed a laugh. "No way."

Ian, Sam, Everly, and their boss, Roman, had all been on different military Manhunter teams, but their work brought them together from time to time. And no matter where they found themselves, Everly never failed to locate the best donuts in a hundred-mile radius.

In the thirty seconds it took Ian to reach the conference room, his mouth started watering. At the door, he stopped, hands on hips, and pinned her with a look. "How in the hell did you find *your* caliber of sinkers in this frozen wasteland?"

Leaning back in her chair, Everly popped the last piece of a donut into her mouth, crossed her arms, and offered a superior smirk. "I'm just that good, Heller."

"She is, man," Sam declared around a mouthful of apple fritter. He licked his fingers, muttering, "She really is."

"I'll be the judge of that." Ian made his way around the table toward the box. "Got any crullers in there, girl?"

She frowned. "Cru-what?"

Ian tipped back the lid and found three perfect crullers among half a dozen other fried delicacies. He grinned at Everly and pulled one of the tender pillows of sugary goodness from the box. "I think I love you."

He dropped into a chair and stuffed the heavenly fried dough into his mouth.

Every bakery made crullers a little differently, and they were all good. But this kind was his favorite—light, airy, melt-in-your-mouth moist. The sugary softness exploded in his mouth, and Ian moaned with pleasure.

"Okay." Roman strolled in and dropped a packet of papers in front of each of them. "Forget the donuts."

"*Forget* the donuts?" Ian said around the last bite of his own. "There are crullers in there, dude."

Roman's gray eyes homed in on Ian with the intensity of a laser. "You better not have eaten the chocolate one."

He opened his arms wide. "How long have we been friends? Have I ever—and I mean *ever*—stolen your chocolate cruller?"

Roman smirked. They both knew Ian had no scruples when it came to crullers.

"What was I thinking?" His boss slapped an information packet hard against Ian's chest. "Sounds like you made unexpected inroads with Savannah and Jamison Bishop today."

Ian shot a look at his conniving teammate. That girl was always stirring shit. "More like a less-than-friendly discussion." He glanced at Sam, their tech genius. "Get anything interesting from the bugs in either of the Bishops' offices?"

"They are seriously the lamest law enforcement group on the planet," Sam complained while dusting fritter crumbs from his hands, his mouth, the chest of his black sweater. He'd let his stubble grow into an almost-beard that caught everything. "No practical jokes, no good-natured ribbing."

"Is that a no?" Ian asked.

Before Sam could confirm, the tap of high heels halted the conversation. Everyone turned their attention to the stairs. Gianna Bliss slowly came into view and immediately started toward the conference room. Ian had met her a couple of times while he'd been in the military when she'd come to brief the team on the high-value targets they'd been tasked to capture or kill. At that time, she'd been with the CIA.

Since then, she'd swapped out chasing foreign bad guys for the homegrown kind, living and operating in the US. She must just have stepped off one of the FBI's private jets. Dressed in a navy power suit, she was probably fresh from one of those high-level DC meetings. She held a trench coat over one arm and a briefcase in the other hand. If her attire hadn't screamed *This is serious business*, her expression would have.

And she wasn't alone. Liam Moore was with her. As Mason's handler, Liam had reported him missing and been on the op with the Manhunters when they'd located his body. But today, instead of fatigues, he was dressed in a suit, looking just as professional, just as somber, as Gianna.

Roman turned to face her. "This is a surprise."

Gianna paused at the door and exhaled in one hard breath. "There's been a development."

"Must be significant for you to jump the jet," Roman said.

"It is." Gianna tossed her trench coat over a chair and dropped her briefcase on the table. She was one of those stunning women who stopped traffic—tall, lithe, confident. She was also wickedly intelligent. Everything other women both envied and loathed. To top it off, she was one of the few women with power in DC.

As the director of the Joint Interagency Task Force, Gianna led a group of agents from various law enforcement departments on tenuous black-ops missions. She reported directly to the director of the NSA and the president. And she used the Manhunters when critical missions needed finesse, raw power or went awry—like one of her undercovers getting killed under suspicious circumstances while hunting a counterfeiter.

"Liam," Roman greeted.

"Roman." Liam took the closest available seat. Then glanced around the table with a nod to the others. "Heller, Slaughter, Shaw."

When Liam's attention returned to his boss, Gianna, Ian, and his teammates shared a silent glance, confirming the new tension in the room.

Gianna pulled a file folder from her briefcase and tossed it on the table with a slap. Papers and photos spilled out.

Ian homed in on the images first—the gruesome photos from the remnants of a plane crash. He reached for one showing a charred piece of the plane's tail, and every shred of joviality he'd been feeling just moments ago fled.

"Flight one-twenty-one?" He lifted his gaze to Gianna. "The seven-forty-seven that went down in New York last month?"

"Killing all three hundred and thirty-four people on board and one hundred ninety-eight people on the ground," Gianna confirmed, "including one of my colleagues. Tens of millions in damage to a city that's already seen too much tragedy."

Sam and Everly had also pulled several photos from the melee, documenting the carnage.

Ian asked what everyone wanted to know. "What does that have to do with this mission?"

"We just received confirmation that the terrorists who blew up this plane are linked to the smuggler distributing passports from *here*—this little dot on the map," she said. "The four terrorists' passports have identical flaws in their printing and the same hacker's code in the RFID chip. And all four passports originated from employees working for Bishop Mining."

A shock wave traveled the length of Ian's spine. His teammates wore equally surprised expressions.

"After checking with Interpol," she said, "we've confirmed that the same errors were seen in passports used by terrorists who have attacked across the globe—London, Paris, Brussels."

This op just got very interesting.

Everly shot him a sassy I-told-you-so look.

"Just to clarify," Ian said. "The terrorists manipulate Canada's soft spot for refugees and immigrate there, then search out like-minded men—if not men from their own terrorist cells—and open themselves up to recruitment by Bishop for cheap labor in the work-visa program? After a year in the mine, they grab a US passport and hit the road?"

"They also crash planes, blow up buildings, and target large venues with modified semiautomatic weapons," Gianna added.

Ian raised his brows, shook his head, and tossed the photo back into the pile. "That's fuckin' devious."

"And fuckin' terrifying," Everly added as she scowled at a photo.

"The media know something is up," Gianna said. "We've managed to keep a lid on the details, but I don't know how long that will last. The public is petrified, and the media is fueling the fear with speculation a little too close to home."

A heaviness settled on the room. Everyone there knew that when a country's sense of safety and security was threatened, the economy plummeted. People canceled travel plans. They stopped spending their money at cinemas, restaurants, and malls. They avoided crowded arenas like concerts and sporting events. And they held everything dear very close—including cash. Add to that an angry public demanding answers for the horrific loss of life, and you had the perfect storm for every politician.

And the politician breathing down Gianna's neck happened to be the leader of the free world.

"Is there any sign of the ledger?" Gianna wanted to know. "It just went to the top of our priority list."

"No," Ian said. "We searched both offices at the sheriff's station and Bishop Mining top to bottom and inside out. Whatever ledger Mason was talking about isn't in either office."

"We'll search and wire up both homes," Roman assured her. "We haven't gotten anything from the bugs in the wife's home, but Ian's made positive inroads with both her and son."

"Good," Gianna said, focusing on Ian. "Once the divorce is final, she won't be able to hide behind spousal privilege when she's on the stand. Having someone she can trust and lean on now might be a treasure trove of information."

The conversation had just gone off the rails. "Wait. What?"

"Dig," she told Ian. "If we're not getting anything directly from the Bishop men, mine the ex-wife for dirt. Messy divorces always yield valuable fruit. Use the information to flip Hank or Lyle or both. I want that ledger. I want Lyle and Hank Bishop. I want everyone who had anything to do with Mason's death and the counterfeiting, even if they only knew about it and didn't disclose. Everyone within reach is going down. Hard."

Her phone rang. Gianna picked up her trench and her briefcase and strode out of the office, answering her phone with a crisp "Bliss."

"I guess she's under a little pressure," Sam spoke first.

Gianna had closed herself in Roman's office and paced the length of the glass wall with her phone to her ear.

Roman exhaled slowly, his jaw muscle jumping. "Liam, why don't you fill in some of the gaps regarding Mason's mission?"

Liam sat forward and met everyone's gaze in turn. He was a clean-cut, lean blond. A pretty boy who looked like he fit better in an office analyzing data than in the field getting dirty. If Ian hadn't seen the man rappel into that mine with his own eyes, he never would have believed Liam capable.

He pulled another folder from a briefcase and passed stapled packets of information to each Manhunter.

"What's the background on this ledger?" Everly asked.

"A guy in the mines told Mason that Bishop kept a detailed list of some kind that contained the name of every person he'd issued a fake passport to. His name was Tully, and he was due a passport, but Bishop was dragging his feet, so he went to Bishop's office for a chat. Only Bishop was in the toilet, so the guy got nosy and found an open ledger on his desk with names and dates. Bishop walked in before he could memorize anything, but from working in the mine, he'd recognized names of coworkers, and dates corresponded to the days they started. In light of the new link between terrorists and the passports, that ledger doesn't just contain the names of people who are guilty of passport fraud—"

"They're potential terrorists," Everly finished. "What happened to the guy, Tully? Can we talk to him?"

"He's disappeared."

"Disappeared?" Ian asked. "As in he was fired, quit, left town?"

"We suspect he's dead. The day after his conversation with Mason, Tully was called back to Bishop's office to pick up his passport and never returned to work. Never cleaned out his apartment. Never picked up his final paycheck. Never contacted his family again."

"They thought he saw something that could have taken them down and killed him," Everly said.

"Looks that way," Liam confirmed.

"But why go to the trouble to hide Tully's body and not Mason's?" Everly asked.

"Two people getting close to the scheme at the same time?" Roman said. "Mason may have been a warning to the others."

"Why would Bishop keep that kind of information in a paper ledger?" Ian mused. "Kind of nineteenth century."

"Pen and paper keeps the information out of a hacker's reach," Sam said.

"But it's so...concrete, so...permanent," Everly said. "Even Third World warlords are more tech savvy."

"Bishop's no warlord," Roman said. "He's a fuckin' miner. But if he caught Mason trying to grab the ledger after Tully had seen it, he'd have moved it or just gotten rid of it altogether by now."

Ian leaned forward and rested his elbows on the table. "If you can tie the false passports you already have back to Hazard, why not just arrest Bishop and pressure him to give us the ledger and the name of the counterfeiter?"

"Because everything we have is circumstantial. We have no evidence of Lyle counterfeiting or even being the person who gave out the passports to employees. According to other miners, Baulder does that."

"So Bishop keeps his hands clean," Ian said.

"We need that list," Liam said. "Those names are our top priority. We need to track down every person who was given a passport to nail the terrorists among them. Those who weren't involved in terrorism are still guilty of passport fraud. They'll be willing to talk for a reduced sentence, and they'll be able to pin Bishop as the mastermind."

"What about Mason's killer?" Ian asked. "And the counterfeiter?"

"We want them too, but the list is the key to finding these terrorists and stopping them before they kill more Americans."

"This is a pretty big deal," Ian said. "Why was the operation so small? Why was Mason the only one undercover?"

"At any one time," Liam said, "there are over a thousand terrorist threats throughout the United States. Before we connected the known terrorists' passports to Bishop Mining, this was considered a small operation. My resources were tied up in bigger, deeper, more dangerous operations. Discovering the link between the terrorists on flight one-twenty-one and men who worked for Bishop pushed this operation into the red zone. Gianna shuffled resources around. I've been freed up to join you here. I'll be working with Sam, developing background and intel."

"What kind of leverage can we get on Bishop from his ex-wife?" Roman asked, his gaze alternating between Ian and Everly.

"There's a lot of animosity between them," Ian said. "And they've been living apart for, what?" He glanced at Sam. "Two years?"

"Three," Sam said.

"I just don't know what kind of information she would have considering the two of them have been apart so long."

"Or she could know everything," Everly countered. "Maybe his crimes contributed to the divorce. She probably knows things that would help. Things she doesn't even realize have power."

"We could offer both Savannah and Rosen a way out," Ian suggested. "They might jump at something as simple as relocation and work somewhere else in Montana."

Roman nodded. "Rosen could be our eyes and ears inside the department. The ex could provide intel or evidence on Bishop's ethical improprieties. Let's start with Rosen," Roman told Everly. "Propose the scenario. See how he responds." Then he looked at

Ian. "Since you've already made headway with the ex and son, stay focused there. Trade roles with Everly. Build trust. See what you can get while holding your cover."

Ian cut a look at Everly—who was smiling like a little shit. "Whoa, boss. No one's going to believe me as a waiter in a café."

"We don't have the luxury of time here," Roman said. "Make it work."

"I saw a help wanted sign at the mechanic's shop a few storefronts from the café," Everly offered with a flutter of lashes. "You'd make a great grease monkey."

Ian gave Roman a pleading look. "Come on—"

"Do it." Roman scooped up the contents of the folder Gianna had scattered across the table. "And do it fast."

Roman turned out of the conference room and headed toward his office.

Ian glared at Everly, who was still smiling. "You little—"

"Don't say anything you can't take back," she said in a singsong.

"I did some preliminary background on the ex," Sam told Ian. "Her father is an unknown entity. Her mother is alive, but they appear to be estranged. Mother lives in Los Angeles, and get this, she's been a devout Scientologist for over a decade. She's married and has more children with the new husband—all working within the Scientology movement. I'll hack her VPN today." He rubbed his hands together and grinned. "Anyone want to place a wager on what I'll find?"

"Not me." Everly stood and tugged on her parka. "I've already hit my jackpot." She shot that gleaming grin at Ian. "I always wanted to be a miner, and you know I play better with boys. Don't think I'd know what to do with a girlfriend. And kids? *Eesh.*" She faked a shudder, then met Ian's gaze again. "Look at this as a chance to brush up on those flirting skills."

On the way out, Everly patted Ian's arm. "Oh, and I hope you like Pepto-Bismol pink. Your side of the duplex interior is covered in it."

"Payback's a bitch, Shaw," Ian yelled at her back.

Everly kept walking with the sway of triumph in her step. "Bring it on, Heller. Bring it on."

∼

ROMAN HATED this damn office space. With all the glass, he had nowhere to collect his thoughts without anyone watching.

He paused at his office door. Gianna had finished her call and now stood at the window, looking out at the blanket of snow, one arm crossed over her middle, the other hand rubbing her temple. She'd shed her suit jacket, and her hair had come loose from the sophisticated coil. Strands hung in loose spirals along the sides of her face; a few wisps trailed the nape of her neck.

Longing hit him low and hard. Longing to press his lips to that spot on the back of her neck. To feel the curve of her spine against his chest. For the millionth time since their one and only night together, Roman wished he'd slowed down and savored. But they'd been so hungry, hurting so badly...

He let his eyes close on the bittersweet memory and whispered, "Fuck." Then pushed the door open.

Gianna glanced over her shoulder with a look that took him back two years. A look of pain, of hopelessness, of pleading that pierced his heart. She only let the vulnerability show for a split second before she recovered. "Sorry. I lost it a little with the team in there."

He didn't respond. What could he say? She'd lost her lover in that plane crash, a former assistant district attorney in DC. When the silence carried, he managed a rough "It's understandable."

"I'm getting pressed from every side—the president, the secretary of defense, Congress, Homeland Security... Not to mention my own rabid need to catch these guys. All those people. So many lives..." She exhaled heavily. Her shoulders sagged, and her brow pulled with sadness. "Roman..."

The softness of her voice, the turbulence in that one word, twisted his gut. But he couldn't do this. He couldn't want her, because he couldn't have her. Not the way he wanted: heart and soul. She'd spent one night in Roman's bed. Then turned around and spent two years with a fancy suit. Roman had found a way to work with her, but he wouldn't make the same mistake twice. This time around, he couldn't give her what she was looking for —distraction, a warm body, solace.

"I've got Everly on Rosen," he told her. "She'll work him as a CI and find her way into the mines."

Gianna turned, a single line appearing between her brows. "A woman in the mines? Isn't that...I don't know, odd? Wouldn't that increase suspicion?"

They were back to business. Good. This, Roman could do. "There are six other female miners. It's not all that rare."

"Six out of, what? Six hundred?"

"Everly's not great with kids, and Savannah Bishop is devoted to her son. Ian's already befriended the kid, which gives him an in with the mom. It's the fastest route. We've already got audio surveillance at her home. Sam and Liam will continue digging into the digital trail."

Her clear hazel eyes stayed sharp on him, but thoughts churned in the background. Her mind was busy calculating, assessing, strategizing. That was Gianna—always thinking. Which made him wonder—for the hundredth time—where her mind had been during their night together. Had she been thinking of another man then, the way Roman thought about Gianna when he was with other women now?

Finally, she exhaled, lowered her gaze to the floor, and nodded. "You know your people. I trust your judgment."

"Give us a week or two," Roman told her. "We'll have enough evidence for warrants at the least."

"We need more than warrants. If the forger gets spooked—"

"He'll disappear," Roman finished. "And we'll be back to square one. Believe me, I want this guy too. But like you said, if we spook him, we'll lose him. Just give us a little time."

She exhaled, nodded, and moved to the chair where she'd tossed her jacket. "Keep me in the loop?"

"Always." He stepped forward to hold her blazer while she slipped her arms in. Her scent floated on the air, and the soft spicy floral scent lightened his head. One whiff and memories slammed him—a series of film clips flashing through his mind. Skin on skin, breaths hot and quick, moans of pleasure, erotic whispers. Roman's heart rate jacked up. Fire erupted through his body in a way he hadn't felt in years. Two years, to be exact.

He helped with her trench, letting it fall over her shoulders before he stepped back—way back—shoving one hand into the front pocket of his slacks and running the other over his damp face and into his hair.

Gianna turned with a soft smile. He could have made himself believe the look in her eyes was longing, but he knew it was most likely regret or pity.

"You look good," she told him.

God, she made him ache. "You too."

She tipped her head. "Are you good?"

"Yep." His answer was immediate and confident. It was also a total lie. "I'm great."

She nodded. "We'll talk soon, then."

He forced a smile and a little twang into his voice. "Yes, ma'am."

She laughed, just a light sprinkle of humor that quickly died. "Roman..."

"Don't worry. I've got this." He pulled the office door open, needing space to get his head straight. "Your Gulfstream awaits."

But she didn't move. Her hand pressed against his chest, and the feel of her touching him, reaching for him, nearly dropped him to his knees. "Stay safe."

"Of course." His voice came out ragged.

She nodded, but her gaze kept scanning, looking for...something. "Promise me."

The woman didn't just steal his breath, she ripped it from his lungs. He covered her hand and gave it a squeeze. "I promise."

~

SAVANNAH PACED the hallway outside Hank's office, waiting for Lyle to exit. The last thing she needed was to see them both twice in one day, but she needed to confront this custody issue head-on.

The older man's voice rose, and his tone prickled the skin on the back of Savannah's neck. He was angry, hammering Hank about something he hadn't done to Lyle's expectations, she was sure. Some things never changed. Lyle was still an abusive bastard—physically and mentally—and Hank still allowed his father to degrade and rule him.

But that was Hank's problem now. Savannah didn't care what either of them did as long as it didn't affect Jamison—which was the real problem. Because as long as they were both in her son's life, Jamison would be exposed to their abuse. It wasn't too bad now; Jamison was a great kid. But as he grew and became his own person, as natural rebellion progressed, Savannah could see conflicts that would erupt in physical punishment and emotional abuse.

No way would she let that happen.

"It's too soon." Hank's lowered voice drifted through the glass. "People are watching. They're still nervous over Mason's death. Rumors about a killer among us are still flying."

A fist of uncertainty tightened in Savannah's chest. She

leaned against the wall just beyond the window and focused on the conversation.

"If I don't deliver on my promises," Lyle said, "more than Mason's death will be flying around the gossip rings."

"Keep your voice down," Hank told him.

"Make the pickup tomorrow night at eight, son, or I'll find someone to run against you in the next election."

Savannah pulled in a sharp breath. Lyle wouldn't make that threat lightly. Without Hank in a position of power, Lyle also lost power.

"I'll text you when they're ready," Lyle said. "Drop them at my house after you pick them up. I have to deliver at the end of the week."

The door to Hank's office jerked open. Lyle barged out of the room, saw Savannah, and stopped dead. His expression was familiar—furious and indignant. "What the fuck do you think you're doing?"

She straightened and crossed her arms. "Waiting to talk to Hank."

He took one menacing step toward Savannah. Her gut hiccupped with fear, but she held her ground. "Looks like you're eavesdropping."

"Only someone with something to hide would think that."

Hank stepped into the hall, scowling. His gaze jumped from Lyle to Savannah. "What the hell do you want?"

She forced her voice steady. "To talk about our son—unless that's too much trouble."

"Fuck," he bit out, turning back into his office. "What the hell now?"

Savannah stepped around Lyle, glad to be out from under his icy stare, and entered Hank's office. "I'm sorry discussing Jamison is such an inconvenience."

"Shut up." He dropped into the chair behind his desk and scanned the paperwork scattered there.

She was so sick of being treated like shit. She deserved so much better. Ian's crooked smile flashed in her head. Yeah, that. That's how she should be treated.

But then, Hank used to have a charming smile too.

He cracked a pen against his desk. "*What?*"

"You told me to shut up." She forced her spine to steel. Forced attitude through the fear. "I know from past experience that if I speak without an invitation, I end up with your knuckles against my face."

He gave her the you-fucking-bitch stare and stabbed a finger toward the door. "Shut that door."

She ignored him. "I won't be here long. I just wanted to point out the irrationality of fighting for full custody of Jamison."

"Don't start."

"You can't even hold up your end of visitation now. You've agreed to take him one night every two weeks, but he hasn't spent any time with you in months."

"I'm a little busy"—he gestured to his desk—"in case you haven't noticed."

"That's my point." She dropped the attitude and brought up a compassionate tone. "You're always busy. Your job is important. The town depends on you. Taking full custody of Jamison would hinder your availability to the people who need you most."

He pushed from the chair and approached in that menacing way that—in another life—would have had her backing away. Now she stood firm and held his gaze, even while her insides trembled.

"Don't fuckin' pretend you care," he said, his voice low and rough. "*You* don't tell *me* how things work. *You* don't tell *me* how to spend my time or how to raise my son." He lifted his hand, and Savannah flinched. But instead of hitting her, he jabbed a rigid finger against her chest. "*You* don't walk away from *me*."

"Stop stabbing at me." Even as the words came out, she braced for a backhand against her cheek. "It hurts."

He dropped his hands to his hips. "I told you that if you divorced me, you'd lose Jamison. And I'm a man of my word."

"You also said you'd honor and cherish me on our wedding day."

His eyes narrowed. "I also said until death do us part."

A stream of ice coursed down the center of Savannah's body.

"If you want our son in your life every day," Hank told her, "you'll move back into our house."

It took Savannah a few long seconds to find her voice. "You know that's not going to happen, and you know you can't take care of Jamison on your own."

He lifted both hands out to his sides and stepped back, then turned toward his desk, assessing his paperwork dismissively. "We're done here."

Savannah left the office feeling the same way she always felt walking away from Hank—disgusted and dirty...but still terrified. Someone outside their relationship might not have considered the *"Until death do us part"* comment a threat, but Savannah knew that was exactly what it was.

Once she'd exited the station, she pulled her phone from her pocket and saved the recording on her way to the car. She sent one copy to Audrey, one to Misty, and another to her own email.

She stuffed the phone back into her pocket and slid into the car with a muttered "You're not the only one building a file, asshole."

5

Savannah guided Jamison's hands as he slid a cookie sheet into the oven. "Be careful of the racks and the sides."

He pushed the metal sheet onto the rack, let go, and jumped with excitement, almost knocking his head into Savannah's. "I did it."

"You sure did."

"You're a star." Misty held up her hand. "High five, dude."

He slapped her hand. "Thanks for the recipe, Aunt Misty. Oatmeal chocolate chip is Bailey's favorite."

Misty laughed and crouched in front of Jamison, gripping his arms. "She's going to fall head over heels for you, buddy. Girls love it when you do special things for them."

He wrinkled his nose. "She's not my girlfriend. And it's just a playdate."

"If you say so."

"Mommy." Jamison turned. "Can I bring some to school for my class?"

"You bet." She anticipated his next question. "And I suppose you'd like to take some out to Deputy Corwin."

A spark of fear touched Jamison's eyes, and his smile evaporated. He thought about it for a second, screwed up his face in a torn expression, and said, "Not really."

Surprised, Savannah said, "No? Why not?"

"He wasn't very nice to you the other day. And he was really mean to Mr. Ian."

Misty lifted her brows at Savannah.

"That's very true." She ruffled his hair. "Go play until the cookies are done."

Jamison bounced out of the kitchen toward his room, but stopped before he reached it, calling, "Mom? Can we bring cookies to the new neighbor too?"

"New neighbor?" Savannah and Misty said in unison, meeting each other's gaze.

They met Jamison at the picture window, where he looked at an old beater of a truck sitting in the driveway reserved for the tenant next door.

"When did that show up?" Misty asked. "It wasn't there when I got here, was it?"

"No." Savannah put her hands on Jamison's shoulders and steered him toward his room. "Let's see how many cookies we have before we go promising them all away."

With Jamison settled on his floor, deep in a fantasy scenario starring his Star Wars action figures, Savannah pulled the door almost closed and returned to Misty's side. The storm had passed through over the last two days, dumping record-setting snowfall. But the day broke with clear blue skies and sunlight sparkling off the fresh snow like pixy dust. Savannah used to love this time of year. Now, she hated everything about Hazard.

Okay, everything but seeing Ian in the diner every morning. He'd become her reason to smile over the last few days.

"Have you seen anyone yet?" she asked. "Maybe it's just a maintenance guy."

"No. But judging by those boxes in the back of the truck, I'm betting it's a new mucker moving in." Misty heaved a sigh and crossed her arms. "I'm disappointed our waitress fell through. I was looking forward to another single girl our age in town."

"Yeah," Savannah agreed. "I was looking forward to having a female neighbor for a change."

Lyle pulled in at least half his workers by offering an employer-sponsored work visa for the first year. He got cheap labor for people who needed a way into the US, mostly from Canada. But as soon as they'd completed their year of service, the majority of them left town. Savannah didn't know if they went back to Canada or moved on to find other work in the US, but she didn't care either. Mining was a hard job, and the pay sucked until the three-year mark, when they got their first substantial raise. Even then, they moved slowly up the scale, with the lifers being the only ones who made a decent living wage. Bishop was a cheap sonofabitch on top of a mountain of other shortcomings.

And that just meant the caliber of men in town also sucked. Drifters, lowlifes, drinkers, druggies, felons... She prayed whoever moved in next door wasn't a young partier, a creepy old man, or a criminal.

"I shouldn't have to worry about who's moving in." She clenched her hands into fists and glanced over her shoulder to make sure Jamison was still playing in his room before adding, "I should be on my way out of this place. Just when I didn't think I could hate Hank any more."

She shook her head and stared out the window, willing someone to come out of the duplex next door so she could put at least one fear to rest. "Just the other day, Lyle was bitching about how Hank had to spend so much time saving the world, he couldn't be expected to feed Jamison a decent meal. Now he's supporting Hank in a custody battle? With Hank's schedule, he wouldn't see Jamison any more if he had custody than if I were to bring him here twice a month. I swear, everything is such a battle with him. Every damn thing."

"Lyle's the worst kind of— No." Misty held up a hand. "*Hank* is the worst kind of bastard. But Lyle is right up there in Hank's asshole."

"I'm so tired," Savannah admitted with a sigh. "I've been fighting so long, sometimes I just want to throw my hands up and yell *Uncle*. Imagining another thirteen years of this... God."

"Don't give in. That's what he's counting on, wearing you down."

"And driving me into bankruptcy. I don't have a rich daddy paying all my legal bills."

"If he throws another wrench into the works and you find you have to stay, I'd really like you to consider moving in with me. I know neither of us can do it now, but I could have those second and third bedrooms cleared and sanitized in two weeks, tops, if I knew you and Jamison would be in them. I'd stuff everything into the barn and add extra locks so Jamison didn't get into anything and hurt himself."

Savannah smiled at Misty. The thought was sweet and generous, but hardly realistic. Misty's father had died over six months ago. He'd been an eccentric man, an inventor of silly, strange, mostly useless gadgets. Only one of those inventions had sold, but it had given him enough money to raise Misty alone and live out his life on his small ranch following his useless passion of inventing. It hadn't been enough to leave anything for Misty. Anything but a house where he'd hoarded furniture, appliances, equipment, supplies, books—you name it. Anything that caught his eye—whether bought, found, or scavenged.

Now, Misty worked extra shifts to keep her head above water and spent her spare time slowly moving through the junk to clean out the house in hopes of selling it one day. And she made a little extra by selling some of her father's bizarre junk online.

"I've seen that barn," she said, teasing Misty. "There's no room to stuff anything anywhere."

"You underestimate me."

"No," she said with a sigh. "No, I don't. I have no idea how you deal with everything."

"We do what we have to."

Amen. Savannah nodded, but her tension skyrocketed as she wondered if she'd be able to do what she'd have to do if Hank was granted custody of Jamison.

"You're not going to lose him," Misty said, reading Savannah's thoughts. "I'll steal him myself before that prick gets him. My Aunt Carmen has a cabin in the mountains outside Coeur d'Alene. He'd never find us."

"Oh," she sighed with a whimsical little laugh. "A hidden cabin in the woods. You know you've hit bottom when that sounds heavenly."

Maybe it's time to run.

The thought crept into her head again, and her heart picked up speed.

"You know I've been dreading your move to Missoula," Misty said, "but I hope you also know I'd do everything possible to support you if you choose another way out."

Like running.

The unsaid words hung between them.

Savannah gave Misty's arm a squeeze. "I do know. Thank you."

"I want what's best for you and Jamison. You both deserve peace, security, and love in your lives. And you certainly aren't getting any of that here."

Savannah released a breath, her heart growing heavy. She returned her gaze to the window but let her eyes blur over the blue sky and white mountains. It wasn't that she didn't think she could do it. Savannah had already walked away from an abusive man, something she'd never imagined she'd have to face. And she'd walked away from their marriage, something she'd never dreamed she'd have to do. And—if the custody arrangement had been settled with the divorce—she would have taken Jamison and settled a few hours away and faithfully brought him to see Hank every two weeks.

But she didn't have confidence in her ability to disappear. At least not from a man like Hank. He would come after her armed with his fury, his unscrupulous methods, his law enforcement connections, and his father's nearly unlimited resources.

"If it was just me," she told Misty, "I'd already have changed my name and my appearance. I'd have gotten a new passport, a new driver's license, a new digital life—however the hell one goes about doing that. But I would have figured it out, and I'd have vanished from the face of the earth as Savannah Bishop. I'd have moved somewhere completely different—Hawaii or Europe or Central America—and started all over. But it's not just me."

"I know," Misty said, her voice heavy with the same futility plaguing Savannah.

She thought of her beautiful gem of a boy in the next room. He didn't just need her, he trusted her, loved her, looked up to her. She couldn't let him down.

"I know Hank's been an asshole, but he's still Jamison's dad, and he wasn't always such a bastard," she said, as much talking to herself as to Misty. "Do I think he deserves to be a dad? Not the way he's been acting the past few years, no. But I also don't feel like I have the right to take Jamison's father away from him completely. I don't want Jamison growing up with the same holes in his life that I had. And ripping him away from everything he knows, changing his name, lying about his father and running to a place he's never been?" She shook her head. "I can't begin to imagine the damage that would cause a little boy. The thought breaks my heart."

Misty nodded, her expression clouded with misery. "I never thought it would come to this."

"And that's a huge concern too—not knowing exactly what Hank—or Lyle—is capable of or to what lengths they'll go if I leave Hazard, trying to escape completely. Hell, I can't think about escaping Hazard permanently when I can't even take Jamison to Splash Mountain in Missoula." She exhaled, the stress heavy on her heart. "They have contacts throughout the state. Access to nationwide databases. The backing of law enforcement. Look at the petty, manipulative bullshit he pulls around here for absolutely no reason other than to mess with me. What do you think he'd do if I tried to take Jamison?"

Misty didn't have an answer.

"I keep hoping Hank will wake up one day and stop fighting," she admitted, feeling foolish and hopeless. "That he'll finally realize we were just wrong for each other or find another woman and move on with his life. Let Jamison and me move on with ours." She shook her head with tears pushing at her eyes. "But it's obvious now, that's not going to happen."

To hide her tears, Savannah moved around the living room, picking up Jamison's toys.

"We'll figure it out, Savannah. You have Audrey and me..." Misty let the words trail off. Savannah didn't have to look at her friend to know she'd just realized that Savannah's entire pool of support consisted of an overworked attorney who lived three hours away and a well-meaning but resource-and-cash-poor friend. "I bet Mark knows something about getting a new identity. He told me he had to jump through some sketchy hoops to get into Lyle's work-visa program."

Savannah's gut clenched. She dropped a sofa pillow and spun. "No. Absolutely not." Misty's boyfriend of three months was a great guy, but he wasn't exactly the brightest crayon in the box. "Rumors spread like wildfire in the mines. You know that. Those guys gossip like high school girls. If that got back to Hank, or Lyle..." She trailed off, sucking a slow, terrified breath into her lungs. "Please promise me you won't talk to Mark."

"You're right. I'm sorry. I won't say anything." Misty gripped Savannah's arm and met her gaze deliberately. "But, listen, Savannah, if or when you are ready to take that step, you tell me, and

I'll find a way to get you what you need. We'll figure it out together."

Savannah covered Misty's hand with her own. "Thank you."

"How much cash do you have saved now?"

Savannah's mind veered toward the hidden hollow panel in the depths of her closet securing her savings. She lived off her meager income from the café and cashed all the checks that came from the court-mandated child support Hank paid by way of a garnish on his paycheck. Then she squirreled the cash away in a secret spot. She'd been doing that from the moment she got the job at the café.

"Last count," she said, "Twenty-one thousand four hundred thirty-two dollars."

Misty whistled through her teeth. "Damn impressive, girl."

"Thank God for Audrey's tenacity. If Hank weren't being forced to pay, I wouldn't have a penny. And he wouldn't give a damn how that affected Jamison."

"I have no idea how you do it," Misty said.

"Yes, you do. The same way you do. We scrounge, cut corners, and work our asses off. I know it sounds like a lot of money, but if I end up using it, that will be because I vanish. I can't collect child support if I vanish. That cash would burn through my pockets."

The oven timer dinged, and Jamison zoomed out of his room. "They're done! They're done!"

Misty laughed, her gaze following Jamison as he ran past them into the kitchen. "Even Karen doesn't get that excited about cookies."

Savannah helped Jamison through the process of moving the cookies from the hot pan to the cooling racks. Then, together, they finished off the dough with one more sheet of cookies.

Once they were in the oven, Jamison jumped, both fists in the air, yelled, "Yahoo!" and ran from the kitchen.

Savannah laughed, dropping pots and pans into the sink. "That kid is the freaking light of my life." And she wasn't about to let Hank take him. She glanced at Misty. "You're working tonight, aren't you?"

"Yep." She sighed. "Eighth day in a row. *Cha-ching.*"

"Would you mind if I walked over and borrowed your car?" Her stomach tightened as she worked up a lie. Okay, a partial lie. Jamison often went to Bailey's house if he wasn't in school while Savannah was working. She tried not to use her back door too often, as it was currently her own escape from constant prying eyes and she didn't want to lose that. But she needed to get out alone to follow Hank. "While Jamison's at his playdate with Bailey, I wanted to run some errands, and I just want to do them without Nastimeister Corwin in tow. I'll sneak out the back and walk over."

Misty smiled. "Of course. Whatever you need."

"Mommy!" His excited call from the living room interrupted. "Mommy, look!" His words were punctuated by the sound of his hand knocking on glass.

She and Misty returned to the living room and found Jamison at the window, vibrating with excitement and alternating between knocking and waving to someone outside.

"Mr. Ian," he called through the glass. "Mr. Ian."

An electric zing stung Savannah's gut. She put her hand on Jamison's shoulder and peered through the window to where a man stood in the street beside a tow truck from Mo's Garage. He wore a navy-blue parka and a baseball hat.

"Honey, that's not—" Savannah started. But Jamison cut her off with more yells and clacks against the window.

"Jamison." She caught his hand just as the man turned toward their house. With his face hidden beneath the brim of a ball cap, Savannah couldn't tell who it was, but Jamison was grinning and waving.

The man shifted, angling toward them. He pushed his ball cap up and smiled. It *was* Ian. He waved, then finished his conversation with Mo.

Savannah was still trying to figure out what was happening when Misty's giddy voice pulled her attention. "Oh my God. Finally. *Finally* the universe is on your side."

"How do you figure?"

"Duh." She gestured toward the window. "Your new neighbor?"

Savannah shook her head, unwilling to buy into the connection between Ian appearing on her street to him being her new neighbor.

When she glanced back at the street, Mo's truck had driven away, and Ian walked toward the other side of the duplex, shedding his parka and continuing to return Jamison's incessant wave. Then he leaned into the truck, grabbed a box, and headed inside.

"Oh jeez..." she breathed, her eyes sliding closed. She had to live next door to the sexiest guy who'd come to town in ages? "I'm afraid I just lost a year's worth of sleep."

Misty burst out laughing, immediately connecting Savannah's complaint with the very real tossing-and-turning problem a man like Ian could create for a woman.

Ian living on the other side of their shared wall. Sleeping... changing...showering with just six inches between them.

"Dear God," she muttered.

Jamison, oblivious to the new turmoil, whirled and grasped her hands. "Can we bring him cookies?" he asked, bouncing on his toes. "Can we? Can we?"

Misty doubled over with laughter while Savannah dropped her head back and groaned.

She and Jamison layered cookies on a paper plate, and Misty said her goodbyes and left for work. Jamison ran to grab his jacket from his bedroom, eager to visit Ian, while Savannah gnawed on her lower lip over the new issues their neighbor presented.

She pulled her own jacket from a hook by the door and glanced out the window again, her gaze holding on the cruiser

stationed out front. Hank had surely already been alerted to her
new neighbor. Her visit next door with Jamison in tow would go
directly to Hank's ear. If nothing else, she should let Ian know
what he was in for if he stayed in the duplex—the same thing
others had endured while living there: constant scrutiny, no
privacy, manipulation, and coercion, to say the least. Ian's already
tense relationship with the department after the confrontation at
the café wouldn't do him any favors.

"Ready." Jamison popped up next to her, the plate of cookies
in his hand, a big grin lighting his face.

The sight broke her heart a little. He yearned for a male role
model. Craved positive reinforcement from a male figurehead.
Instead of getting it all from his own father or even his grandfa-
ther, Jamison was searching for it in a stranger. A stranger who
would soon turn his back on them like every other man in town.

"Come on, Mom," he said, reaching for the door. "You're
so slow."

Savannah covered his hand. "Hold on a sec. We need to talk."
She dropped into a crouch and searched for the right words. "You
need to remember that Ian is an adult with his own busy life. He's
going to be working long days and will probably be really tired
when he gets home. Just because we're bringing him cookies
doesn't mean you can jump over there any time you want to visit.
And you absolutely *do not* leave the house without telling me."
She gave him a stern look. "Are we clear?"

Her warning didn't dim Jamison's grin any. "Crystal."

Damn, those freckles over his nose, the sparkle in his smile,
his unrelenting hope. She ruffled his hair. "Kid, you slay me."

When they stepped onto the porch, Savannah realized it was
much nicer outside than she'd thought. The sun beat down and
the snow insulated the area, creating a microclimate of spring
bliss. Snow dripped off the eaves and melted over the sidewalks.
The plow had come by earlier, and a strip of the road had been
cleared.

Savannah left her mittens in her pocket and her jacket unzipped for the short walk. As they approached the strip of revealed asphalt in the street, Corwin looked over from his patrol car. He rolled down his window, smiling at Jamison. "Hey there, little man."

Savannah glanced down at Jamison, saw the cookies, and realized the man thought they were for him. But Jamison looked right at Corwin, then turned at the road, continuing to Ian's without a word. Savannah experienced a collage of feelings from pride to fear. When it was obvious Jamison wasn't going to acknowledge the deputy, Corwin's gaze turned on Savannah—and it was anything but friendly.

Sure, blame Mom. Everything is my fault.

"Karma's a bitch," she told Corwin.

News of this visit would go straight to Hank. Savannah was in for a real headache. She was feeling jumpy by the time they reached Ian's door. She stood back as Jamison climbed the porch, much the way she did when he went door-to-door selling chocolate for his T-ball league.

Jamison shifted the cookies into one hand and lifted the other to knock. The door opened before his hand met the wood, and Ian stopped short, surprising all three of them.

"Well, hi there." He looked down at Jamison with a curious expression, then his gaze made a quick sweep of Savannah.

She'd seen him just hours ago when he'd been in the café for breakfast. Over the last few days, they'd built a warm familiarity. But she swore the man got better looking every time she saw him. He was in the same jeans and long-sleeved waffle thermal as this morning and every inch of fabric showed off assets Savannah wished she could investigate intimately.

"Hi, Mr. Ian." Jamison lifted the plate. "We brought you cookies."

"I see." His gaze flitted to Savannah again. "Is this one of those fund-raiser things?"

"No," Jamison answered. "It's because you're our new neighbor."

Ian planted his hands on his hips. A smile lifted the corners of his mouth. "Heck, if I'd known fresh cookies came with this place, I'd have moved in last week."

"They're oatmeal chocolate chip," Jamison told him. "My Aunt Misty's recipe. The best *ever*."

"Sold, partner, sold," Ian said, taking the plate. "That's awfully"—he looked at Savannah, and a little more smile reached his eyes—"*hospitable* of you."

She returned his smile, too pleased he'd remembered their conversation from the day before.

And while they were staring at each other, Jamison crooned, "Ooo, a bat," and slipped past Ian and into the house.

That broke Savannah's concentration. "Jamison," she scolded, "get out here. You don't just walk into someone's house uninvited."

"Oh, it's all right," Ian said.

"He knows better." She inched closer to the porch. "Jamison—"

"Look, Mom." He stood in the doorway, holding an aluminum bat. His gaze jumped to Ian. "This is a big bat."

"But it's light, right?" He stepped back and opened the door wider to Savannah. "Come on in. I'll put these in the kitchen."

A spark of uneasiness nagged beneath her ribs. When she hedged, Ian disappeared in the direction of the kitchen with Jamison following like a tail.

"Jamis— *Grrrr*." She was caught in an awkward place, moving forward only when neither Jamison nor Ian reappeared instantly.

She stepped into the duplex and closed the door to the cold air. The space was the mirror opposite of hers, which meant the largest bedrooms—her bedroom and his—shared a wall. Something she really shouldn't think about.

"Just for a minute," she said. "Jamison, come here right now."

He appeared at the front door with a mitt and baseball.

"Jamison," she scolded. "Those aren't yours. You don't touch things without permission."

"Mr. Ian said it was okay."

Savannah exhaled and glanced round, wincing at the paint job. The sheer intensity of the pink strained her eyes. The living room floor was draped with tarps, and a bucket of paint occupied one corner.

"Someone's finally going to paint," she said as he came back in. "I wondered how others could live with this color. They said they got used to it and didn't even see it after a while, but somehow I find that hard to believe."

"Right?" he said, also grimacing at the room with a shake of his head. "How do you not notice this? It hurts to look at it."

She resettled her gaze on him. All six-foot-two muscled inches. "I guess you got ahold of Mr. Baulder."

"I did."

Jamison knelt on the floor at their feet, fitting his hand into the mitt and tossing the ball to catch it. Savannah pushed her hands into her back pockets, uneasy with the nerves tingling in her gut. She hadn't spoken to a man she was attracted to in so long that even after seeing him for four days in a row, her stomach still floated whenever they talked. "I guess that means you'll be staying around awhile."

He tilted his head, his brows pulling together.

"The one-year signing agreement," she explained.

"Oh, right. That feels sketchy to me."

"I think so too, but I guess it's how he keeps his labor force from bugging out."

"That right there tells me something's wrong."

"You're intuitive," she said. "But you still took the job?"

"No. I've lived with term agreements my whole adult life. I want to be free to come and go."

"I'm confused." She glanced around the living room. "You're painting but not staying?"

"*Pffft*. I wouldn't paint if I wasn't staying. At least for a while. This place was cheap, and when they agreed to let me paint, I took it."

"Are you going to look for other work in town or...?" She cut herself off. "I'm sorry. It's none of my business. I didn't come over to grill you."

"Doesn't feel like a grilling." He shifted on his feet and leaned one shoulder against the wall. "Feels like small-town hospitality."

She laughed.

"I'd ask you to sit down, but..." He lifted his chin toward the empty living room with a smirk.

"Are your things coming soon?"

"I don't have any. Everything I own is in the back of my truck."

Okay...that seemed odd. "You travel light."

"I've been in the military."

"Ah." She drew out the realization. "What made you settle here? Is your family close by?"

"Nope. Dad disappeared when I was a kid, and Mom passed away about six months ago."

"Oh... I'm sorry."

"Thanks," he said, a little subdued. "I like to hunt and fish and backpack. Thought this would be a good place to relax my first year out. Heard about the jobs available at the mine and thought I'd give it a try."

She fished her mind for other places he could work, but since everyone in town kept their distance, she didn't have any ideas. "Since that fell through, what made you decide to stay?"

"Mo."

"Mo Barley?"

"Yeah. Met him in town. He's a vet, we got to talking, and he hired me."

"At the garage?"

Ian nodded. "I did a lot of mechanical work in the army. Felt like a good fit."

Savannah smiled, tucked her fingers into the front pockets of her jeans, and leaned her shoulder against the wall, mirroring Ian. Jamison was content to toss and catch the ball over and over. He'd always been good at occupying himself, and he loved listening to adults talk. But Savannah was enjoying it too. This was the first decent conversation she'd had with a man in a damn long time. Initially, Ian seemed to have a lot of rough edges. But talking with him felt as comfortable as chatting with her coworkers at the café. It felt good. Better than it probably should.

"I think you'll like working for Mo," she told him. "He and his wife are good people."

"That's the impression I got."

She smiled. "I'm glad you're staying." The words flipped a switch in her brain and her smile vanished. Her stomach chilled. "But, yeah, about that..." She glanced at Jamison, then back. "We should probably talk later."

He held her gaze for an extended moment, silent and still. His gaze eventually lowered to Jamison. "Are you up for fielding some grounders?"

Jamison's whole body stiffened, and he looked up at Ian as if he were a Greek god come to life. "Yeah." Then his gaze jumped to Savannah. "Can I, Mom?"

She looked toward the road. "I don't know. There's still snow..."

But Jamison jumped to his feet, swung the storm door open, and ran to the porch with the mitt and ball.

Ian pushed off the wall, picked up the bat, and met her gaze. "It'll give us time to talk." He cocked his head toward the door. "Come on."

Jamison was already running to the quiet street bordered by snow berms. Ian strode down the walk, and Savannah lost her train of thought as she watched. He moved with force and ease.

His shoulders were wide and hard, stretching the thermal material. And, damn, this wasn't the first time she'd noticed his amazing ass. Not the flat ass of a bean pole or the lard ass of a beer belly, but the high, tight ass of a man with muscle. She freed herself up at the diner every time he finished a meal just so she could watch him walk out.

"Might want to move your patrol car." Ian's words snapped Savannah out of her lust-filled thoughts, and she found him talking to Corwin, who'd stepped out of his vehicle. "Wouldn't want to dent that spiffy paint job."

"Holy shit," she muttered under her breath. Corwin slanted an angry look at Savannah before speaking into the radio on his shoulder and dropping into his car again. She'd bet her next paycheck this event was being translated straight into Hank's ear. "Just what I don't need."

But Ian and Jamison were already in position in the street, and her son was so excited to have someone to play ball with, he couldn't stand still.

"Okay," Ian called to Jamison. "Watch the ball and keep your mitt on the ground."

As Savannah made her way to the street, Ian tossed the ball in the air and tapped it with the bat. The ball bounced, then rolled along the wet asphalt toward Jamison. He stopped the ball with his mitt and grinned like he'd hit a home run.

"Good job," Ian said. "Now aim for my hand."

Jamison's grin faded. "Won't it hurt without a mitt?"

"Nah, my hands are like leather. Come on."

When Jamison hesitated, Ian glanced over his shoulder at the cruiser, then turned back to Jamison with "I warned him. If he doesn't move, it's his own fault. Toss it."

Jamison looked at Savannah.

"You're better than you think," she encouraged.

Jamison hauled his arm back and threw the ball straight to

Ian. The leather slapped Ian's palm, and he laughed. "Whooo-we. You've got an arm on you, kid. Ready?"

Ian coached Jamison through a couple more grounders. Once they'd found a rhythm, he turned to Savannah, his expression curious. "So, what's with the surveillance?"

"Yeah," she breathed, exhaling her stress over the topic. "That."

He hit another grounder to Jamison. "There's either an inordinate amount of crime in this sleepy little town, or you've got a problem with your ex."

"Can you guess which?"

He grinned.

She glanced at Corwin's vehicle. "Unfortunately, my problems with him also seem to become the problem of anyone who's nice to me."

He didn't respond, just encouraged Jamison with "That's it. Good job."

She lowered her voice. "I think it's only fair for me to tell you that if you decide to stay in the duplex, he'll make trouble for you." The guilt of how this affected those around her felt heavy in her chest. "I'm really sorry. I—"

"You stopped apologizing for your ex a long time ago, remember?"

Her air leaked from her lungs. "Seems to be a hard habit to break."

"Would help if he wasn't such a prick."

Savannah laughed, and the load on her shoulders lifted.

Jamison's next throw went wild, and Ian lunged left. The leather slapped his palm just a foot from the cruiser's rear window. Savannah's breath caught.

"Whoa," Ian said with a grin. "That was a close one."

He was quick, agile, athletic. And damn, that smile of his, one she didn't get to see often enough, was so sexy.

"Okay," Savannah said. "I think that's enough for today. My nerves are fried."

While Jamison complained and danced in the street, begging Ian for just one more grounder, Ian asked Savannah, "What's your ex so afraid of?"

"Losing control."

"Hasn't he already lost it?"

Savannah cut a look at the patrol car. "Does that look like freedom to you?"

Ian studied the car for a long, quiet moment. "My mom always told me you can't control what others do; you can only control how you react to it." He tossed the ball a foot in the air and caught it as Jamison ran toward them. "Why do you stay?"

"Sometimes there's too much power holding you down to have control over how you react."

"That's just flat-out wrong." A slow, sultry smile lifted his lips and heated his eyes. "But I'm feeling damn lucky you're staying put next door."

He held her gaze, thoughts churning behind his eyes. If they were anything like the ones rolling through her own head, the two of them should erupt in a fireball of spontaneous combustion. Savannah hadn't had thoughts like this in years. The raw power of them made her shaky.

Luckily, Jamison ran up to them, breaking the tense spell. His face was flushed, eyes sparkling, grinning ear to ear. It was the happiest Savannah had seen him in months.

He looked from Ian to Savannah, vibrating with excitement. "Can we paint now?"

6

E verly scanned the dingy office as Tim Baulder read over her résumé. She didn't expect to find anything labeled "Terrorist Ledger" lying around, but...hell, criminals were notoriously stupid.

The space reflected the man so perfectly, Baulder could have melted into the grungy fixtures. In his late fifties and forty pounds overweight, Baulder wore his dark hair, threaded with gray, too long and too limp. His skin had aged heavily during his years working outdoors, he hadn't shaved in about two weeks, and his sweatshirt and jeans were threadbare in places. In contrast, his navy parka with the Bishop Mining logo embroidered into the left upper chest looked brand-new.

"I'd say mines aren't the place for a woman," Baulder said, his gaze roaming the résumé, "but it looks like you've grown up in one."

"I've always worked best with men. Have four brothers," she lied.

"Your family still in Alberta?"

"They are."

He looked up from the paper, eyes narrowed and hard.

"These guys are rough around the edges. Pretty girl like you is bound to get harassed."

"Nothing I haven't dealt with before. Definitely not anything I can't handle."

"Awful sure of yourself."

Everly gave him a smile. Baulder was not impressed. He just turned his scowl back to the paper, shook his head, and finally leaned back in his chair with a restless air, like he was beyond ready for this interview—all ten minutes of it—to be over.

"I've got an admin position open," he said. "And an HR position coming up next month when the girl goes on maternity leave."

Everly swallowed a guffaw. Movement in the hallway beyond the office drew Everly's gaze. Lyle Bishop wandered in from the cold, pausing at the secretary's desk to collect messages.

Just the man she wanted to see.

When he turned and walked past Baulder's open doorway, Everly said, "I'm not looking for an office job, Mr. Baulder. I'm far more qualified for a management position in the field."

As expected, a woman's voice with that bold statement in a man's world stopped Bishop in his tracks. He scowled into the office. Everly gave him a flirty smile and swung her crossed leg as if she were wearing heels, not work boots. The fucker responded just like every man swayed by a grin—he turned toward the office and leaned his shoulder against the jamb.

"Those are bold words coming out of such a feminine woman's mouth."

Everly laughed and glanced down at herself in the most unfeminine outfit she'd ever worn—outside of fatigues, of course—an old, solid sweater, worn jeans, and steel-toed boots. "The more feminine I get, the bolder the words. Just imagine."

Bishop grinned. "Then it's a good thing for us you're not in stilettos."

"Hey, boss." Baulder stood and stretched. He moved like a man whose body had been injured and worn.

Bishop sauntered into the office, picked up Everly's résumé, and propped his ass against the edge of Baulder's desk. The two men were a study in contrast, Baulder overweight, wrinkled, and worn; Bishop lean and fit, youthful for his sixty-something age.

"Miss Everly Farrell." He let the words trail off as his gaze skimmed the paper. His amused grin transitioned into surprise. "Well, well..." He looked up, pinning her with a new expression, one of challenge. "What brings you to our humble company, Ms. Farrell?"

"Reputation, location, and work, I hope."

"You're a little...overqualified. Aren't you?"

"Only if you prefer to hire bottom-of-the-barrel employees."

He chuckled, pushed from the desk, and tipped his head toward the door. "Come on into my office. I'm sure you'll be able to tell me exactly where you think you fit in here."

Hooyah. She hadn't expected to get an in with Bishop so soon.

Everly stood and offered her hand to Baulder. "Thank you for your time, sir."

She followed Bishop to another office at the end of the hall. Still a rangy old hole with fake wood paneling and dirty industrial carpet, but bigger, with organized shelves, a clean desk, and a window that offered a truly stunning view of the jagged mountains that dwarfed Hazard.

She stood at the window, arms crossed, her back to Bishop. Couldn't hurt to have the man a little distracted for this conversation. "What a view."

"Sure is."

The tone of his voice—low and gruff—made Everly smile. Mission accomplished. When she turned, she found Bishop's gaze right where she'd wanted it—on her ass.

He looked up and met her gaze, unashamed of where his eyes had been. "Have a seat, Ms. Farrell."

"Call me Everly." She hated the cover name of Farrell, but she wouldn't have it long. She eased into a chair across from his desk, rested her elbows on the arms, threaded her fingers over her lap, and smiled.

She let her gaze travel leisurely over the bookcases and filing cabinets, but she didn't expect to see the alleged terrorist ledger here either. Sam had already scoured this place top to bottom when he'd placed the bugs.

"Everly." His tone was silky smooth, trying the word out as if he were tasting it. "Very nice." He tossed her résumé onto his desk and tapped a few computer keys before pulling a thumb drive from his laptop. Leaning back in his chair, he wrapped the short cord attached to the thumb drive around his wrist, then secured the bracelet by connecting the metal ends.

No fucking way. A geyser of giddy excitement pulsed through her body.

That was the ledger. He'd transferred the information from paper to computer and put it on a private drive. A drive he carried on him. No hacking. No discovery. No chance of loss. No risk. She'd bet her lovingly restored '93 Harley Heritage Softtail on it.

"Everly?"

"Yes," she responded, realizing she'd missed his question.

"Tell me about yourself."

"Thirty, Canadian, grew up working in the mines with my dad and brothers."

"Looks like you've had your share of jobs all over the world. Canada, Dominican Republic, Mexico, Africa?" He met her gaze again, eyes sharp and narrowed. "What are you lookin' for at our little mom-and-pop mine?"

"I've done my research. Bishop Mining is hardly a mom-and-pop establishment. Your gross annual revenue rivals that of mines three times your size. I'm qualified for several positions— team leader, mine foreman, project manager." She paused. "But I'm particularly interested in a position as safety officer."

"Safety officer," Bishop echoed, tipping his head. "Why?"

"Because you need one."

"We have one," he countered with challenge in his gaze.

"You need a new one."

He crossed his arms and held her gaze as thoughts churned through his dark eyes. The man had a menacing expression when he was serious. She could see how others would be easily intimidated by him, but Everly would have paid to be given the green light to fight him for the bracelet right then.

"How do you figure?" he asked.

"The mining world isn't all that big. And when you've been in it for as long as I have, traveling as I have, you get to know a lot of people. People who move around and climb the ranks. I happen to have an acquaintance who works for the Department of Labor in Mine Safety and Health Administration. He's told me that your latest death here, on top of the high number of severe machinery-related accidents over the last two years, has them looking at you for a serious investigation of safety practices."

That perked him up. "We haven't had a death—"

"It's all over town, boss. Someone named Mason?"

"He didn't die in a mining accident." Bishop's voice rose as he sat forward. "He was somewhere he wasn't supposed to be, on his own time, doing God knows what—"

"He was an employee of Bishop Mines. And his body was found in one of your tunnels. That makes his death one for the MSHA books."

Bishop dropped back in his chair, gaze sharp, mouth tight. "I haven't heard from MSHA."

"You will. Soon," she told him. "Sorry to be the bearer of bad news. But I really am here to help. One of my brothers died in a mine accident. A stupid accident that could have been prevented with minor precautions, which led me to become an expert in mining safety. Hiring me on as your safety manager would go a long way toward mollifying MSHA. Just like most government agencies, they're short staffed and overworked. I could make a call to my guy, let him know I'm on the job, persuade him to give me some time to get our ducks in a row. I could keep MSHA off your back and save you money at the same time."

"Save me money how?" He was definitely listening now. Looking at her as an information source rather than a sex object.

"Every dollar spent in prevention saves you three to six dollars in avoidance. And for every dollar you can see spent on injuries and illness, there's another five to fifty dollars in costs you don't see. By taking me on as your safety officer and letting me work my magic, I can save you money on both the visible and hidden costs associated with injuries—from workers' compensation and insurance to equipment damage and legal fees. And that doesn't account for the invisible benefits gained by providing the safest work environment possible like employee morale, longevity, and retention."

He threaded his fingers over his lap and regarded her with both awe and suspicion. "You talk a good game, little girl."

She smiled, purposely ignoring the nickname many women would have considered a slight. Everly was sure that had been purposeful on Bishop's part, checking to see if she'd rise to the bait.

"No, sir, I *play* a good game. In my last position as the safety officer at Prescott Mining in British Columbia, I brought home the Canadian Top Performer award for a combination of the highest productivity rate and the best safety rating. I'm proud to say that Prescott went from one of the worst safety offenders to maintaining a zero-incident accident rating for the last fifteen months in a row."

His eyes had narrowed. "That's impressive. So impressive, it's almost unbelievable."

It was, in fact, beyond unbelievable—it was untrue, at least the part about Everly having anything to do with that success. But with Manhunters spliced into Prescott Mining's switchboard, she knew she'd have the references to back up her lies.

"Please call my former boss for confirmation," she suggested. "But don't be surprised if you're stuck on the phone while he negotiates to get me back."

"Why leave such a successful job?"

"I've put them on the right path and trained my replacement to keep them there. I'm ready for a new challenge."

Bishop rested his elbows on the arms of his chair, clasped his hands, and ran his thumb across his bottom lip. "Your offer is tempting."

"But?"

"But my current safety manager is a lifelong friend. We grew up together, worked my family's mines together, much the way you did with your father and brothers."

"Loyalty. I respect that." She paused, then threw in the wrench. "But loyalty won't get MSHA off your back."

"What if I hired you to train him to attain your level of success in the realm of safety?"

After a moment, Everly said, "I'd be open to that arrangement —if I enjoyed the same benefits as others who signed a year-long contract with you."

"Ah." He chuckled and dropped his arms to his chair. "Now I see. The work-visa program."

"More specifically, what comes at the end of the work-visa program."

His suspicion was back. "You have a history as a nomad. You're still young. What would make you want to settle in the States permanently?"

In translation: Why would she want a US passport?

Everly held his gaze for a long moment, working up her emotions so she came off as sincere. She lowered her gaze and cleared her throat. "I have a son. He's seven, and he has cystic fibrosis." She met his gaze again. "Up until a year ago, our medical coverage in Canada covered his needs. But the disease has progressed to a level where he needs specialty care. I'm sure you've heard of the limitations in our health care when people are in need of urgent care from a specialist."

"I have quite a few Canadians working for me," he said. "And they tell me that the rumors regarding lousy Canadian health care aren't true."

"Then they've never had aggressive cancer or needed urgent surgery or struggled with a rapidly worsening disease. Don't get me wrong. General, routine health care in Canada is good. But my son is beyond that level of care. There is an amazing specialist right here in Montana, teaching at the medical school in Bozeman."

"I admire your dedication to your son."

"I don't need admiration, Mr. Bishop. I need a job that can supply me with the means to stay in this country to get the best medical care for my boy. And I promise you, I'll make it worth your while by bringing exemplary safety and increased profit to Bishop Mining." When he still hesitated, Everly said, "How 'bout this? I'll work the first month free. If you like what you see, you can put me on salary and pay me for the previous month. If you don't, I'll walk away, no harm, no foul."

Bishop laughed and shook his head. "I sure like the way you think."

He offered his hand across the desk, and Everly's gaze fixed on the USB bracelet. The latch had a safety lock. It wouldn't be coming off by accident. If she took it from him now and the names weren't on it, she'd have blown the whole mission.

Patience.

Bishop grinned at her. "You've got yourself a deal."

SAVANNAH SAT at the curb outside the sheriff's department headquarters, idling in Misty's Subaru. The car was almost as beat-up and worn-out as Savannah's, but the heater still worked, so she couldn't complain. Her heart thumped hard and quick. Her mind toiled around all that could go wrong with this little escapade. But she had to be proactive if she didn't want to live the rest of her life at the whim of a narcissist. If she wanted to keep her son.

It was time to turn the tables on Hank. Time to hunt the hunter. The task might be well outside her expertise, but she'd learned a thing or two over her years with Hank. And wouldn't it piss him off to know she was using his own techniques to plan a counterattack?

She checked the dashboard clock and found it only two minutes later than the last time she checked: 7:44 p.m. Sighing, she adjusted the heater vent to blow warm air on her feet, rested her head against the seat, and let her eyes close for a moment. "You can do this," she murmured. "You *have* to do this."

A muffled voice in the distance pulled her eyes open, and she found Hank jogging down the front steps of the station, talking on his phone while he pulled on his parka. By the time he reached his cruiser, he'd finished his call and stuffed his phone into the pocket of his jacket.

Savannah's heart skipped, and she second-guessed her idea to follow him. She couldn't even imagine what he'd say—or do—if he caught her. But that thought reminded her exactly why she was doing this: so neither she nor Jamison would ever have to worry about Hank's moods or abuse again.

With renewed purpose, Savannah slid low in the driver's seat as Hank pulled out of the station parking lot and turned toward downtown. There were still a few cars on the road at this hour, and it was fully dark, so she felt relatively safe following a few car lengths back. But a few minutes later, when he pulled into the empty parking lot of the Episcopalian church, Savannah had to drive past and double back. She pulled to the curb half a block away, close enough to see that Hank wasn't in the cruiser but had left his car running.

"What in the hell could you want in there?" she murmured.

The adorable little church stayed open until eight every night, but Savannah knew Hank hadn't ducked into the building to pray. He reappeared within minutes, carrying a small, dark bag.

"What have you got?" she wondered. Though even if she found out what he was doing here, even if she discovered it was something illegal, unethical, or immoral, she'd have a damn difficult time proving it in any way that would give her leverage. At least not in this county.

She was disheartened that this escapade hadn't netted her any more usable information. But knowledge was power. And Savannah needed every ounce of power she could get. Maybe, in time, those ounces would add up to something substantial enough to get out from under his control. She wouldn't know if she didn't try.

So when Hank returned to his car and left the parking lot, headed toward downtown, Savannah followed.

Another few minutes' drive and they were on Main Street. Hank parked again, this time across the street from The Busy Bean, his favorite coffee haunt. Excitement darted through her veins. This was her chance.

She quickly found a spot at the curb several cars back, shut off the lights but left the car running, and waited as Hank crossed the street and slipped inside the coffee hut just before close. As soon as the shop's door shut behind him, Savannah hopped out of the car and hurried to the sidewalk, crouching to hide herself behind other parked vehicles. When she reached the passenger's side of the cruiser, she searched for Hank inside the shop and found him leaning on the counter, flirting with one of the pretty girls who worked there.

Perfect. His coffee would take at least fifteen minutes. Now, if Hank's other habits just held up...

Savannah reached for the passenger's door handle. The cold metal cut right through her mittens. She said a quick prayer and pulled on the lever. The door opened, and a thrill spiked through Savannah. Hank's arrogance had paid off for once. He believed he was invincible.

"Yes," she whispered before taking one more look at the café, then bending to search the cruiser's interior.

She found the bag almost immediately. He'd left it on the passenger's floorboard. Her heart skipped as she pulled the bag onto the seat. It was light, maybe a pound or two. The bag itself wasn't dark, as she'd first thought. It was a clear ziplock bag—the contents were dark.

She reached in and grabbed what felt like rigid booklets. Dragging one out, she tipped the dark cover toward the overhead light. The gold embossing flashed back at her with the word PASSPORT and the seal of an eagle.

Savannah grabbed a few more booklets. All passports. She opened one to the identification page and found a photo of Benjamin Reiz. Confused, she pulled out another, this one for Omar Sarak. And a third for Martin Clark.

"What the hell?" she murmured. Her mind was still spinning while she dragged out her phone and took quick pictures of the three passports, then the bag filled with them. She had no idea what this meant, but her gut told her it was wrong.

She scrambled to put everything back the way she'd found it. She needed to get back to the car before—

The passenger's door flew wide, and cold air washed her back. Savannah gasped just before a hand clamped over her mouth. Panic broke open, spilling through her chest. Her captor pulled her back against a body like steel and dropped to a crouch. Her fight response was automatic, and she twisted and pushed to get the man off her.

"Shh," he whispered at her ear. "It's me, Ian."

Savannah's fear receded, but uncertainty lingered. Her heart kicked in her chest and hammered in her ears. She tried to tell him to let her go, but her demand came out a garbled nothing behind his hand.

"He's coming," Ian murmured at her ear, releasing the hand around her waist to shut the car door quietly. "Be quiet, or we'll both end up in jail tonight."

The sound of Hank's boots clomped on the asphalt. A surge of fear cut through her body like ice. Instead of pushing against Ian, she curled into herself, and his weight pushed her closer to the sidewalk.

Her breath came in short pants. She tilted her head toward the ground to conceal the telltale billows in the air. She swore she felt every heartbeat kick her ribs as Hank got into the cruiser. Swore time slowed as she waited for the engine to start. Then for him to pull away from the curb.

Once he was gone, relief swamped her. She would have crumpled to the ground if Ian wasn't there to pull her to her feet.

"Where's your car?" he asked.

She glanced that direction. "There."

"I don't see—"

"It's Misty's."

He wrapped his arm around her shoulders and started that direction. "What in the fuck are you trying to do? Get yourself hurt?"

She didn't answer, her mind a jumble of thoughts in the wake of the adrenaline rush.

Ian walked her to the driver's side and pushed her in with "Don't go anywhere" before rounding the car and climbing in the passenger's side.

"What are you doing here?" she asked.

"I was at the grocery store," he told her. "A better question is what the hell were you doing?"

She shook her head. "I don't want you to get—"

"Involved? Too late. Why would you take a risk like that? You have to know he'd jump at the opportunity to throw you in jail."

"I... I..." How to explain? She took a breath. "I overheard him fighting with Lyle about something Hank was supposed to do tonight at eight. I thought I could catch him doing something I could use against him in a custody hearing."

Ian exhaled hard. "Well, did you?"

She shook her head and gave a shrug. "I don't know. He had a bag of passports in his car. He picked them up at the church on Ninth and Main. I can't see how I would use that against him."

Ian's expression shifted, and the intensity of his focus shivered down her spine. "Passports? Are you sure?"

She dragged her phone from her pocket and pulled up the images she'd taken. "You tell me."

He took her phone and inspected the images, enlarging them to view the photos and names, asking, "How many were there?"

"I don't know, maybe ten or twelve?"

"Do you know these guys?"

"In the passports? Sure. Everyone comes into the café at some point."

He glanced up. "How long have they been in town?"

She heaved a breath and looked out the windshield, thinking. "About a year, I guess."

Ian nodded and tapped on the share function.

"What are you doing?" she asked.

"Forwarding them to myself. I might be able to do some research. These may be more valuable against Hank than you thought."

"I don't see how they can help either one of us, but, whatever. I've gotta go. I have to pick up my car and get Jamison at a playdate."

Ian handed her phone back. When she took it, he used his free hand to cover her own. "Savannah, please don't do this again. If you have suspicions, need information, or want to track Hank, come to me. I have experience in this kind of thing, and it would be better for me to get caught. You have Jamison to think about."

She didn't know what to think of that offer. She certainly didn't know him well enough to trust him in that way, but she nodded, ready to get her son and get home. "Thank you."

7

Ian was knuckles deep in the engine of a sheriff's cruiser when his cell rang. He put the ratchet down, wiped his hands on a rag, and glanced around for Mo. His temporary new boss was in the office, so Ian picked up the call from Everly.

"Hey." He wandered toward the heater near the partially open bay door. "What's up?"

"I'm in at the mine. Start tomorrow. I just talked to Sam. Reiz and Sarak are Bosnian. Clark's Canadian," she confirmed the team's suspicions. "None of them have ever possessed a US passport, nor do any of them qualify for one. But none are on any terrorist watch list."

Still, excitement tingled through his gut. One step closer.

"No irregularities have popped up on Hank's financials yet," Everly told him, "but Lyle has been sending a monthly stipend to an anonymous bank account—through Bitcoin."

"Fucking Bitcoin." The virtual-cash payment system was a favorite among privacy-seeking individuals. "Next thing you'll tell me is that they're using a mixing service."

"*Ding-ding-ding*, you win."

Ian swore and leaned his shoulder against the wall. Bitcoin's anonymity was hard enough to hack, but add a company that served as an escrow account, mixing all incoming funds before distributing them again, and you had a virtual money-laundering service. One that was beyond difficult to track.

The image of the little black box sitting near Savannah's computer popped into his head. Ian's brain made quick, automatic connections, but the idea of Savannah paying Lyle Bishop for anything made him balk.

He still found himself saying, "Not the same company—"

"That Savannah uses for internet privacy?" Everly said. "No."

He exhaled with relief. A second later, a sheriff's cruiser pulled into the driveway at Mo's.

"I gotta go," he told Everly before disconnecting and returning to his work.

Mo came out of the office. He was in his midfifties, but like so many others in this part of the country, the man looked older. His crown of salt-and-pepper hair showed beneath the rim of his knit cap, and his jaw hadn't seen a razor in days.

He took one look at the customer and told Ian, "Good time to take lunch, son."

Ian lowered his head to peer through the gap created by the open hood. Hank Bishop sauntered toward the garage bay in uniform, rocking his black felt cowboy hat into place.

Fuck that. "I've got a lot of work here, Mo—"

"Lunch is a better use of your time. This won't take long." He held Ian's gaze an extra moment before turning to Hank. "Afternoon, Sheriff."

"Mo." Hank stopped at the driver's door, his hard warning gaze on Ian. "We've got some business to discuss."

"Ian," Mo said with a go-on tilt of his head.

Retreating went against everything Ian believed in. Everything he was made of. But he straightened from the car and settled the ratchet in the toolbox at his side. "I'll just grab a quick bite."

Wiping his hands with a rag, Ian exited the back door, leaving it slightly ajar. He pressed his back to the exterior wall and rested his head near the gap. Without the cranking space heater warming the garage, the cold sank into Ian's bones.

"How's business?" Hank asked.

"Busy. What can I help you with, Sheriff?"

"I'm just gonna get right to the point, Mo. You need to fire him."

Fucker. Even though Ian had known it was coming, the order still pissed him off.

"Why's that?" Mo asked.

"Just tell him you made a mistake. That you don't need him."

"I didn't make a mistake," Mo hit back, deepening Ian's respect for the man. "And I do need him. My arthritis is actin' up. Can't do everything I used to."

"Find someone else," Hank told him.

"I've tried two other guys with half his experience. Neither worked out. I'll oversee him until I know he's reliable, but being he's just out of the military where he worked on anything with an engine, I'm guessing he knows even more than I do."

"I don't care how much experience he's got. I don't want him working on sheriff's department vehicles."

Motherfucker. The man knew exactly how to exploit a weakness.

"You know somethin' I don't?" Mo asked.

"Not anything I can repeat. Just trust me—you don't want him here."

"If he's bad news, he'll show his colors soon enough."

"I haven't made myself clear." Hank hooked his thumbs in his duty belt and leaned toward Mo, his voice clearly carrying a threat. "This is not a discussion. It's an order. *Fire. Him.*"

"I've been running this shop since you were in diapers, Hank. And I own my own business so I don't have to take orders. The fact that you think I will is both arrogant and disrespectful." Mo lifted his chin in defiance. "This about Ian working on the cars? Or about Ian living next door to Savannah?"

"Just fucking fire the guy, Mo." Hank's voice dropped, raspy around the edges with frustration. "Or I'll find another garage to handle the maintenance contract for the department's vehicles."

"Fuck," Ian whispered.

"Good luck with that," Mo told him. "I doubt you're going to want to drive every car in your fleet to and from Whitefish for maintenance."

Ian didn't need to hear any more. It was almost three o'clock, and he hadn't stopped to do anything but piss since six a.m.

He took a side street so he didn't have to enter the garage again and walked to the diner. As soon as the thought of food and Savannah entered his mind, he was starving. For both.

He approached the café, disappointed when he didn't see her car. But when he walked in, he found her standing near the counter, pulling off the apron around her waist where she carried pens, straws, and an order pad.

The bell signaled his arrival, and she glanced over. Her face lit up, creating a sparkle in her eyes. "Well, hey there." She turned away from Misty and leaned her hip against the counter. "Didn't see you this morning. Are you making yourself breakfast now that you have a kitchen?"

Damn, she had a great smile. Considering all the hell her ex-husband and ex-in-laws had put her through, how many men came and went in this town, he didn't know how she could take to him so fast or be so friendly. If he were in her shoes, he'd be homicidal, which would be a very bad thing for everyone, considering how much training he'd had in killing people.

He also knew that if Savannah ever found out who and what he really was, he'd never see her smile at him like this again. The thought created a pang in his gut. A painful one. Ian needed to check his barriers.

"I burn water," he told her. "I wanted to get a jump start on my first day with Mo. But now I'm so hungry, I could eat the bear that left tracks behind the house."

Her smile melted away. "What bear?"

"There were tracks in the snow when I took the trash out this morning." He could see her mind turning. Hoped that information would give her pause when she thought about bailing out the back window with Jamison again.

"Oh," she said. "I didn't see them."

"Don't worry, I'll build an enclosure. That might not keep them from sniffing around, but it'll keep them from making a mess."

"Okay. We're a little tight on cash for materials, but I'm happy to help build it. I can handle a hammer well enough."

"I don't doubt that." He'd bet she could handle more than a hammer. Divorcing an abusive, overbearing man. Raising a boy on her own. Living in this frozen wasteland. Battling powerful in-laws. Yeah, he'd trust her to get the job done. "I need to wash my hands. Will you be here when I get back, or are you leaving for the day?"

"My shift's over," she said. "But I'll get you started. Coke?"

"And water. Thank you. Be right back." In the restroom, he washed his hands and face, returning to find Savannah carrying two glasses toward the nearly empty dining room. He glanced around. "Where do you want me?"

"Anywhere you'd like."

"Now there's a dangerous proposal," he muttered under his breath. He'd first and foremost like to be in her bed. But other places instantly came to mind—the kitchen counter, the shower, the floor... He slid into a chair at the nearest table. "Do you have time to join me?"

She set the drinks on the table, and her gaze jumped to his before it traveled around the café. Finally, she exhaled, rubbing her hands down the thighs of her jeans. "Sure, I guess. For a minute."

Savannah eased to the edge of a chair across from him as Misty wandered up to the table. Her hazel eyes moved between them, and a slow smile lifted her mouth. "You two look good together."

"Misty," Savannah snapped, almost before Misty had finished the remark.

She held up her hands. "Just sayin'. What can I get you, handsome?"

He ordered a burger, and Misty returned to the kitchen.

"Sorry about that," Savannah said, still on the edge of her seat, as if she were about to jump to her feet. "She's a consummate matchmaker. It never ends."

"Doesn't bother me." He picked up his water glass.

She tipped her head. "It seems like not much does."

He shrugged and drank down half the glass of water. "Life's too short to get ruffled by the little stuff."

She smiled. Seemed to relax a little. "So, Mo finally let you out of the cave to eat?"

"Yeah." He laughed and set his glass down. "He's got one busy shop."

"Only game in town."

"True." Maybe he'd have a job when he returned to the shop after all. He sat back with a sigh, letting his sore muscles relax.

She glanced around before lowering her voice to ask, "Did you find out anything about the passports?"

"Only that they're forged."

She sucked in a surprised breath. "Are you sure? How can you tell?"

"I sent the information to a friend I served with overseas. He does contract work for the government now. He looked into the names of the men in the passports and found that not only weren't they eligible for a passport, none of them had even applied for one."

She met his gaze steadily, but her mind was in another place. "Misty told me she'd heard of ways to get a fake passport."

"How would Misty know?"

"Her boyfriend works in the mine. Word travels."

"Why would Misty think to tell you that?"

Savannah refocused, shook her head, and averted her gaze. He saw the lie coming before she even answered. "Just conversation."

"Savannah."

She pulled in a deep breath and exhaled slowly. "We were just tossing around worst-case-scenario ideas." She stared at the table. "I can't lose Jamison."

He wanted to reassure her, promise her she'd never lose him, but Ian didn't have enough information to offer her that reassurance. "I can understand. He's a great kid. And you're a great mother."

Her smile was quick but shy. "Thanks. He's..." She shook her head. "He's everything to me. My whole world."

"The way it ought to be." He paused before testing deeper waters. "Do you have family in town?"

"Oh no." She shifted in the chair, rested her forearms on the table, and leaned forward, dropping her chin into one hand. "I don't really have family. I mean, my mom's still alive, but she has another family. We parted ways a long time ago."

"Did you grow up here?" he asked, easing her toward confiding in him.

"No. Los Angeles, then Michigan."

"What brought you here?"

"Hank." A shadow darkened her eyes, and her gaze went distant. "We met at U of M."

"University of Michigan?"

She nodded. "He was a different man then."

"What changed?"

"Moving here." She met his gaze, serious, sober. "This place, his father, the job. All of it. Over the last few years, he's become a man I don't recognize at all."

"Why do you stay? Why not move to another town where he can't harass you?"

She laughed, but the sound wasn't humorous. "I think you've figured out by now that he wouldn't take to that idea." She shook her head. "Besides, that's a looooong, messy story."

"I'd like to hear it." He leaned forward and rested his arms on the table, holding her gaze. He knew this was a long shot, but if he could get her alone, somewhere she felt safe, he might get a lot of information. "Over dinner? Sometime this weekend?"

Her gaze jumped to his, surprised. Color flushed her cheeks. "Oh..." She shook her head. "Um..."

"Mo told me about some hole-in-the-wall in Whitefish I have to try. Says it's the best barbeque in the state."

A smile quivered over her mouth. "Smoke." She nodded. "It's amazing. Haven't been there in so long..."

"Does Jamison ever stay with his father?"

"Rarely." The mention of Hank killed her smile. "He uses work as an excuse to get out of taking him. He's supposed to take Jamison Friday night, but he hasn't come through on anything in so long—"

"Friday's perfect," he said before she could give him a definitive no. "Pick you up at six?"

"Like I said, he's not the most reliable when it comes to Jamison. Besides, I don't really, you know, date."

Her rejection niggled beneath his ribs, a sure sign he was crossing that professional-personal line. Ian reined in his desire and refocused. She was a source of information, nothing more. "Because Hank doesn't want you to date?"

Her gaze slid away with traces of embarrassment and disappointment. "No. Kind of. It's...complicated."

"He's your ex. You're a free woman. An attractive, sweet, free woman." Her gaze jumped back to his, assessing, as if she didn't believe him. "And I'd really like to get to know you better."

She smiled, threaded her fingers, and rested her hands on the table. "I like you, Ian. I really do. Every other man in town lets Hank bully them into compliance. Which is why I'm saying no." She shook her head. "This is your fresh start, and I don't want Hank to ruin it."

"You mean like trying to get me fired on my first day?"

Her spine straightened; her eyes widened. "What?"

"I only left the shop to get something to eat because Hank was giving Mo an earful about me."

"No." She breathed the word, clearly stricken.

"Unfortunately, yes."

"Oh my God, I'm so—"

He pressed his index finger to her lips to halt the apology. They were soft and supple. And Ian had an urgent and immediate need to feel them under his own.

His gaze dropped to her perfect lips beneath his thick, rough, calloused finger, and something raw and primal clawed low in his gut. He couldn't deny it—he wanted her.

When she didn't move away from his touch, Ian forced himself to lower his hand. But it drifted to hers, covering hers with a reassuring squeeze. Again, she didn't pull away.

"No more apologizing for him," Ian told her. "You make Jamison take responsibility for his words and actions. Hold Hank accountable. He's a grown man who makes his own choices. In truth, he's nothing more than your average bully; you said it yourself. But he's messing with the most important things in your life —your freedom and your son. It's not right. I don't care how he tries to hurt me, I'm not backing down. Believe me, baby, I've dealt with assholes far worse than Hank."

The endearment had come out automatically, but it felt right. He was on a slippery slope into dangerous territory with this woman. If he didn't watch his step, he'd find himself in a landslide.

"So, dinner," he said, more a statement than a question. "Friday."

She lowered her gaze to their hands and stroked the side of his little finger with her thumb. The gesture was so sweet, it pinched something deep in Ian's gut and spread tingles up his arm. Her gaze met his again. "It would take planning..."

He grinned, far too happy with this small measure of progress. "Then you're with the right guy."

SAVANNAH CHECKED her appearance for what felt like the hundredth time. She slid her hands down the front of the wrap-around sweater she'd borrowed from Misty. It was so soft, she couldn't keep from touching it. It also made her waist look small, her breasts full. Coupled with her one pair of nice jeans and a trendy pair of Misty's boots, Savannah saw a different woman looking back at her from the mirror in the living room. A trendy, sexy woman.

Misty had insisted she wear her hair down, and added a touch of makeup to Savannah's eyes, cheeks, and lips. The overall effect made Savannah remember what life had been like before everything went south with Hank. When she was carefree in college. When she had friends and fun in her life. When her whole future lay ahead of her. When anything was possible.

The tingle of impending tears tickled her nose. She tugged at the white cami peeking from under the sweater, trying to cover a little more cleavage. "I should cancel."

Misty looked up from the puzzle she and Jamison were working on. "What? *Why?*"

She glanced at Jamison and found him oblivious, his tongue stuck out at the corner of his mouth as he tried to find the perfect fit for a puzzle piece. Instead of meeting Misty's gaze, she looked at herself again. "What's the point?"

Misty stood from where she sat on the floor at the coffee table and stepped up behind Savannah. Her friend had plugged in her portable speaker to her cell phone, and a mix of country and rock played through the living room.

"Nerves are normal." Misty's voice was low, for Savannah's ears only. She reached around and drew Savannah's hair off her shoulders, letting it fall down her back. "It means you're alive. It means you like him."

"It means I could get hurt," Savannah countered. "Or that I could hurt someone else."

"You told him to come around back, right?"

"He figured it out by himself. It still surprises me that he hasn't run screaming from Hank's threats."

"It doesn't surprise me. You're worth it. And the fact that he's jumping through the hoops Hank creates only mean's he's willing to take the risk for you. The least you could do is return the favor." Misty wrapped her arms around Savannah's waist and rested her chin on her shoulder, meeting her gaze in the mirror. "Because without risk, there's no life. You've lived in captivity long enough." Then she grinned and lowered her voice another notch. "And if you cancel on sex on a stick, *I'm* going to dinner with him."

Savannah laughed and elbowed Misty. "Shut up."

Her friend stepped back and stroked Savannah's hair one more time. "I will. Just watch me. He's way too hot to be stood up."

Savannah grinned at Misty's tease and turned away from the mirror. A knock sounded on the back door, and Savannah's smile stiffened. An effervescent sizzle coursed through her chest—nerves, excitement, fear.

She met Misty's gaze. Her friend shot Savannah a bright, excited smile. Jamison popped to his feet. He was dressed in his shoes and his jacket, ready to hit the road. "Mr. Ian's here, Mommy."

And he ran through the kitchen to the back door.

"Hey, buddy." Ian's rich voice drifted into the house and jumbled Savannah's stomach. "You look like you're ready for ice cream."

"Come see my puzzle."

He was as excited to see Ian as Savannah. The fact that she'd seen him every day didn't seem to diminish the thrill either. In fact, they seemed to have developed a silent method of communication. A look, a smile, a simple word or phrase conveyed mutual interest and pleasure over seeing each other.

Ian walked through the kitchen, his hand on Jamison's head, his gaze on her son's exuberant face. Savannah suddenly didn't have anything to do with her hands and stuffed them in her back pockets.

He wore dark jeans, boots, an inky thermal beneath his parka. A day's worth of stubble darkened his jaw, but his hair looked wet, like he'd just stepped out of the shower. The thought lit a spark beneath Savannah's ribs. As he passed through her small kitchen, she was reminded of just how big he was—easily six two, easily two hundred pounds of muscle. The sight of this sexy man, in her house, willing to jump through hoops just to spend a couple of hours with her, kicked off a flurry of emotions—disbelief, gratitude, excitement. And again, fear.

But she'd taught herself a long time ago that if she didn't face the fear and do what terrified her anyway, she'd never grow. Never escape. Never be free.

Ian grinned down at Jamison, his eyes glittering with joviality over her son's excitement. In that moment, she felt herself fall a little in love with the man.

When he looked up, his gaze traveled over Savannah and his smile transitioned into something other than amusement. Something more like surprise edged with desire. Jamison grabbed his hand and tried to pull him toward the coffee table, but Ian didn't seem to even hear him. He just stared at Savannah, his smile hot and wildly seductive.

"Wow," he said while Jamison added traction to his grip on Ian's hand. "You look great."

She smiled. "Thanks. You too."

"Come see," Jamison said, undeterred by Ian's distraction. "Aunt Misty helped me get the frame done."

Ian smiled, amused by Jamison's demands for attention. He finally sauntered through the living room, said hello to Misty, and stood over the coffee table, looking at Jamison's puzzle. He dropped into a crouch and made suggestions for a few piece placements, letting Jamison revel in the thrill of making the connections himself. Savannah's heart softened a little more.

Misty cleared her throat. When Savannah tore her gaze from Ian and Jamison to meet Misty's gaze, she mouthed *Yum* with an expression as equally astonished as Savannah felt every time she saw the man. And that made her laugh.

Ian glanced over his shoulder with a grin that made Savannah's knees weak. "What are you two giggling about?"

Savannah pressed her lips together and shook her head.

Misty sat on the edge of a chair and pulled on her snow boots. "I'm in the mood for a banana split. What about you, Jamison?"

"Watermelon sherbet," he said, followed by both him and Misty saying at the same time, "with the candy seeds."

While everyone readied themselves to go their separate ways according to plan, what-ifs tumbled through Savannah's mind. What if this date was a major fail? What if they started a relationship but her infatuation fizzled? What if his interest faded? What if Hank became too much of a pain in the ass for Ian to deal with? What if she fell for him but he bailed on her? What if he cheated? Lied? Broke Jamison's heart? Broke hers?

Misty stood and tossed her jacket around her shoulders,

pushing her arms into the sleeves. "Don't" was all she had to say
to bring Savannah's mind to a halt.

Savannah pulled in a deep breath and let it out slowly,
clearing the negative thoughts from her head.

Ian pushed to his feet, turned, and gave Savannah a steady,
reassuring smile. "Ready to do this?"

"Yeah!" Jamison was the first to yell, popping to his feet.
"Misty's going to show me her dad's bubble machine."

Ian lifted a brow. "Bubble machine?"

"My dad had a few screws loose," Misty said. "He was a
mostly amateur inventor. The farm is chock-full of the strangest
gadgets. In honor of Jamison's overnighter, I pulled his bubble
machine from the barn and played with it until I got it working
again."

Savannah said her goodbyes and stood in the partially open
doorway, waving, as Jamison and Misty climbed into Misty's car.
She felt Ian come up behind her. Hidden from the deputy's sight,
Ian ran his hand up Savannah's back, under her hair, and gave
her neck a gentle squeeze.

Every inch of her body reacted like he'd thrown an ON
switch, lighting her up.

"You smell so good." His murmur sounded soft in her ear just
before he pressed a kiss to the top of her head. The gesture was so
sweet, her eyes fell closed, and her chest swelled. Savannah
leaned back and found him there, a rock of stability and strength.

What would it be like to have this in my life every day?

She couldn't begin to imagine and cut herself off from fanta-
sizing about something that had such a slim chance of happening. She shored herself up and gave a final wave as Misty pulled
away from the curb.

Ian's hand slid down Savannah's back again, then around her
hip, his forearm stretching across her waist and pulling her fully
up against him. She pulled in a sharp breath of surprise, of pleasure. "I haven't been able to stop thinking about you."

The moment was so decadent, her eyes closed again as she soaked in the feel of him. The sensation of being wanted. The sound of the cruiser's engine turning over pried her eyes open. Deputy Sandberg flipped on the headlights and pulled away from the curb.

"Did he follow?" Ian's voice sounded low and rough.

"Yes."

"Are you still interested in trying Smoke?"

Even though everything in her wanted to turn in Ian's arms and kiss him until neither of them could think about anything other than getting naked, she said, "Yes. We should go before someone comes to take Sandberg's place."

"Roger that." Ian stepped back, releasing her. When she turned, he took her hand and started toward the back door, pausing to press the button on the television, turning it on. "Little noise will add to the illusion that you're home."

He pulled her through the kitchen and out the back door to his waiting truck, which was already running. Opening the door for her, he helped her into the warm interior and rounded the hood to the driver's side.

Instead of securing his seat belt, he scooted to the center of the bench seat and cupped her face with one big warm hand. "I need to get this out of the way or I won't be able to think about anything else all through dinner."

He slowly drew her forward, his gaze lowered to her mouth. Savannah pulled in a quick breath of surprise just before his lips pressed hers. She instantly hyperfocused on the moment. To the feel of his firm lips against hers. To the way he kissed her, tilted his head a little more, and kissed her again. The warmth of his tongue as it slid over her bottom lip, into her mouth, teasing her until she met it with her own.

She'd long forgotten the feel of a man's mouth on hers. Wondered if anyone had ever kissed her so seductively before. Considered changing her mind about going anywhere...

He pulled back long before she was ready and left her tantalized and aching. She smiled and pressed a hand to his cheek, brushing her fingers over the stubble and reveling in the wholly male feel of it. "Now *I* won't be able to think about anything else all through dinner."

He grinned, quick and bright. "My job here is done."

And he moved behind the wheel, secured his seat belt, and put the truck into Drive, all while smiling at her like they had a new secret.

8

So far, so good.

Ian was surprised by just how receptive Savannah was after all she'd been through. What he continued to put her through. Her resiliency, warmth, and trust humbled him. The only thing that kept him from feeling like a complete user was the fact that he was intensely attracted to the woman.

He shut down his emotions, compartmentalizing this outing as his job. He was doing his part to catch and stop terrorists who killed thousands of innocents. None of this was real. Savannah was out with the man she thought he was, not the man he really was.

Once he'd turned onto the main road headed out of town with no tail, Ian patted the seat next to him. "Slide on over here, beautiful."

She hesitated, then unfastened her seat belt, moved to the center of the bench, and belted herself in beside him. He loved having her close. Loved the easy, feminine heat of her. The jasmine-and-sunshine smell of her.

He squeezed her knee and let his hand rest on her thigh. "It was nice of Misty to take Jamison tonight."

"He loves her. She's always pulling some new crazy gadget from her father's stash to entertain him. She's a good friend. My only friend, really." She smiled at him. "Thanks for this. It's the first time in years I've felt like a real person."

He squeezed her knee. "My pleasure."

She leaned into him and covered his hand with hers.

Ian threaded their fingers, fighting to concentrate on the job and not how *damn right* this felt. "So...the story."

"Story?" She glanced at him.

"Yeah. The reason you stay in town instead of moving away from your shithead of an ex."

"Oh, that." Her gaze returned out the window. "If you don't discover the answer to that question before we reach the restaurant, I'll tell you then."

So they were conducting the same test—to see how far outside the county line they could get while her surveillance teams thought she was home. Interesting. The gears of Ian's mind turned. Was he merely a means to an end? An unwitting accomplice in her attempt to run? It shouldn't bother him—especially given he was using her the same way—but it still did.

"What did you major in at Michigan?" he asked, going for something nonthreatening to open routes of communication.

"Child development. Thought I might like teaching. What branch of the military were you with?"

"Army," he said, even though there was no right answer to that question. The Manhunters were an entity unto themselves. Men and women recruited and trained for extraction and elimination and funded by the classified black-ops budget. Most likely the same budget that funded Roman's team. "Why aren't you teaching school here?"

"I didn't finish my degree. Hank was a couple of years ahead of me. He was going to find a job in Ann Arbor after he graduated so I could finish, but his mom came down with early Alzheimer's.

He moved back to be with her and support his dad. I thought I'd transfer to a college here and finish up with some online classes or outreach programs."

"What happened?" he asked.

She shrugged and stared out at the pavement illuminated by the headlights. "I got caught up in taking care of his mother. Hank got caught up in the job. I got pregnant."

"So, life."

She smiled. "Yeah. Life. I still want to go back to college at some point. If I return to Michigan, I'll only need a year to finish. If I go somewhere else, I'll probably need two years. Not sure if I still want to be a teacher, but I want to get my degree."

"You'd make a good teacher."

"What makes you say that?"

He shrugged. "The way you are with Jamison. The way you treat your customers. You're patient, good-natured, positive. Kids need that."

She thought for a moment. "You're great with Jamison." She hesitated, then asked, "Do you have kids?"

"Me?" He laughed and shook his head. Kids meant having a woman. Women required maintenance, security, trust, an emotional investment. None of that suited his lifestyle. "No. No kids."

"I guess it would be hard to have a family when you're in the military."

"Takes special people to make that work."

"Why did you leave? You can't be old enough to have retired."

"The military has special programs for certain branches and units. When they're downsizing, they allow retirement with fifteen years in. My mom got sick, and I took leave to care for her. When it was time to go back to work, my job had been given to one of the kids coming in at eighteen and nineteen."

"That's not right."

He laughed at her indignant tone. "It's a young man's game, but I miss it. They offered me a job as an instructor, but after being in the field so long..." He shrugged. "I don't know. It doesn't exactly suit me."

As the county line approached, Ian checked his rearview mirror. No other lights shone on the highway, and a smile curved his lips. He might just get a decent date out of the night after all. "What happened between you and your mom?"

"Oh..." She drew out the word with a whimsical smile. "That's a little bizarre."

"I've seen bizarre. Try me."

She exhaled. "She's part of the Church of Scientology."

"Really." He hoped he sounded as surprised as when he'd heard it the first time.

Savannah nodded. "I actually grew up in the movement. I don't know how familiar you are with Scientology, but when adults enter the church, they give up their children to be raised by others. They brainwash you from the very beginning. Feed you lies, make you fearful of outsiders, and raise children to serve the congregation and spread the message. The day we walked into that compound in Los Angeles, I lost my mom. I was only six. I rarely saw her, and every time I did, we didn't act like mother and daughter. It's really strange. Not something many people can even believe let alone understand."

"What a bizarre way to grow up. When did you leave?"

"When I was eighteen. To make a long story short, I had to pretend I was devout up till the very day I escaped. If I wasn't, they would have stopped me."

She shook her head, her gaze distant, her voice soft, as if she were reliving those years. "I still wonder how I missed this coming with Hank. It's humiliating, really. I escaped one cult just to land in another. I fell in love with the idea of the opportunity to make his family my own. I was starving to belong. The ironic thing is that, looking back, I think my experience in Scientology made me more susceptible to Hank's manipulation and Lyle's intimidation."

"Sounds like it might help you escape again."

She sighed. "I don't know. I was young then, immortal. And I didn't have a little boy to think about. Once I had Jamison, all my priorities changed. It took a few times of Hank crossing the line before I realized Jamison and I weren't safe with him. It's been a long road, but leaving is the best damn decision I've ever made."

He squeezed her hand. "That explains a lot."

"Like what?"

"All your strength. I see it every time I'm with you. It's palpable. I bet that pisses Hank off too. Bullies rarely take well to confrontation."

"I don't know how strong I am. I try. Sometimes I succeed, sometimes my fear still wins out. He's a hard force to outmaneuver day after day, week after week..."

Her words trailed off. Her gaze drifted out the window.

Just when Ian was going to ask her to go on, a reflective surface caught his eye. The door of a cop's car. A sheriff's department four-by-four, parked off the road. The vehicle's headlights were turned off, but the parking lights still glowed.

Savannah saw it too. She released Ian's hand and turned to look out the back window. A tense silence filled the cab. Ian found her hand again and brought it to his mouth for a kiss. Holding her gaze, he let their joined hands rest on her thigh again. "We're fine."

She didn't respond, but he could read the doubt in her expression. The same doubt filling his chest. Half a mile back, the cruiser's lights flipped on, and the car glided onto the highway.

Ian bit back a sigh. Confrontation was inevitable. "Do you have something on Hank?"

"Have something?" she asked.

"Something that would hurt him if it got out. He wouldn't be the first dirty small-town sheriff, and he's obviously got something going on with those passports."

"What do you mean?"

"Small towns are notorious for their backwoods justice." He split his attention between the approaching cruiser and the dark, snowy road stretching ahead. "They have little to no supervision and maintain handshake oaths among politicians to keep the dirt under the rug. Often they aren't held accountable for unethical or illegal action until it reaches the media. And even then, the boys' club of law enforcement usually creates an impenetrable blue wall of silence."

As if the cop knew Ian was bad-mouthing him, the car's blue and red lights flashed on.

"Damn," Ian muttered, not exactly surprised, but still annoyed that the rumors were true.

"Shit," Savannah whispered, sinking back in the seat. "How did they know?"

The impatient, intermittent trill of the cop's siren cut through the night, but Ian took his time slowing to pull over. He gave her knee another reassuring squeeze. "Let's not get ahead of ourselves."

"I'm so sorry." Savannah eased to the far side of the bench seat and buckled up again. "I should have known this wouldn't work."

"It's not your fault," he said, searching for a reassuring tone when he was royally pissed these pricks made her life so miserable. "And it doesn't have to be a big deal."

He put the car into Park and rested both hands on the steering wheel. Ian followed the cop's progress in the side mirror.

When he recognized the man, Ian's stomach sizzled: Hank Bishop.

This ought to be fun.

Hank paused beside Ian's door and tapped one knuckle on the window. "Open up."

Ian rolled down the window with an overly solicitous "Good evening, Officer."

The freezing night air swept in, chilling his face.

Hank put both hands on the window ledge and bent to look through the cab, scowling at Savannah. "What have we got here?"

She jackknifed forward in her seat, twisting to get a better view of Hank. "What—?" Her question never made it out before anger took over. "You said you had a city council meeting tonight. Did you seriously cancel on your son just to harass me?"

"Did you seriously send our son to a friend's house for the night just so you could whore it up with this—"

"Whoa," Ian told Hank. "Don't go there."

"Don't tell me how to talk to my wife."

"Ex-wife," he corrected.

Hank's frustration transitioned into arrogance, his grin all-knowing and condescending. "You two going to Smoke, huh?" His gaze jumped back to Savannah and hardened. "We used to go there all the time, didn't we, sugar?"

"Don't, Hank—" she started.

"But that's way out of bounds now, and you know it." He stepped back, one hand on his duty belt, one on the butt of his weapon. "Out of the car, Heller."

"Hank, stop—"

"*Step. Out.*" Hank demanded, cutting off Savannah's warning.

Common sense told Ian to turn on the humility and let this asshole think he'd intimidated him. And while that might be the best thing for the mission, it would go against all his beliefs, all his values, all his training.

Military Manhunters didn't back down. Period.

But he was a civilian Manhunter now. He should be evaluating every shade of gray between black and white.

He reached for the door handle.

Savannah slapped a hand to Ian's arm. "No," she told him, then looked at Hank. "We're going home."

"Not until Heller and I have a little come-to-Jesus meeting," Hank said. "Get out of the car, or I'll drag you out."

"Chill, man." Ian pulled on the door handle. "I'm getting out."

"No." Savannah's nails dug into Ian's forearm. Her eyes were wide and terrified. She looked past Ian to plead with her ex-husband. "Leave him out of this, Hank."

"Too late for that, isn't it?"

Ian closed his free hand around Savannah's wrist and pulled her hand away, meeting her eyes. "I'll be fine." He lowered his voice. "Stay here."

"He's..." she whispered.

"I know," he assured her. "Believe me, I know."

Ian stood from the truck. The icy air sliced through his jacket.

The driver's door hadn't even closed behind Ian when Bishop threw the first punch. Ian had seen it coming, could have avoided it, but he forced himself not to react.

The bastard's fist smashed against his cheek. Pain cut through the left side of his face, but in all honesty, it was hardly anything to write home about. The guy didn't have the strength or technique to do much damage.

Savannah's scream sounded muffled amid the low thrum of blood in Ian's ears.

He easily remained on his feet, but fake-stumbled a couple of feet away to put a little distance between them.

"You must not be using your dash camera tonight." Straightening, he wiped the back of his hand over the corner of his mouth and chuckled. "Bullies always operate in the dark."

Fury replaced the smug look on Bishop's face. He hauled his arm back for another punch. Ian ducked, spun, and stepped back. Hank's momentum turned him in an arc, and he fell against the truck's fender.

Ian's blood gushed hot. His reflexes tingled to life, but inner conflict raged between could and should. He put his hands up, palms out. "Man, let's talk this out. It really doesn't have to be—"

Bishop came at him again, and this time his reflexes overrode the shoulds in his head. He leaned away, dodging Bishop's fist and planting his own in Bishop's gut. He added an uppercut to Bishop's jaw, snapping the man's head back, then retreated to a safe distance.

At least safe for hand-to-hand combat.

But Bishop drew his weapon.

Ian wanted to roll his eyes, because now he was going to have to get serious.

"Hank, don't!" Savannah yelled, her voice edged with shrill panic. "Jesus, *stop this.*"

"Shut up," he yelled back, then told Ian, "Jail or hell? You decide."

"Great line. But I'm not interested in either."

In his peripheral vision, the passenger's door swung open. Savannah boldly strode right toward Bishop.

"Get back in the truck."

Ian and Hank yelled it in stereo. Ian was sure he'd look back on this moment and laugh. But probably not for a long time.

He grabbed her arm and stepped in front of her, still facing Hank.

"Put your gun away." Savannah's icy order matched the weather.

"Don't fuckin' tell me what to do," he bit out.

"*Do it.*" Her voice shook a little. "Or I'll break out the pictures from Halloween three years ago."

Both Hank and Ian looked at her.

"What fuckin' pictures?" Hank said just as the same thought crossed Ian's mind. "You're full of—"

"And I'll circulate them all over town. All over the media. No one will ever look at you the same again." She was trembling, her arm shivering in Ian's grip. "Your deputies, the mayor, the city council, the entire community—"

"You crazy bitch," Hank yelled. "You don't know what the fuck you're talking about."

Ian wanted to pick up Savannah and carry her back to the truck, but he let the confrontation draw out a little longer, curious about these pictures.

"I'm talking about an emergency room visit Halloween night," she yelled, her eyes bright with anger. "I'm talking about twenty-six stitches and bruises in five different shades of purple. I'm talking about medical records documenting your drunken rampage. I'm talking about *the reason* I walked out on you."

Bishop's expression shifted from fury to concern. "You don't have any fucking pictures."

"Want to test that theory?" she spat at him. "Go ahead. Take Ian to jail."

"Whoa now, hold on," Ian tried to add a little levity to the moment. "I'd really rather just go home—"

"I hoped I'd never have to expose you as the bastard you are and myself as the pathetic idiot who gave up everything for you," Savannah spoke over Ian and stepped out from behind him. "Hoped you'd somehow snap out of this violent, narcissistic streak. But you've pushed me too far, Hank. You're not going to hurt Ian just because you can, and you'll *never* take Jamison from me." Her hands fisted as she leaned closer to Bishop, clearly unintimidated by the Glock still pointed their direction. "Try and watch how fast the news and the photos spread. Watch all the hero worship you enjoy around this town dry up. And before you think of just getting rid of me, know Audrey has everything. She's been begging to use it against you for years."

Holy shit. This woman wasn't just smart, she had balls.

The next few moments seemed to stretch into an eternity. An eternity with the fuse to a bomb burning shorter and shorter. Ian shifted to put his body between the two again, but kept his mouth shut. Savannah had this handled on an emotional and intellectual level. But he kept his muscles coiled tight, ready to take over on a physical level if Bishop didn't holster his weapon in the next five seconds.

Four. Three. Two.

Bishop lowered his arms.

Ian turned to Savannah and met her gaze deliberately. "In the truck. *Please.*"

She hesitated. Cut another look at Bishop.

"You heard him." Bishop holstered his weapon and stabbed his finger toward the truck. "Get back where you belong."

SAVANNAH'S HEART hammered against her ribs like she'd just finished a snowball fight with Jamison. Only without the happy high that fun left behind. Now, all she felt was scared. Scared and embarrassed and guilty.

She let Ian walk her to the passenger's side of the truck, but never took her gaze off Hank. Before she got in, she cautioned Ian, "Watch your back with him."

He nodded. "No doubt."

Once Ian made it back to the driver's side, Hank said, "Your days are numbered, Heller."

"Everyone's days are numbered, Sheriff. Some of us just get more than others."

The way he stood up to Hank was so...shocking. So unexpected. Confrontational in the most respectful way. Savannah never dreamed something like that could be so sexy on a man.

Ian slid behind the wheel. Then, while Hank stood in the deserted road, hands on hips, glaring at them, Ian swung the truck in a U-turn and started back toward town.

Goodbye, Smoke.

Goodbye, freedom.

Goodbye, hope.

Savannah couldn't stop wondering how Hank could use

what she'd just told him against her. He'd find a way. She just had to figure it out first if she was going to protect herself and Jamison.

Thoughts of Jamison had Savannah pulling out her phone.

Just checking in. Is everything okay? she wrote.

"Texting Misty?"

She looked up from her phone. "You always seem to be one thought ahead of me."

"It's a gift."

She would have laughed if her stomach wasn't knotted. If his jaw wasn't ratcheted tight, his lips pressed into a grim line. Savannah worried about Ian's safety now that Hank had seen them together. And she hated to think of how Ian viewed her now that her dirty laundry was strung out right in front of him.

"What kind of phone is that?" he asked. "I thought you had an iPhone."

"Oh." She looked down at the cheap device. "It's one of those pay-as-you-go phones."

His gaze drilled into hers. "A burner?"

She was starting to feel boxed in again. "I guess some people call it that."

"Why do you have two phones?"

She heaved a sigh. Man, she really didn't want to get into this right now. "Can we talk about this another—"

"He's got your phone bugged?"

"No," she answered in a knee-jerk reaction. "I mean, I don't see how he could. I always have it with me."

"Where is it now?"

She rolled her eyes. "It's at home. I meant I always know where it is. I don't just leave it out where someone could get to it."

"Why did you leave it home and take a burner with you tonight?" he pressed. "I can't help if you don't talk to me, Savannah."

She stared out the windshield, considering. She wanted to

confide in him—really bad. But she'd stopped trusting anyone but Misty and Audrey years ago.

"Misty told me there's a way to remotely tap into your phone so someone can listen to your calls. I've snuck out on my own before. They don't watch the back of the house because my car's always out front, and there are only so many men Hank can spare from regular duty. Besides, I can't exactly get very far on foot this time of year, so they're more concerned with my use of the car. I coordinated with Misty to take Jamison to Splash Montana in Missoula. But somehow, they still knew where I was. Every time I'd reach the county line, one of his deputies would be there to turn me around. Every time I'd buy something off Amazon aimed at keeping my privacy, the orders vanished before they reached my porch or they were canceled, but I didn't cancel them."

She heaved a sigh, her expression frustrated and lost. "I changed all my passwords, but that didn't help. Misty said he was probably tracking me with my phone and my computer. She ordered the disposable cells to her home and brought them to me. She also bought something that scrambles my computer activity. I don't know how it works, but it keeps Hank from interfering with my purchases and internet searches." She shook her head, furious. "But he's obviously found another way to track me, because there was no way he knew about tonight. I'm starting to think he implanted a damn GPS chip into me while I was sleeping or something."

"He's not that sophisticated," Ian said. "I think he's just listening in on your plans."

She tossed her hands up. "*How?*"

"Do you really have those pictures?" he asked.

The change of subject threw her for a second. "Of course I do. I'd never risk your safety with a lie."

He cut a look at her, but Savannah couldn't read it. "Why haven't you used them before this? *Long* before this. To get him to leave you alone or get yourself out of town?"

His voice was level, making it hard to read his emotions. "Because something that happened years ago, with no witnesses to prove Hank was the person who hit me, will not stand up in a Hazard County court. I need more. I was saving it in the hope it would work as a last-ditch effort, as an emergency get-out-of-Hazard-free card, hoping his reputation in town means more to him than his need for revenge and control."

"Then why'd you use it tonight?"

"Because he was pointing *a gun* at you," she said, her voice rising with frustration. "Maybe you're used to that after being in the military, but my heart just about jumped out of my chest."

He stared at her for another moment, then returned his gaze to the road with a soft "Fuck" under his breath.

"Are you mad?" she asked, then quickly followed with "I mean, it would be totally reasonable if you were. I am, and if I were in your place, I'd be really—"

"No," he cut her off. "I'm not mad. Not at you. At him, yeah. At this situation, you're damn right. I can't stand the way he's got you cornered in this little town, trapped between Canada, the Blackfeet Reservation, and the Rockies with your only way out through him. And I'm royally *pissed off* that you had to use your ace in the hole to save my sorry ass."

He exhaled hard, as if he had more to say but wouldn't let himself. With his elbow on the window ledge, Ian wiped his hand across his mouth and shook his head. "I'm sorry," he said, his voice a soft rumble now, filled with apology and compassion. "Like I said, I'm not angry with you. I'm angry *for* you."

Savannah experienced a quick, deep tug of connection. The way he'd cut to the heart of the biggest obstacle in her life validated her in a way she'd never experienced. She felt...*seen*. She hadn't realized—until that very moment—how minimized she'd felt all these years. How she could see so many people day in and day out, but not one acknowledged her struggle. Yet, Ian had been in town two weeks, and he'd not only recognized her problem but was incensed over the injustice of it.

Warmth blossomed low in her belly. She hadn't had anyone but Misty give a shit about her in so long, the gratitude filled her until her chest tightened with it.

Her phone chimed with a return text. We're great. Don't worry. Focus on your hottie.

Savannah breathed a little easier. She knew Misty would die protecting Jamison; she just didn't want it to come to that. And after seeing Hank draw his weapon on Ian, she was grateful Misty had weapons and knew how to use them.

"Everything okay?" he asked.

Savannah released a long breath. "Yeah. They're fine."

She looked out the passenger's window into the darkness for a long moment. A sense of vulnerability washed over her. A sensation that was far too familiar.

"Hey," Ian said, his voice soft as he patted the seat beside him. "Come here."

She unbuckled her seat belt and slid to the center of the seat again. A smile tipped his mouth and relaxed his features. He lifted his arm, and she slid into place beneath it as if it were the most natural thing in the world. His muscled arm pulled her close and gave her a squeeze, and the whole atmosphere in the truck eased.

"Everything's okay," he said. "We'll figure this out. It won't be like this forever."

She angled toward him and curled her fingers into his shirt. With her head on his chest, she murmured, "Thank you. I can't remember the last time someone stuck up for me." She exhaled. "But can we not do that again? I about had a heart attack."

He kissed her head. "He would never have gotten off a shot."

She wasn't sure what that meant or how Ian would have stopped it from happening, but that didn't matter. She just never wanted to be in that situation again. Though considering all the

steps they'd taken to make sure they got out of the house unde-
tected, yet still had been caught, Savannah couldn't see a way out
other than cutting herself off from the only man who'd ever stood
up to Hank.

"I can hear the gears turning in your head," he told her. "Talk
to me."

She rested her head against his shoulder. "How did he know
where we were going? I didn't tell anyone but Misty. And we
didn't talk about it on the phone."

Ian didn't answer immediately. The silence felt heavy, like a
weight on Savannah's shoulders.

"I'll check the house when we get back," Ian said.

"Check it for what?"

"Bugs."

She glanced up at him. "Bugs?"

A little grin flashed over his mouth but disappeared before
she could appreciate it. "The listening kind, not the crawly kind."

Her mouth dropped open—first to reject the idea, then to
question, and finally, "Oh shit" popped out.

She scoured her mind for everything she'd said and done
over the past few months. Repeated, "Oh, *shit*" and dropped her
head into her hands, covering her face.

He squeezed her shoulders. "Try not to worry. What's done is
done. How you move forward knowing, that's in your court now."

She felt the walls closing in on her again. The way they
always did whenever Hank took aggressive action against her—
like filing for sole custody of their son.

She couldn't do this anymore. She couldn't stand the stress.
The fear. She wanted out. "Do you know how I could get one of
those false passports?"

His gaze jumped to hers. "What?"

"Okay, maybe not a passport. Maybe a birth certificate? Something that I could use to create a new identity?"

"That's...drastic."

"Believe me, I've tried everything else." A little bubble of panic inflated in her gut. "And he's filed for custody of Jamison."

"*What?*" Ian's caustic laugh filled the cab. "That's a fucking joke."

"Judges in this county won't think so."

"Let's take this one step at a time. You've got a good start with those passports you grabbed. And I know you're stealthy about recording interactions with him and his deputies. Now I know you've got pictures. We need to sit down and put everything you have together."

She snuggled closer and lifted her lips to his jaw. Having his arm holding her close, his warmth surrounding her, made her feel positively giddy, despite the bullshit Hank continued to pull. And, God, he smelled so good, all clean and citrusy fresh. The stubble on his jaw felt foreign but exciting against her lips. She kissed him again. Moved lower, kissed him again. Lower, kissing his neck.

A deep growl sounded in his throat, and he held her tighter. "Baby..."

Warmth tingled through her chest. After so long without any male attention, the endearment felt good on her heart. And his hard body felt amazing against hers.

She kissed him just below his ear, then took the lobe between her lips and sucked.

Another sound rolled through his throat. "Savannah."

His voice was rough with desire and warning, and her body flared to fiery life. She felt safe and wanted, allowing her to take a chance.

She slid her hand across his belly and around his side. Bent one knee and laid it over his thigh. Pressed her face against his neck and opened her mouth over his skin, tasting with her tongue.

"Jesus Christ," he rasped. "I can't think when you do that."

"Mmm," she hummed against his skin. "You taste good."

It had been so damn long since she'd been this close to a man. Since she'd even wanted to be close to a man. She was aching by the time he pulled the truck into the alley behind their duplex.

He parked behind his unit, shut down the engine, then twisted toward her. He tightened his arm around her and cupped her face with his other hand.

Instead of kissing her the way she wanted and expected, he just stared at her, scanning her face, his gaze lingering on her mouth. "I'm going to check the house."

He combed her hair off her face and kissed her, just a firm press of his lips. But that wasn't enough for Savannah. She desperately needed an escape. She slid her tongue along his lower lip. Ian responded immediately, meeting her tongue and groaning into her mouth.

Then he abruptly pulled out of the kiss, leaving Savannah dizzy.

"Hold that thought," he said.

He rounded the truck and helped Savannah from the car. On the walk to the back door of her duplex, he pulled out his phone and tapped into an app. An image of a dial filled the screen. He wrapped his arm around her shoulders and leaned close. "This will detect the magnetic fields used by audio and video surveillance units. Don't talk until I tell you it's safe."

Nerves tingled to the surface again, smothering the sexual need he'd rekindled.

He let her unlock the back door, then wrapped her hand in his and entered the house first, pulling her close behind him. It felt strange to return to a house with the lights on and the television playing.

Once the back door was closed, he paused and lifted his phone, scanning the room in a slow circle. The pointer that lay on one side of the circle labeled zero bounced a tiny bit.

After scanning the room, he met her gaze and shook his head, indicating there were no bugs. A little tension leaked from Savannah's shoulders. On one hand, she really hoped Ian was wrong. She loathed the idea that Hank had been listening to, or worse, watching her. On the other hand, it would explain how he was always one step ahead of her and give her more control over what he heard and didn't hear.

Ian let go of her hand and continued into the kitchen. His phone made a static sound, the pitch changing as he moved the phone over various surfaces.

Savannah crossed her arms and stepped into the kitchen, seeing the space with new eyes. Nervous eyes. She rubbed a hand over her face, turned, and wandered into the living room. She stood in front of the window, looking out at the black night and the cruiser parked across the street, waffling between fury and hopelessness.

She worried the edge of her sweater between her fingers as Ian made his way through the living room and hallway.

He'd gone through the entire house in minutes. Minutes that felt like lifetimes to Savannah. When he came up behind her and put a hand on her back, she jumped.

"Sorry," he whispered at her ear. "Let's talk outside."

She turned, and Ian took her hand in his again, drawing her from the house out the back door. The cold, quiet night closed in. Ian wrapped his arms around her, taking the brunt of the cold and lending his body heat to keep her from shivering.

"I found one audio-video surveillance unit," he told her.

"Video?" Her stomach clenched as his mind raced back in time, trying to remember everything she'd said or done that could have alerted Hank to her plans. "Where?"

"The hallway. The camera is a micro CCTV unit pointed toward the living room. Even with a one-hundred-eighty-degree view, it only monitors the living room and the hallway. Because of the floorplan, the bedrooms, kitchen and laundry room are video-free zones."

She exhaled, relieved Hank couldn't see inside her bedroom, grateful he hadn't found her escape hatch out the back. "Still, that's sick. What about the audio? How good is it?"

"Hard to tell. Most units like that are designed to monitor one room well. But since the house is small, I'd guess it could pick up most conversations at a normal volume. The farther from the unit, the more degraded the quality."

"Shit." She buried her face against his chest.

"It's not always on. It's remotely controlled by calling in and activating it."

"I don't care." She looked up at him. "I want it out."

He stroked her back with one hand, her hair with the other. "If we take it out, he'll know we found it, and that would only make him increase security on the house. You don't want that. Besides, his illegal surveillance might be something you could use in court against him."

She exhaled and closed her eyes, wishing she could force all this ugliness away. "I can't live like this."

"Why don't you get some things and stay at my place tonight? I'll take the sofa. We can talk out a plan."

His suggestion added a whole new and confusing element to this mess. She didn't want to drag him into a problem that wasn't his. But she found herself grabbing hold of a lifeline no one else had offered.

She nodded and turned toward the house. But Ian turned her back.

"Just do what you always do. Act like you're getting ready for bed. You need to make sure whoever's watching thinks I'm out of the picture and you've returned to your normal habits."

"Then how—"

"After you turn out the lights, get into bed. Move your pillows around to make it look like you're there. Wait ten minutes, then slide out and stay as quiet as possible as you leave. My back door will be open."

Her stomach jumped. "God, this is crazy."

He tipped her head back and smiled. "Just think of it as sneaking out of your house as a teenager to meet your boyfriend."

That made her laugh. Savannah had never had that opportunity.

Ian kissed her forehead, opened the back door for her, and said, "See you soon."

9

Ian paced his kitchen with his phone to his ear. He kept glancing out the window of the back door for signs of Savannah.

"She's freaked out," Ian told Roman. Sam and Liam were also on the line. "Reasonable, considering."

"If she kept pictures of the abuse," Liam said, "you can bet she's got more ammunition tucked away."

"Sam," Ian said, "what have you gotten off her VPN?"

"Some Amazon shopping—can't believe they deliver to that frozen hole—nothing of particular interest," Sam said. "And a lot of Google searches. How to disappear without a trace is a popular theme. As is psychobabble about boys growing up without fathers and post-traumatic stress disorder related to abuse and control."

Ian closed his eyes, tilted his head back, and rubbed a hand over his face. He hated—*hated*—the idea of Savannah struggling through this alone, with the internet as her only source of information about a very complicated and risky endeavor.

"Bishop is out of control," Ian said. "And since I came on the scene, he's escalating."

"If she gives you something solid on Bishop," Roman said. "She won't even need to go into witness protection, because the bastard will be in jail. Mine her."

Ian didn't like the sound of that last comment. He found himself falling into the same category as Hank—manipulating, lying, and spying. He'd much rather be dropped in the middle of nowhere to trek a hundred miles in the desert heat and take out his target with a double tap from a distance. But if taking out Bishop could help Savannah get out of this situation and create a new life, he'd just have to deal with it.

Shadows moved outside. "I've gotta go."

Ian signed off and opened the door for Savannah. She'd changed into sweats and was huddled beneath a parka, her cheeks bright pink against a pale face and big, scared eyes. Her arms were crossed over a file folder held against her chest.

He shoved his phone into his pocket as she stepped inside. "Are you okay? You look a little—"

"Who was that?"

He closed the door at her back. "The friend I sent the passport photos to."

Hope sparked in her eyes. "Did he find out anything?"

"Not yet."

Her breath whooshed out. "I brought the papers, but I've been thinking about this." She started pacing. With her arms crossed, holding the evidence Ian desperately needed tight against her chest, she didn't look like she planned on staying. "You've been so great. Amazing, really. To help me, a stranger, with all my stupid problems—"

"Savannah—"

"But I need to step in and stop you. This has gotten way out of hand. This isn't your fight, and I'm not going to drag you down."

"You're not—"

"I swear Hank slips closer to the edge every day."

"Listen—"

"After tonight, I don't know what he's capable of anymore, and I'm not going to let you—"

He took her face between his palms and silenced her with his mouth. She covered one of his hands with hers but didn't pull away. When she sighed, he tilted his head and kissed her again, deeper. Her lips relaxed, and she kissed him back. Her fingers curled into his shirt. Her body eased against his. Before he knew it, his hands had slipped into her hair, his tongue into her mouth. She tasted so sweet, so honest.

He forced himself to pull away. But when he looked down into her heavy-lidded eyes, his heart squeezed. Ian was definitely getting in too deep.

Still, he had a job to do, and staying close to her was a significant part of getting that job done. He just had a very fine line to walk.

"Pushing me away isn't going to keep either of us safe," he told her. "Only closing ranks will do that."

Concern crept into her gaze. She lowered her head, pressed her forehead against his chest, and heaved a troubled sigh. Her warm breath penetrated his shirt and sent tingles over his skin. If he didn't move away from her now, he was going to take this too far.

He released her and turned toward the kitchen. "Are you hungry? It's almost eight already. I can't compete with Smoke, but I could make you..."

He opened his fridge and surveyed the contents—which didn't take long. He had beer, milk, bread, and peanut butter.

Savannah came up behind him, set the file on the counter and slid her arms around his waist, pressing the front of her body to the back of his. She was warm and soft, and Ian breathed a moan as he slid his hand over her arm. "Sorry, baby, I don't have much. All I can offer is a peanut butter sandwich."

She laughed with her cheek pressed to his back. "Jamison would be thrilled."

He closed the fridge and stroked her arms at his waist. "Want to try another restaurant closer to home?"

"No," she said on a sigh. "I've got exactly what I want right here."

Ian closed his eyes and searched for strength. For the will to send her to his bed—alone. He hadn't quite found it before she released him, moved to the counter, and lifted her butt to the edge beside the file folder. They still weren't eye to eye, but she spread her thighs and wrapped her legs around his hips, pulling him into her. She locked her arms behind his neck, and Ian rested his forehead against hers, his hands gripping and releasing her waist.

"You're amazing," he said. "You know that?"

She huffed a laugh. "Pathetic is more like it."

He shook his head and pushed a strand of hair behind her ear. "Problems don't make you pathetic. They either break you or strengthen you. And you're one of the strongest women I know."

"Thank you." She searched his face, her expression open and curious. Her hands stroked down the front of his thermal, and her touch tingled over his skin. "I've forgotten what it's like to talk to a person who's not under Hank's control."

Ian was seeing a whole lot of gray in this situation. All the black and white from his military days was gone, blending so seamlessly, the line of right and wrong disappeared. He knew what he'd been told to do. He knew what he wanted. Those, at least, meshed—get close to her, get her to confide in him. But there was another gray area that Ian could see becoming a problem as this mission came to an end. He'd lied to her, surveilled her, used her to get information on Hank.

He was thinking about all that when Savannah tilted her head and kissed him. God, her lips were sweet. Soft. Supple. Maybe getting one long, deep taste of her would quench his thirst temporarily. Maybe showing her some rough passion would give her second thoughts about crossing that line between friends and lovers.

He wrapped one arm low on her hips, pushed his other hand into her hair and held her head as he deepened the kiss. Savannah moaned and fisted his hair. The sound pushed Ian to the edge. He kissed her deeply, passionately, aggressively. Licked into her mouth while he rocked his erection into the apex of her thighs.

Instead of putting on the brakes, she met his passion and answered his lust with desire. That had backfired. Big time. Because the way she gave herself over to him short-circuited his brain.

She released his hair to fist the back of his thermal and pulled it over his head. Her hands stroked his back, his sides, his belly, lighting him on fire. Then they slid to the button of his jeans. This situation had just turned into a freight train, careening downhill with no brakes.

Ian broke the kiss. "Savann—"

"I want you," she murmured as she pushed a hand into his open jeans and stroked his cotton-covered cock. "God, how I want you."

Searing pleasure stole his words, his thoughts, his resistance. "Jesus Chri—"

She tilted her head and kissed him again, her mouth open and willing, begging him to respond. There was no right answer here. If he gave her what she wanted—what they both wanted— she'd hate him later. If he didn't, she'd hate him now.

Later. Later was the better option here. Because maybe, just maybe, if Ian could deliver Savannah the kind of freedom she longed for and deserved right along with the hell the Bishops deserved, Ian's betrayal might sting a little less.

He lifted her from the counter, and she wrapped her thighs around his hips, locked her arms around his neck, and kissed a path toward his ear. Fireworks shot across his skin as he navigated the hallway like a drunk.

In the bedroom, he pressed one knee to the bed and laid her back. He brushed her hair from her face. "I've wanted this from the first time your sassy mouth put me in my place."

She reached for his pants again. "I'll make sure to sass you more often."

He caught her hand before she touched him and he lost it again, and pulled on the sleeve of her jacket. It was his turn to drag off some clothes.

Her jacket hit the floor first, then her sweatshirt. He flipped the clasp on her bra and pulled it from her arms, tossing everything aside. And when he refocused on Savannah, her hair was a tangled halo on his white sheets, her face flushed, her eyes heavy lidded and hot. Her breasts were just the right size to fill his hands. Her waist was small, her stomach flat, her skin smooth.

"God, you're beautiful," was all he managed before his hands and mouth touched and tasted every part of her—throat, chest, belly, ribs, and finally her breasts. They were supple and full, with perfect pink tips, and he loved the way she shivered and moaned when he licked and sucked at them. He loved the way she combed her hands through his hair, her fingers tightening as her pleasure rose.

His focus had narrowed to include only Savannah. Savannah and her wildflower scent, her petal-soft skin, and the pleasure he could bring her—at least in the moment.

He dragged off her sweatpants, panties, and snow boots. And then he paused and looked at the grand result: Savannah Bishop gloriously naked. Naked and in his bed. Naked, in his bed and reaching for him.

Ian had never experienced a rush like this. So overwhelming. So intense. He had a ravenous need to sink into her and drive them both to ecstasy. With any other woman, he would do just that. He'd also be out the door before his breathing had returned to normal. But this was different. So different. He didn't know how or why exactly, at least not while the majority of his blood was pooled below his belt.

He forced himself to slow down. To taste every inch of her body.

"Ian," she complained, fisting his hair to pull his mouth to hers.

Instead, he pushed two fingers into her wet heat. Her back arched, and her hands slipped from his hair. The guttural moan that rolled from her throat set him on fire. And, God, she was perfect. Velvety and slick and tight. Savannah lifted her hips into his touch, and a current of excitement ripped through his body. She was so beautiful. So sexual. So needy, open, and hungry. He wanted to take his sweet time with her. Wanted to learn every curve of her body, taste every inch of her skin, torture her with pleasure until she begged him to take her.

Savannah sat up and took his face in both hands, pulling his mouth to hers. She was so hungry. And when he lost himself in her kiss, Savannah pushed his jeans lower and took his cock in both hands. Lightning cracked through him. He moaned into her mouth, closed one hand around her wrist, and pulled. But she didn't let go. Her fingers tightened around his cock, and Ian had to grit his teeth and use every ounce of restraint not to come in her hand.

He tore his mouth from hers. "Savannah..." His impatient tone made her smile. A sexy, seductive smile he felt all the way to his bones. "Baby, slow down."

She rolled him to his back and straddled his hips. Dipping her head, she kissed him and murmured, "You wouldn't be saying that if you hadn't had an orgasm in half a decade."

That information hit him sideways. He hadn't wrapped his brain around it before Savannah pulled his cock from his pants and stroked him.

All thoughts evaporated in the stars shooting off behind his eyes. "Fuck, Savannah—"

Warm, wet heat enveloped his cock, cutting off his words. Ian's hips bucked, and he opened his eyes to the sight of Savannah pushing his cock deep into her mouth, eyes closed, her face glowing with the kind of pleasure that made Ian teeter on the edge of control.

"God dammit." He cupped her face in his hands and drew her mouth off his cock. "Baby, do you want me inside you?"

Her eyes fell closed, and her forehead creased on a breathless "*Yes.*"

"Then you've got to stop, or I'm going to finish before I ever get close."

He gripped her waist and flipped her to her back. Ian didn't waste any time giving her what she wanted. He slid down the bed, pushed her thighs wide, and covered her sex with his mouth.

Savannah choked a sound of ecstasy. Her eyes rolled back in her head, her mouth dropped open, and her hips lifted to his touch with a guttural "Yeeeeeeees."

The woman blew his mind. He wanted to spend all night getting to know her every pleasure point and exploiting them until he'd heard all her sounds of pleasure. Until her body glistened with sweat. Until she begged for relief, then passed out from exhaustion in his arms.

For now, he knelt on the floor, pulled her legs over his shoulders, and her pussy to his mouth. He pushed his fingers deep, teasing her G-spot with his fingertips. With his other hand, he parted her folds, exposing her most vulnerable pleasure point. Ian met her gaze and held it as he laved slow licks across her bared clit. Savannah shivered. Her muscles coiled tighter and tighter.

Ian pressed his hands to her inner thighs and spread her wide, stretching her muscles and holding her open. Just to look.

To lick. To tease. To brand her with the kind of pleasure that would burn him into her memory.

"Come for me, baby," he rasped. "I want to watch you shatter."

He covered her with his mouth, sucking and licking. Savannah fisted the sheets on a scream, and her body convulsed with pleasure as she spilled on his tongue.

A wave of wicked satisfaction swept through Ian. While her body shivered with aftershocks, he pressed his face to her belly, kissing her and breathing in the scent of her satisfaction. His cock throbbed for the same kind of release.

Ian kissed a trail to her breastbone, resting there a moment while her fingers combed through his hair. Then she shifted her leg, and her thigh rubbed his cock.

Lust surged through him, and he groaned, sliding up until his hips were between her thighs and they were face-to-face. She smiled up at him, and he kissed the tip of her nose, then her lips, chin, and neck. She wrapped her legs around his, caressed her hands up his back. Skin to skin, she pulled his mouth back to hers.

Ian moaned and pulled away. "I need my wallet," he smiled down at her, "but I don't want to leave you to get it."

She slid a hand over his cheek. Her heavy-lidded eyes sparkled, her full mouth tilted in a smile. "I promise I won't go anywhere."

He flattened his hands on the bed flanking her shoulders, pushed up, and leaned over the side of the bed to dig a condom from his wallet.

Savannah took it from him. "I haven't used one of these in a long time."

"This isn't a good time for trial and error," he teased, trying to grab it back.

She pulled it out of reach. "I guess you'll just have to employ amazing willpower, won't you?"

She ripped the packet, pulled out the condom, and met his

gaze deliberately as she reached between them. She stroked him with one hand and the other rolled the condom on, all while her sexy gaze never left his. The excruciating pleasure flashed hot in his lower body, rising through his belly and chest, tingling down his limbs.

"Are you...purposely torturing me?" he asked from between gritted teeth. "Or do you need some help? Because I can't take much more of—"

Her fingers pressed the base of his cock. "I love this needy side of you."

Ian exhaled heavily, rested his sweaty face against her neck, and muttered, "I definitely need you."

She laughed, a light, breathless, trickling sound that faded as she grew serious. Her eyes softened into the color of stormy seas. "I can't wait to feel you inside me."

His heart thudded hard. He kissed her, met her eyes, and, because she still had her hand wrapped around his cock, rasped, "Lead the way, baby."

She shifted her hips and rubbed the head of his cock along her slick folds while her tongue slid across her lower lip. The combination forced desire through his veins. When she buried the head of his cock in her warmth, Ian swore they shared a simultaneous shiver. All while their eyes remained locked on each other.

The impulse to rock his hips took over, and he pushed deeper inside her. Savannah took a sharp breath, and Ian eased back, then thrust again. Her body opened for him and immediately reformed a tight seal. The pressure and heat of her body, the hunger and awe in her gaze, urged him deeper. He gripped her waist and held her gaze as he continued to forge his path.

Savannah closed her eyes, dropped back, and arched, pushing him home.

"Oh, God..." Her raspy, reverent whisper touched him.

And when her eyes opened again, new emotions shone there.

Emotions he wasn't ready for—affection and vulnerability. They hit him dead center in the chest and tugged at his heart. A sensation he hadn't felt in decades spread through him. He couldn't call it love, because he'd never been in love. He'd been infatuated. He'd been in lust. But this was different. Very different.

And when he moved inside Savannah, all kinds of emotions whipped up, clouding all thought. He focused on her pretty face and the pleasure etching her features. On the way her body rocked his world. On the sexy sounds rolling from her throat.

He wrapped an arm low on her back and slowly pulled her into a sitting position, easing back on his heels so she could straddle his lap. Her weight pushed him deeper, and the velvety squeeze made him moan.

Savannah tossed her hair off her face, stroked her hands over his shoulders and down his arms, then threaded their fingers. Ian used his thighs to lift and his glutes to thrust, and Savannah rode him hard through her next orgasm. When she peaked, Ian released her hands and gripped her hips, holding her there as her body squeezed and squeezed and squeezed.

His own climax was pounding at the base of his spine for release. "One more," he told her, lifting one hand to her head, holding her blue gaze, and giving his all to his resumed thrusts. "Give me one more, baby. Come with me this time."

Savannah's hands clawed at his shoulders for balance, her face pressed against his neck. Her hot breath bathed his skin, and her moans rippled through his chest, a flame to the explosion of his orgasm. He held her hips tight, thrusting deep and fast.

"Ah, God… Ia—" The power of her orgasm cut off her words, and Ian let go.

His release ripped through him, hips to chest. He echoed Savannah's cry, and relished wave after superheated shock wave of pleasure, until the climax passed, leaving them both sweaty and breathless.

She grew heavy on his lap, and Ian kept a tight grip on her as he waited for their breath to slow, for Savannah to move, or for his own need for space to creep in. But she never moved, and space was the last thing Ian wanted.

Long, silent moments passed. Ian's lower legs fell asleep. Still, he didn't want to move. He didn't know when or if this chance would ever come again, so he rode it out as long as possible.

Savannah took a deep breath and released a long, satisfied sigh. "I don't want to move."

Ian laughed. "I was just thinking the same thing."

He lifted her head to look into her eyes and laughed.

"What's so funny?" she wanted to know.

"You look so..."

"Satisfied?" she said with a wicked little curl to her lips. "Go ahead, Mr. Heller, bask," she said, leaning her head into his hand. "You deserve it."

"*We* deserve it," he said. "I didn't do that alone."

She opened her eyes, lifted her head from his hand, and cupped his face. Her blue eyes slid over his expression. Her fingers traced his features. The gesture was so tender, her expression so loving, Ian's chest tightened with an unfamiliar sensation. One that scared him a little.

Then she kissed him, a gentle press of lips, over and over— his mouth, chin, cheek, forehead, and the tip of his nose before she brought her mouth back to his for a deep, slow kiss that warmed him from the inside out.

Finally, she lifted her body from his, then collapsed against the bed with comical relief. "I hope you don't mind if I stay here for a week. I don't think I'll be able to move again until then."

Ian rolled to his side, draped an arm over her waist, and pulled her close. She slid an arm around his neck and her fingers into his hair.

"God, I wish I could memorize this moment," he murmured. That foreign, powerful sensation tightened his chest again. "You're so beautiful."

Savannah grinned and stroked his cheek. "You're not so bad yourself, handsome." She closed her eyes, sighed heavily, and breathed, "Wow."

Yeah. That about said it all, didn't it?

Too bad that wasn't the only thing they needed to talk about tonight—and he knew without a doubt, their next conversation would change the entire mood.

10

The smell of something delicious finally pulled Savannah from Ian's bed.

They'd made love twice more before their growling stomachs sent Ian over to Savannah's side of the duplex to raid her fridge. Now, at midnight, he was in the kitchen cooking something to eat.

Savannah stood, picked up one of Ian's T-shirts from a folded pile of laundry and slipped it over her head. She wandered through the living room, noting the blankets and pillows on his couch, and smiled. Neither one of them would be using those tonight, but she appreciated his offer to sleep on the couch early on.

Now, he stood at the stove in his thermal shirt and jeans. His shoulders were wide, their corded muscle stretching the fabric. A sigh slipped out of her as she thought back over the last few hours, a wild whirlwind of lust, sweetness, passion, intensity, and release. More than she'd ever imagined and something she was fully aware might never happen again. Even if she hated the thought of this being a one-time event, she had to admit it made a lot of sense in her situation.

She might as well get as much of him as he'd give while she was here.

Savannah came up behind him and slid her arms around his waist, flattening her hands on his taut abs.

"Hey there." He slid a hand over her forearm and smiled over his shoulder. "I thought I was going to have to wake you up to eat."

"It smells heavenly. What are you making?"

"French toast."

"Mmmm, one of Jamison's favorites."

"I hope it's one of yours too."

She released his waist and stepped up beside him at the stove. "It is."

He set down the spatula and turned, pulling her toward him by the waist. His smile still made tingles of excitement skitter over her skin. "With butter and syrup, I hope. I stole those too."

She laughed. "Did you leave me anything?"

He lowered his head and skimmed the tip of his nose down the length of hers, murmuring, "Maybe," before he kissed her. A slow, sweet press of his lips that lingered until Savannah thought they might be putting food on hold again.

But the sizzle of the pan broke the trance, and Ian quickly saved the French toast. "Whoa, that was close."

He pulled a plate warming in the oven and added the toast to a ridiculous pile of eight slices.

"Who in the heck are you cooking for?"

"Me, mostly," he admitted with a grin. "I figured you for about two pieces." He leaned over and kissed her again. "You helped me work up an appetite."

When he said things like that, she got all giddy inside. Being with him created a constant inner battle between hope and reality.

After buttering the toast, he picked up the plate and the syrup and set them on the table in the kitchen. He'd already moved the file folder to the windowsill and put out forks, knives, and—

"Is that my orange juice?" she asked.

He gave her an um-yeah look. "I promise to make a store run tomorrow and replace everything."

She laughed and waved his offer away. "Don't worry about it." She moved toward a chair with "It's the least I could contribute to the best night of my life."

She'd meant the comment to come out flippant and sarcastic, but as she approached the table, Ian grabbed her arm and yanked. Savannah fell off-balance with a squeak and dropped into his lap sideways.

"Really?" he murmured. Something soft flashed in his eyes. "I keep wondering if my head's in the clouds, thinking it's been a-freaking-mazing."

She wrapped her arms around his neck. "Yes. Really. Hands-down best ever."

He lowered his head and kissed her. Then kissed her again. He pulled back and tilted his head to kiss her deeper...and his stomach rolled with a thundering growl, stopping him cold.

"First things first," she said with a laugh.

When she patted his chest and leaned forward to stand, Ian held her back. "Where do you think you're going?" He picked up a fork with his free hand. "This is a full-service joint." He drizzled syrup over the French toast, cut a piece of the bread with the side of the fork, and held it dripping over the plate. "Open up."

"Ian—"

The toast was in her mouth, syrup dripping down her chin before she could say any more. She was laughing when he licked the syrup off her chin, then kissed her.

Savannah chewed and was surprised by a burst of flavor. The exterior of the bread was crisp, the inside warm and soft, and a mixture of sweet syrup, rich vanilla, and spicy cinnamon coated her mouth.

She made a sound of surprise, then relished the bite by chewing slowly. While she took her time, Ian dug in, eating an entire piece in the time it took Savannah to finish one bite.

"That," she said, eyes wide, "is amazing." She licked her lips. "I thought the café had the best French toast, but Karen's obviously got some competition. What did you do?"

He gave her a comically stern look and pointed at her with the fork. "Never leaves this kitchen?"

"Deal."

"Pinky swear?"

She laughed. "Where'd you hear that?"

"Jamison."

The walls around her heart were taking a serious beating right now. "Pinky swear."

"Vanilla, cinnamon, sugar, and cream in with the eggs."

"Decadent," she said. "Sugar, huh? Never would have thought of that."

"It caramelizes and creates the crunchy coating," he said, feeding her another bite.

"Mmm. So good."

They continued to eat in comfortable silence, Ian feeding her another bite as soon as she'd finished the one before, until she held up a hand. "I can't eat any more."

"Good," he teased with a sparkle in his eye. "More for me."

She let him finish off the toast in peace while she ran her fingers through his hair and caressed the planes of his forehead, nose, jaw.

With one piece of toast left on the plate, he put his fork down and looked at her with a furrow between his brows. "I've been thinking."

Her stomach fluttered. "I don't know if I should be excited or terrified."

He laughed, his grin primed to superstun. He squeezed her waist. "Funny." He took a sip of juice, and when he looked at her again, he'd grown serious. "This thing with your ex."

"No, no, no," she whined, closing her eyes to shut out reality. "I don't want him anywhere near this night."

"That idea went down the drain when he pointed his service weapon at me."

A chill vibrated down Savannah's spine. That very image played against her closed eyelids. She forced them open and exhaled heavily. "Okay, what were you thinking?"

"He's into some bad stuff." His voice was light, as if this bad stuff wasn't all that big a deal. He stabbed another bite of French toast and said, "Counterfeiting passports, selling or distributing counterfeit passports, that's serious stuff. With evidence, he'll go away until Jamison is well into adulthood."

Savannah's stomach jumped again. And again, she wasn't sure what emotion lay behind the buzz. "Evidence is the key word there. I don't see how I could get any."

"You already did."

"Those pictures don't prove anything."

"They prove those three men were given fake passports."

"But it doesn't prove where they came from," she argued. "And nobody would believe where I found them either. Around here, nothing I say is valid."

"I'd back you up."

"I wish it was that easy."

He went quiet, twirling a square of French toast in the syrup. "You're a savvy woman," he said, looking up at her again. "You consistently document your conversations with him, knowing his ego will get the best of him and he'll spill damning stuff."

She shrugged, unsure where he was going with this. "Live and learn."

He nodded, then angled the empty fork toward her. "What if you already had incriminating evidence against him and didn't even know it?" He lifted his brows. "Hell, you might be able to send him to jail tomorrow. What would it feel like to have the weight of him off your back?"

Her eyes slid closed. "Heaven." She looked at Ian again. "Unfortunately, I don't have enough. If I did, he'd already be gone."

"How do you know? You didn't think you had anything with the photos of the passports either, but they could turn out to be very powerful. Just because you don't know how one thing connects to another doesn't mean you don't have enough evidence to nail him."

She frowned. "I don't understand."

He put the fork down and lifted a strand of hair off her cheek, tucking it behind her ear. "Why don't you let me take a look at everything you've got—pictures, audio, video, personal notes?" He slid the tip of his index finger along her jawline. "I bet you've got way more than you think you have."

A persistent sparkle of hope gleamed somewhere deep inside. She'd been collecting every little detail for this very reason—to get enough to amount to something. But she'd learned over and over again that hope was a fickle bitch.

"I've given everything I have to Audrey. She doesn't seem to think any of it is enough to sway a judge in a criminal court. She also said a lot of it wouldn't be allowed as evidence."

"Audrey is focused on making sure Jamison stays with you. I'm focused on putting your ex away and giving you total freedom. Audrey is looking for evidence that would stand up in court. I'm looking for evidence that could be used as leverage to make him surrender. Audrey is a small fish in a big pond—the same pond where Hank swims. My contacts are the sharks that swim anywhere they smell blood."

"Who are these contacts?"

"Buddies from the military who have retired and moved on to bigger and better things—FBI, CIA, Homeland Security, Secret Service."

"What kind of work did you do to have such high-caliber buddies?"

"What do you mean?"

"I thought only special forces, like Navy SEALs, became Secret Service."

He grinned. "You've been watching too much television. The SEALs may get the glory, but we all do our part."

She shook her head. "If Hank finds out I've been collecting dirt..."

"That won't happen." He cupped her face and lifted her eyes to his. "He won't lay a finger on you or Jamison as long as I'm around."

She waffled another few seconds, then forced herself to jump. "Okay. If you want to rummage in the junk pile I've collected on Hank, be my guest."

His smile was confident and pleased. "That a girl." He kissed her, set her on her feet, and took her hand on the way to the bedroom. "Let's go burn off that midnight snack."

She couldn't think of a better way to keep reality at bay for at least a few more hours.

∽

ROMAN SAT in his rental with the engine running, the heat on high, his cell pressed to his ear.

"We're making solid progress," he told Gianna, summing up the brief he'd just given her in detail while he'd been watching Lyle Bishop's SUV outside Sugar Daddy's, waiting for the man to finish up with his favorite prostitute, Brandy. "Ian's a great addition to the team."

"Well, he's got a great team leader to emulate."

A smile teased his lips. "Thanks."

If Roman hadn't been sure Lyle would exit the brothel any moment, he would have closed his eyes and soaked in the sound of her voice in his ear. Somehow, the intimacy of speaking to her privately, sitting in the dark, felt wildly intimate. "You sound tired."

She sighed, and the sound shot tingles down his neck.

"Long days," she murmured. "Stress."

He hummed in understanding and fought to clear his mind of the intense desire he shouldn't be harboring for her. Yet kept searching for something else to talk about just to keep her on the phone. "You should have seen that basement, G."

"I wish I'd been there when you found it," she said, her voice a little dreamy. "God, your face. Your expression would have been priceless."

He smiled, enjoying connecting with her like this. They were both intensely dedicated to their jobs. Lived for the successes; suffered through failures. She got him—really got him—like no one else. "It was the coolest setup I've ever seen."

"I hope to be there when you seize it."

He liked that idea way too much. "It would be worth the trip to see it in person."

"All my trips to see you are worth it."

Her voice was soft, and the response surprised him. He was puzzling out her comment and whether or not he wanted to pick up the thread of interest she'd let slip through the well-woven professional fabric of their relationship when a snowplow barreled past.

"Where are you?" she asked.

"Outside the brothel, waiting for Lyle to free up his favorite girl."

"Going to get a little skin with your information?" The slightest edge entered her voice.

"I guess I should take it where I can get it, right?"

She huffed a laugh. "As if you have any trouble getting it."

Another thread slipped through the tapestry. Before Roman

could even toy with the idea of opening up dialogue about her interest in his sex life, Lyle appeared on the porch of the brothel. He said a few words to the security guards there and pulled on gloves, then dragged on a knit cap before starting down the steps with the fluid movements of a man who'd recently been sexually satisfied.

"I can't figure out if I'm more surprised they're bold enough to run a brothel with trafficked women," she said, "or that everyone in town can know about it and no law enforcement agency has shut it down."

"Intimidation, power, and kickbacks," he told her. "A trifecta for sure."

"You've done great work on this case, Roman. You're really close to taking down one hell of a dangerous terrorist ring."

The sincerity in her voice warmed him. "Thanks, but Heller deserves most of the credit. He's got a way of uncovering the nuances of a situation that cracks otherwise unbreachable barriers."

"And you have a way of understanding and placing your team where they work best."

He smiled. "I think my head's going to be too big to get out of the car."

Outside, Lyle turned over the engine of his SUV. Roman closed the door on the compartment of his psyche aching for more of Gianna and switched into work mode.

"He's on the move," he told her. "I'd better get in there before Brandy grabs another customer."

"Keep me posted," she said, her voice businesslike and clipped.

He disconnected, his mind wandering to the edge in Gianna's voice. Since their one steamy night together, Gianna certainly had never shown a flicker of interest in an encore.

When Lyle pulled away from the curb, Roman turned off his engine. He waited for Lyle's taillights to disappear down the highway before making his way across the street to the renovated Victorian.

One of the brawny security guards edged into his path. "I don't know you."

Roman pulled his hand from the warmth of his jacket and offered it to the man. "Tom. I'm new at the mines."

Instead of shaking his hand, the guard smacked his chest. "Arms out."

Roman complied while the other guard patted him down.

"No violence," he told Roman. "If you leave a mark on any girl, I'll hunt you down and break your teeth. Cash only. Leave as soon as you're done."

"Yes, sir," Roman said, congenial.

The guard stepped out of the way, and Roman continued inside. The moment he stepped inside, warmth and the sultry scent of perfume wrapped around him. The dim lighting and deep red décor added to the lush atmosphere, as did the women lounging on the velvet settees flanking a large desk. To Roman's surprise, the women were young and fresh. He'd been expecting the gaunt, strung-out drug addicts he'd seen in other trafficking situations. But the women were sharp and alert.

Two brunettes and a blonde welcomed him with seductive smiles. The lighter-haired brunette eased from one of the lounges and approached Roman.

"Welcome, handsome." Her voice was soft and edged with an unmistakable Russian accent. She pressed her hands to his chest and moved close enough to kiss him. She probably would have if Roman hadn't eased his head back.

"You're new in town." The blonde sounded Bosnian. She crossed her long bare legs and swung one spiked heel. "I would have noticed a silver fox like you if you'd been in before."

At thirty-eight, Roman was the oldest member of the Manhunters, but still too young to be considered a silver fox. At least in his opinion. But he'd grayed early, and women had told him that the mixture of black and white in his hair made it look silvery. He usually kept it cropped too close for the color to matter, but he'd been lazy about getting to the barber, so it was longer than usual.

"Mmm, mmm, mmm. Aren't you just delicious?" The brunette circled him in a languid stroll, her hand trailing across his chest, then his shoulders before she came to a stop in front of him again. Her big hazel eyes dripped invitation. "Will you do me the pleasure of letting me do you tonight?"

The heaviness in the pit of his gut told Roman just how badly he needed to be done, and anonymous hookups were all he had the interest or time for. But he preferred sex arising from mutual attraction, not payment, and with Gianna so fresh in his mind, it was a nonstarter.

"I'm hoping Brandy's free," he said.

The blonde stood and strolled over. She leaned against his side and stroked a hand down his abdomen. A combination of floral and spice floated on the air. A feminine, sultry scent that made Roman think of rolling in the sheets, skin to skin.

"What's that young thing doing to pull in all the sexy older men?" The darker of the two brunettes was Hispanic, and her inquiry purred with challenge. "Brandy doesn't have what we have. And we're available right now."

She sauntered over and wrapped her arm around the blonde's waist. "Why don't you let me and Tara give you a double dose of love?"

Good question. Why didn't he? Had his one night with Gianna really spoiled him for all other women?

Business, Roman. Head in the game. "Thanks, but I've got my heart set on Brandy."

"Did I hear my name?" Another luscious brunette wandered in from the hallway. She was tall and curvy. And, damn, she was young. As in Lyle-could-have-been-her-grandfather young. "Hey, there. You're new."

Roman smiled at her. "And I have similar tastes as Lyle."

Her smile flickered, and her eyes went flat. But she swayed over to him, nudged the other women aside, and slipped her arm around his. "Then come on up to my room. I've got a brand-new set of cuffs with your name on them."

She pulled him into step beside her, continuing through the hallway, then took his hand as she turned to climb a narrow set of stairs. Leading him by the hand, she spoke as if she were giving him a historical tour, not leading him to a bedroom for paid sex.

"This house was built in 1888 by Harold Putman, the town's mayor at the time," she told him in a soft Chechen accent. "He had six children. He and his wife lived a very happy life here."

"That sounds like a little fantasy you tell yourself to feel better."

"A few fantasies never hurt anyone." They passed a guard at the top of the stairs, and Brandy turned down the hallway, leading Roman to the third room on the right. After Roman entered, she closed the door and asked, "What fantasies would you like to play out tonight?"

He wandered through the space until Brandy had moved away from the door. The room had recently been cleaned. The air held a floral, slightly antiseptic scent. When he passed the bed, sliding his fingertips across the comforter. The sheets were warm and smelled freshly laundered.

Roman put himself between Brandy and the exit before he faced her again. "My only fantasy is putting Lyle Bishop in prison."

Her smile slid from her face. All the heat in her eyes turned cold. "You need to leave."

She surged toward the door, reaching for the knob.

Roman caught her arm, stopping her. When she looked up, they were almost nose to nose. "How old are you?"

"Twenty," she snapped.

"More like sixteen."

"Get out," she ordered, "or I'll scream, and security will—"

"You won't scream." To keep her from doing just that, Roman released her and pulled out his Department of Defense credentials. "Because if you do, the only people who come will be the Homeland Security agents waiting outside," he lied. "They'll raid this place and take you all into custody. And you know what happens next: deportation."

Real terror sparked in her eyes. She stepped back and crossed her arms, her fingers squeezing and releasing her arms. "You're right. You're just like Lyle."

"Has he offered you permanent residence in the US if you cooperate? Or to bring your family over from Chechnya? That's where you're from, right?"

She glanced at the door behind him and shook her head. "He'll kill me if I say anything."

"Not if he's in prison."

Her lips pressed into a thin line.

"I know they keep you imprisoned here," Roman said. "I know they took your identification. All your money. And I know they won't let you go until you've paid off your debt to them. They probably threatened to harm your family back home if you ran away."

She shifted on her feet and inched backward.

"None of this is new," he said, keeping his voice soft. "The threats, the power plays, the lies. Traffickers have been using the same old script for decades. But I can change all that for you."

"You lie, just like him," she spit out, clearly terrified. "Leave me alone. I only have a year left until I'm free."

"I bet they told you that last year. And the year before that. There are expenses you have to reimburse, right? Interest that racks up? You won't be any freer a year from now than you are now. They'll keep you here until you escape or they kill you." Roman let that sink in for a long, quiet moment. "All I need is a little help, Brandy. A little help and you and your family will live a free life in America."

When she didn't shoot back another denial, he gestured to an overstuffed chair in the corner. "Now, have a seat so we can talk business."

11

I an pulled his truck to a spot along the street beside the café. He'd begged off early from work with the excuse of a bad tooth and a dentist's appointment. But early was relative. He'd pried himself away from Savannah at six a.m. and headed in early, working a full nine hours without lunch, knowing he'd have to ask to leave at three p.m. As expected, Mo agreed. Now, Ian just wanted to see Savannah before he headed into Whitefish to meet with the team.

He climbed from the car just as Misty exited the back door of the café with a garbage bag almost as big as she was. She lugged it toward a dumpster in the far corner of the rear parking lot. Ian was about to start that way to take the burden for her when a sheriff's patrol car pulled into the lot, blocking Misty's path.

Ian rounded his truck and watched from the safety of the vehicle.

Misty dropped the bag and propped a hand on her hip. "I'm trying to work here."

Hank stood from the cruiser, resting his arm on top of the door between them. With Misty's attention on Hank and Hank's back to Ian, he darted across the street and crept to the corner of the building where he could hear their conversation.

"Now there's a job you're worthy of," Hank said.

"You're such a bastard," Misty shot back.

Ian peered around the corner of the building and found Misty fighting to drag the trash around the cruiser.

"It makes you feel all mighty and powerful to be a shit to all us little people, doesn't it, *Sheriff*?" She said the last with contempt.

"We need to talk," he told her.

"The hell we do." She made it to the front of the cruiser before Hank rounded the open driver's door and grabbed her arm. He yanked her hard enough to make Misty drop the garbage. She whirled on him, furious. "Who in the hell do you think—"

"You need to talk to Savannah," he ordered.

Misty yanked her arm from Hank's grip. "Touch me again and I'll yell 'rape' so loud, your ears will bleed."

Ian smiled. He was grateful Savannah had a friend with guts.

Hank approached her, hands on hips, until he was in her face. "You're going to talk to her, and you're going to convince her to dump that grease monkey."

Ian's smile vanished. He gritted his teeth, swore under his breath. A whole new, heightened sense of protectiveness flowed through his veins after last night. This morning, he'd woken to her soft, warm body pressed against his, and it was as if a light switch had flipped on. He had new goals and new purpose, all related to Savannah and Jamison.

But he still had very real, very substantial hurdles to jump.

"In case you hadn't noticed," Misty said, "Savannah is very independent. She has her own mind. Nothing I say will pry her away from Ian."

A flutter irritated his gut—excitement and dread. He hoped Misty was accurate about Savannah's commitment, but he was also pretty sure there was something he could say that would ruin everything between them. It went along the lines of "I've been lying to you from day one."

Hank stepped into Misty's path.

"See, this is why Savannah would never come back to you. You and your arrogance. You're *such* an asshole."

"You're going to change her mind," Hank told her.

Misty just laughed. "Not a chance in hell."

"You will," Hank's tone deepened and darkened. "Or you'll find the FBI at your barn."

FBI at her barn? That struck Ian as strange.

"Well, that would sure ruin this thing you and Lyle have going, wouldn't it?" she said.

Dots instantly connected, but Ian resisted the picture they created. Like looking at an ink blot, he tried to twist it into something he could believe.

"They sell that shit all over the darknet, nowadays," Hank said. "Your father may have been the only game in town when we started this, but now..." He shook his head. "We can get them anywhere."

"Great. I don't want to do that shit for you anyway," Misty shot back, picking up the bag and walking right into him, pushing him aside with the garbage. "If it weren't for Savannah and Jamison, you'd have been shit out of luck when Dad died. So go ahead, by all means. If you think the darknet would be a great option, go for it. Since the Silk Road went down, every law enforcement agency on the planet tracks the darknet. I'd love to see you get caught."

Holy. Shit. Ian couldn't believe where this was leading.

"Convince Savannah," Hank demanded. "Or you'll lose everything, including your freedom."

Ian couldn't get his mind around Misty as a counterfeiter. Talk about getting blindsided. His mind darted back to what Savannah had told him about Misty's father. An inventor... Useless gadgets of all kinds... Only one ever made him any money... Sounded a lot like that one gadget had been a counterfeiting setup. One Hank had blackmailed Misty into continuing when her father died.

He pressed his back against the wall and looked up at the blue sky. Snow clouds loomed in the distance. Did Savannah know about Misty's activities? Had she helped Misty? He thought back to the night before and Savannah's interest in passports. She wouldn't have asked him if she knew her best friend created them. Would she?

Sickness tightened his gut. Even if Savannah didn't know, she'd find out. At some point, Ian was going to have to tell her. Warn her. Prepare her for the inevitable—losing her best friend to prison. And as soon as he did, he would lose her.

"Fuck me." He rounded the opposite corner and entered the café.

The lunch crowd had dwindled. A couple of older guys sat at the counter, drinking coffee and chatting. Savannah was in the dining room, cleaning and arranging tables for the dinner rush. She was wearing the jeans with the sparkles on the back pockets, but he certainly didn't need the adornment to focus there. Nor did he need any help pulling up the feel of her great ass in his hands the night before.

One night. Barely twelve hours. How could it feel like she'd been his a damn month?

When she noticed him, her face broke out in a smile. "Hey, there. I was just thinking about you."

"Oh yeah?" Ian strolled toward her, took her hand and walked backward toward the hallway leading to the bathrooms. As soon as they'd cleared the doorway, he sandwiched her between his body and the wall and kissed her hard. She made a sound of surprise, then wrapped her arms around his neck and pushed to her toes to kiss him back.

The knots running along his spine eased.

He broke the kiss, and Savannah laughed a little. "Well, hello to you too."

"Been dying to do that since six this morning." He ran his hand over her hair and kissed her again. He dragged her up against his body and swept his tongue into her mouth. God, he wanted her even more than he had last night. He pulled back and asked, "Are you free tonight? To go over, you know, the dirt?"

"I have Jamison—"

"After he's asleep?"

She started to nod then said, "But the bugs—"

He kissed her again. "I'll download a blocker."

She pulled back. "A what?"

"Blocker. It emits a signal that interrupts the bug."

He moved in to kiss her again. She put a hand against his chest. "Why didn't you tell me about a blocker when we found the bugs?"

Alarm bells went off in his head. *Shit.* "I just found it today."

"Oh." She didn't believe him; he could tell by the look in her eyes. "Are you staying for lunch?"

"No. I broke a tooth on a granola bar this morning, and I'm going to Missoula to get it fixed."

"Why go all the way to Missoula?"

"The doc here didn't have an opening, and the one in Missoula uses nitrous oxide gas." He winced. "I'm really a pussy when it comes to dental work."

That made her laugh, and he felt the equilibrium between them restored. She leaned into him and skimmed her fingers down his cheek. "Drive careful. Text me when you get back."

SAVANNAH TURNED to watch Ian walk from the café—all wide shoulders and tight ass. When he got to the door, he shot a "gotcha" grin over his shoulder. Savannah had confessed to her love of his ass the night before, and he was obviously testing her story of stopping whatever she was doing to watch him walk out. He pushed out the door backward and winked at her just before turning to trot down the stairs.

Savannah felt like she'd downed a bottle of sparkling wine, gut fizzing, heart buzzing, head light. She smiled, reveling in the sensations. He was a great guy who also happened to be sexy, sweet, and damn good in bed. She felt like she'd hit the lottery.

His story about the blocker didn't add up, and she didn't know what to think about that.

Misty wandered into the dining room, frowning at her phone.

"What's wrong?" Savannah asked.

"Tell me what Ian's tattoo looked like again."

"His...what?"

"The tattoo on his shoulder. The one of a skull."

Savannah remembered the sight of his broad, naked back, tapering into a tight waist from the night before. "A skull with a dagger through it."

"Did the blade go through the eye socket?"

"Um..." She thought back. "Yeah. Why?"

"Because I've been looking for it online, and I think I found it." She looked up from her phone with concern pulling her brow, turning the device to face Savannah. "Is this it?"

"Yes. Where did you find it?"

"Google images." Still frowning, Misty tapped the screen a few times. "I searched for military tattoos of a skull."

"Why are you making that face?" Savannah asked.

"Because the unit the tattoo is associated with isn't what I expected."

Dread slipped into her gut. Her mind piped up with *I knew he was too good to be true.*

She stopped what she was doing and stepped up beside Misty. Her screen was filled with Wikipedia information on a military group called Manhunters.

Misty read, "An elite group of men recruited for the sole purpose of identifying, capturing, interrogating, and killing high-value targets."

A chill swept through Savannah's stomach.

"The Manhunters report only to their leader, a high-ranking member of the CIA, who identifies targets for elimination. Those killed by Manhunters range from drug lords to scientists, diplomats to heads of government."

The cold leaked through her whole body. The memory of Hank landing a punch to Ian's jaw discounted the whole "elite military team" concept. But then Savannah remembered how quickly and easily Ian had taken the opportunity to get in shots at Hank. And how calm Ian had been when Hank pulled his weapon. *"He never would have gotten a shot off."*

"Savannah," Misty said, pulling her from her thoughts. "Have you talked to him about his work in the military?"

A protective instinct rose inside her. She wasn't ready to believe the worst of Ian. "A little. Not about what he did, just about why he left and what he planned to do now."

"If this is true," Misty said, "you should probably think about ending things between you."

Shock hit, and Savannah pushed back. "What are you talking about? You haven't been able to say anything but great things about him all morning. About how I was *glowing*. How happy you were that I've finally found a good guy."

"That was before I knew this," she said, matching Savannah's vehemence. "Do you really want an assassin around Jamison? Think about it. If he's capable of doing the things they talk about here, what's to keep him from doing it now?"

"Don't call him an assassin, and stop jumping to conclusions. You're quoting Wikipedia, for God's sake. Not exactly the most reliable form of information. Especially not if his team was as elite as that says."

The bell on the door signaled the beginning of the dinner crowd.

"I just don't want you or Jamison to get hurt—physically or emotionally." Misty had lowered her voice. "After living with someone as violent as Hank, the last thing you need is another tyrant in your life."

"Ian's nothing like Hank. He's certainly no tyrant."

"Hank didn't seem like one at first either."

"Good afternoon, ladies." Chuck was a miner who came in every day at the end of shift.

"Hey, Chuck," Savannah called, then told Misty, "Don't tell anyone about this. I'll talk to Ian."

Without waiting for an answer, Savannah continued to Chuck's table with hot coals burning in her gut. She had to make a deliberate, concerted effort to work up small talk.

After putting Chuck's order in, Savannah glanced around the café. When she found Misty helping another customer across the café, she stepped into the hallway to the bathrooms and pulled out her phone. She took a breath and dialed Doctor Dunfy's office then leaned back against the wall with her eyes closed in dread and chanted a quiet "Please, please, please be true."

"Doctor Dunfy's office," the receptionist answered.

"Hey, Sarah, it's Savannah."

After some quick small talk, Savannah said, "I think Jamison may have broken a tooth on a granola bar this morning."

"Oh, ouch," Sarah said. "Poor baby."

"Yeah, who would have guessed, right?"

"I think I've heard everything that could go wrong in a person's mouth at least once, but I'm pretty sure that's a new one."

Savannah's stomach dropped, and she closed her eyes. "Does Doctor Dunfy have an opening this afternoon to take a look at Jamison?"

"Yep. We keep an emergency slot open right before close just for this kind of thing. Can you bring him in at four thirty?"

Damn. Damn, damn, damn. Savannah wanted to scream. Instead, she gritted her teeth a moment, then exhaled. "He'll be coming to the café after his playdate, and I'll take a look at him. If I need the spot, I'll call you back."

"Sounds good."

"Hey, Sarah?" she asked before the girl disconnected. "By chance, does Dr. Duffy ever use nitrous oxide?"

"Sure, but I'll have to check your insurance to see if they'd cover it."

Savannah's heart joined her stomach at her feet. "No problem. I was just curious. Thanks."

Savannah disconnected, closed her eyes, and dropped her head back against the wall.

He'd been lying to her. Savannah was disgusted with herself. She should be able to spot a liar by now.

The bell continued to chime in the diner, cutting into Savannah's worries. She straightened and stocked her apron with straws and pens with a renewed goal of getting the dirt she needed on Hank to end this custody battle, once and for all. Ian might not be a golden boy, he might not even be the kind of man she wanted to continue seeing, but right now, he was the lesser of two evils and her only hope of getting what she needed to keep her son.

12

Ian followed in Roman's footsteps, approaching the barn on Misty's property from the rear. Just past dusk, they had a limited window of opportunity to get in and get out before Misty finished her shift at the diner and returned home.

Roman moved to the back of an outbuilding a few hundred yards from the barn and paused. Ian peered through the night-vision scope on his M4 and scanned the area.

"Clear," he told Roman.

"Alpha team, in position," Roman said, their counterparts approaching from the opposite side of the property.

"Beta team, in position." Sam's voice vibrated over the com line. "And may I just take this opportunity to reiterate my opposition to our team name? Moore and I aren't exactly the moderate, easy-going kind. I'll admit, we aren't withdrawn, resentful Deltas either, but I'd be satisfied with Omega or Gamma. What say you, Moore?"

"Affirmative," Liam said. "I vote for Omega."

"Done." Roman took their sarcasm in stride. "You're officially Sigma team."

"Sigma my ass," Sam muttered. "That's worse than Beta."

"Stop complaining." Everly's voice came over the line from where she'd been stationed to watch Misty. "Any team is better than sitting here watching paint peel. Their internet sucks."

"On three." Roman counted down, and the two teams closed in on the barn with smooth, choreographed precision.

Once they were in position, flanking the barn's double doors, Ian pulled the bolt cutters from his pack, snapped a link on the chain threaded through the handles, and returned to his position behind Roman.

Roman and Sam held their weapons ready with one hand and slid the other into the handles on the doors.

"On three," Roman murmured again.

Ian stepped away from the barn wall, his M4 up, his eye focused through the night-vision sight, mirroring Liam.

"Three," Roman said, "two, one."

The doors flew open with an unearthly screech. Ian and Liam advanced in unison, sweeping the dark interior. Rodents scurried in every direction as flashes of light darted through the scope.

When no other heat signatures registered, Liam and Ian said, "Clear," at the same time, then continued through the space, searching for signs of life.

The barn was packed floor to ceiling with junk—computers, bicycles, appliances, every tool known to mankind. Just junk, junk, and more junk. And the funky, musty, moldy smell of age and disuse.

On the opposite side of the barn, they found a staircase to a second story. Liam led the way up, he and Ian sweeping their weapons over the space, watching through their scopes.

Finally, they lowered their weapons. "All clear," Ian said, exhaling in relief. "At least of humans."

"You two take the loft," Roman said. "We'll look down here."

Ian and Liam pulled Maglites from their gear. With sweeps of halogen, they illuminated televisions, VCRs, and DVD players in one corner. Vacuums, table lamps, microwaves, toasters, hair dryers, and curling irons in another, all in a state of disrepair.

"At least he kept things in some sort of order," Liam muttered.

Ian turned and found the G-man shining his light across a wall where hooks were heaped with electrical cords of all kinds. "Not enough order to find what we came for." He made his way to the banister overlooking the lower part of the barn, testing the wood under his feet before he put his full weight down. "What have you got down there?"

"Washers, dryers, refrigerators," Sam said, "movie projectors, DVDs and VCR tapes, magazines, books..."

The shuffle of paper and the knock of drawers skittered through the barn. Ian made his way down the stairs again. He found Roman in a corner of the barn, sifting through things on a mammoth desk that looked like it would crumble at any moment.

"Anything?" Ian asked, turning to sweep his light over stacks of light fixtures, sewing machines, and space heaters, every appliance gutted for parts.

"Nothing obvious," Roman said on an exhale, abandoning his search of the desk and glancing around.

"Misty just took off her apron," Everly informed them over the com line. "She's closing out her tickets."

"Going through here would take weeks," Ian told Roman.

"We leave in ten minutes," Roman said. "Everyone take one last look around."

Ian wasn't even sure what he was looking for anymore. He shone his light across the dirt floor, wondering if he'd heard Bishop wrong earlier. Maybe there was a deeper meaning to the threat he'd leveled at Misty, insinuating he'd leave something in the barn to frame her. That seemed to be his MO.

"Sorry, boss," Ian told Roman as his Maglite exposed pile after pile of newspapers in a dark corner of the barn. "Maybe I read too much into that conver—"

His boot shuffled across something metal. Something that

created a hollow echo underfoot. He angled his light down and found the corner of a metal plate. Turning a corner, Ian found himself in a three-sided box of decades-old newspapers and standing on something that looked a lot like a trapdoor.

Excitement pulsed through his veins.

He stepped back, crouched, and pulled on a metal ring. The door gave way with surprising ease. Ian's gut tightened. He held the door open a few inches and shone his light into the space.

"Found something."

Before Ian finished the last word, Roman was beside him. "What have you—"

They both fell silent as Ian opened the door, exposing an opening framed in steel, a metal staircase leading into what looked like a large basement.

"What the fuck?" Sam's hands closed on Ian's and Roman's shoulders as he peered past them. "I didn't see that comin'. I have to admit, I thought this was bullshit from the beginning."

"Your 'wrong' score is skyrocketing," Everly teased.

Ian glanced at Roman.

"You found it," Roman told him, "You get to go first."

"Pick up the pace, guys," Everly told them. "Misty just clocked out. She's on her way to her car."

Ian pulled the strap of his M4 over his head and handed the weapon off to Roman, then pulled his Glock nine from his thigh holster, used his other hand to guide the Maglite, and started down the stairs.

At the bottom, Ian swept the light across the space. The floor was concrete, the walls cinder block. He found a light switch and flipped it on, flooding the basement with fluorescent light.

"Holy shit." He scanned the space, jaw unhinged. "*Holy. Shit.*"

"What?" Everly said, excitement edging her voice. "What did you find?"

"Comin' down," Roman said before skipping the steps and

dropping to the floor beside Ian. He took one look and broke into excited laughter. "Holy shit is right."

"*What?*" she asked again. "What is it?"

Liam and Sam pushed their way into the basement, and together, the team scanned the space with shock and awe. Fully finished and meticulously clean and organized, the room was an upscale, state-of-the-art workspace, complete with three industrial printers, half a dozen computers, and twice as many monitors set up around two huge commercial desks. Shelves and workbenches lined the walls holding equipment, paper, plates, ink, and other supplies.

"A top-of-the-line counterfeiting setup," Roman answered Everly, sauntering toward a line of presses and steel printing plates. "That's what."

Misty would be going away for a very long time. Which meant Savannah was going to lose her best and only friend.

And if she had aided Misty in any way, Savannah would be criminally responsible under the aiding and abetting laws. And that would land her in federal prison. She could kiss Jamison goodbye—literally.

The excitement coursing through Ian's veins cooled. He picked up a bottle of ink from the dozens lining the shelves.

"What have you got there?" Sam asked.

"Thermochromic and optically variable security ink," Ian said.

"I've seen my share of counterfeit material," Liam said. "But never anything this sophisticated." He picked up a piece of paper from a stack sitting beside a commercial printer and took a close look, tilting it back and forth under the light. "She's using intaglio methods."

"English, please," Everly complained.

"It's an ancient printing technique still used for passports today," Liam said. "Complex, twisting patterns on the inside pages of a passport created using multiple plates and presses."

"Hologram plates too," Sam said, picking up one of dozens of engraved steel plates. "Look at the detail." He huffed a laugh as he ran his gloved fingers over the metal. "This is intense."

Ian picked up a piece of dark blue plastic used for passport covers. "I thought she might have picked up some passports on the darknet, doctored them, and passed them on to Bishop, but this..." He shook his head. "I never imagined she was capable of *this*."

Which made him second-guess what he believed Savannah capable of—including covering up her friend's illegal activity.

"You either need to contemplate all this elsewhere," Everly said. "Or you'd better get ready to take her down. She's going to pull into the ranch in about fifteen minutes."

"If we arrest Misty now, we'll tip off Hank and Lyle. There's no telling whether Misty kept a record of the passports she's created, but we know Lyle did."

"Hotfoot it, boys," Roman said. "We'll come back for this once we have the ledger. Ian, fix that chain so she doesn't know we were here."

The men filed up the stairs. Sam mulled over an old desk in the corner. At the door, Ian waited as the other's exited. Before Roman passed through the door, he planted a hand on Ian's shoulder.

"You need to prep Savannah for what's coming," he told Ian. "We're going to need her cooperation."

His gut clenched, but he nodded as if he had everything under control. "We'll have it. Sam, get your ass out before I lock you in."

Once Sam cleared the barn, Ian removed the broken link in the chain and locked up the door, then followed his teammates toward their vehicles parked on the main road.

This was a no-win situation for Savannah. She didn't know it yet, but her life just took another turn in its downward spiral.

SAVANNAH SLID her hand over Jamison's brow and pushed his hair off his forehead, then leaned down to kiss him there. She breathed in his fresh-from-the-bath scent and smiled.

Easing back, she took in every detail of his sleeping face, from the freckles across his nose to the way his lips twitched as he dreamt. She'd never imagined she could love this way—so deeply, so completely, so unconditionally.

She would—without any doubt—do anything she had to do to keep Jamison from being ruined by Hank and Lyle. Her love for Jamison was all-encompassing, making her understand the concept of giving her life to save someone else.

Her phone chimed, and Savannah sat back, pulling it from her pocket.

As she suspected, it was from Ian. *I'm home.*

Excitement and dread warred. She exhaled, forcing herself to accept Ian at face value. He might not be all that he seemed, might turn out to be too good to be true after all, might have done unscrupulous things in his past, but he was her only lifeline at the moment. And she liked to think she could still give a man the benefit of the doubt.

Jamison is asleep. Back door is unlocked.

Savannah glanced at Jamison one last time before she closed the bedroom door, then stopped in the bathroom to look at her reflection. The woman staring back looked so much more together than she felt. So much more vibrant and hopeful.

The back door whined open. She turned off the bathroom light and moved across the kitchen soundlessly in her stocking feet. Ian appeared as a looming shadow in the laundry room. Savannah had a sudden, clear image of what he must have looked like to those he'd killed just before he'd ended their lives, and her stomach dropped.

How many homes or offices had he infiltrated just as easily as he'd walked in her back door? How many people had he terrified? How many had he killed? In cold blood? Had there been women? Children?

He stepped into the doorway between the rooms. The moonlight illuminated his outstretched hand, offering his phone. Savannah shook off the nerves and closed the distance. His free hand curled around her wrist and drew her close. Savannah's heart rate spiked, and chills shivered down her spine.

He leaned close and whispered, "Put this on your coffee table. It will block the wavelength for the listening devices."

She did as he said and turned from the living room to find him right behind her. Her heart skipped; her stomach jumped. She stepped back, an automatic reaction she regretted when his expression registered concern.

Savannah swallowed her unease, stepped close, and rested a hand against his chest. His clean scent filled Savannah's head with citrus and man. "How is your tooth? Were they able to fix it?"

"They were." The low vibration of his voice slipped over her, creating another shiver in her belly. This one pleasant. "But my mouth has been missing yours."

He lowered his head and kissed her, wrapping his arms around her at the same time. As soon as she was in his arms with his heat warming her body, all her apprehension melted away. All her doubts evaporated. She leaned into him, and he was there, his strength supporting her. And when she kissed him back, Savannah found emotional bedrock.

Ian broke the kiss, hugging her close. "You're making me want to skip to the fun stuff."

She would have supported that idea wholeheartedly if she didn't have a piano hanging over her head on fraying rope. She was anxious to see if Ian could find solid evidence she could use to keep Hank at bay.

"The sooner we get the dirt out of the way, the sooner we get to the fun stuff." She stepped away and turned for the hallway. "I just need to pull everything together."

When Ian followed her into the bedroom, Savannah realized he was going to see her hiding place. As she opened the closet and removed the floorboards to expose the space beneath, she wondered if she should find a new cubbyhole to stash her dirt. Then hated herself—and even Misty a little—for this new doubt creeping through her head.

"Wow," he said, standing behind her as she dragged up the shoebox holding the papers and CDs she'd collected over the years. "That's quite a stash."

Savannah handed him one box and pulled out another. "I know the CD's are antiquated, and I have the recordings saved to the cloud, but the way Hank operates, I felt like I needed a hard copy too. I hope there's something in here to cut Hank off at the knees." She pushed to her feet, realizing how bad that sounded, and turned to face Ian. "I don't really mean—"

He cupped her face, but his brow was creased with worry. "I know, baby. I know."

"What's wrong?"

He shook his head and turned toward the bed, setting the box on her coverlet. "Just hoping for the same."

He was so sincere. So authentically concerned for both her and Jamison. Savannah would never have investigated his background the way Misty had. She would never have questioned anything he told her. Yet because of Misty's suspicions, Savannah had already uncovered him in a lie. And that made her feel both vulnerable and angry. She didn't care where he'd really gone this afternoon. She only cared that he'd lied about it.

Jamison.

She had to focus on Jamison. And at this point, she couldn't be concerned with how she did that, who helped her or why. After she was sure she'd never lose Jamison, she could worry about Ian and a relationship—if they ever got that far.

At the headboard, she crossed her legs and pulled one of the boxes into her lap. "Okay, let's do this."

He toed out of his boots and joined her on the bed. Leaning back against the headboard, he pulled the other box into his lap and turned his gaze on her. "Try not to worry. We'll find something. He won't take Jamison."

Right now, Savannah was happy Ian was on her side. She pulled the cover off her own box and scanned the CDs. Her stomach clenched. So much hate. So, *so* much hate.

"What are those?" he asked, pulling out photocopies from his own box.

"I transferred my—I guess you'd call them conversations, but they're really arguments—with Hank from my phone to the CDs." And suddenly, she wasn't thrilled at the prospect of exposing the underbelly of her marriage to her new lover. She met his gaze. "I'll warn you now, it's not pretty. And if you don't see me the same after you've heard and seen all this, I won't blame you."

His expression softened, and a smile flickered over his lips. He reached out and squeezed her thigh. "Like I said before, I can guarantee I've seen worse."

If Misty's information about the Manhunters was accurate, and if Ian was in fact a Manhunter, Savannah couldn't begin to imagine what he'd seen. Or what he might have done.

But right now, none of that mattered. Right now, he was on her side, and she forced herself not to think about what he'd be like as opposition.

AN HOUR LATER, Savannah finished sorting the paper documents while Ian listened to the last CD. After fifteen minutes of hearing the first recording, Savannah had given Ian earbuds and insisted he listen to them privately. Hearing the ugliness she'd already lived through made her sick to her stomach all over again. And over the last hour, the Ian she'd come to know transitioned into the man she feared he might be—his eyes dark, expression stern, anger vibrating off him in waves.

She dropped back to the pillows, exhaling as she scanned a copy of Hank and Lyle's bank statement. The document had turned out to be useless in a court run by Tim Baulder's father.

The opposition she faced came into sharp focus once again, and hopelessness edged in. She shouldn't have gotten Ian caught up in this mess. She should have let him remain blissfully oblivious.

Ian exhaled, pulled off the earbuds, and dropped his head back against the headboard, eyes closed. "I need a shower. Your ex is a filthy excuse of a human being."

Hearing her worst fear verified by someone with the training and knowledge to know exactly what filth looked and sounded like felt like a knife in Savannah's gut. She was ashamed she let the abuse happen in the first place. Mortified to look back and see just how long she'd let it go on. Feared how it would continue to affect Jamison as he grew up.

"He threatened to kill you six times." Ian opened his eyes and turned an intense look on her. "*Six times.*"

"More like a dozen. I just didn't get the other half on tape."

"Not funny. *So* not funny."

"Sorry," she sighed. "If I don't laugh, I'll cry."

"Audrey should have gotten you a restraining order a long damn time ago. Didn't she use this in your divorce hearing?"

"Nothing detrimental to a Bishop would be admitted as evidence in a court system greased with Bishop Mining cash and power."

"*You're* a Bishop," he said, his voice tight with restraint.

"By marriage, not blood."

"Fucking unbelievable." His gaze went distant a long, quiet moment. Then he turned that intense stare on her again. "Why hasn't he come through on the threats? Why didn't he kill you a long time ago? It's obvious he would get away with it."

That hit her as a bit harsh, but when she thought of his background, she realized talk of murder wasn't unusual in his world—which made her second-guess the decision to let him into hers.

"I've wondered the same thing in some of my darker moments," she admitted.

His hand closed over her thigh and squeezed. "I'm sorry. I didn't mean it the way it sounded."

She covered his hand with hers. "Honestly, I think he fully believed that I would come back to him. As time passed and his attempts to beg, bargain, threaten, and scare me back didn't work..." She exhaled. "I think he gets closer and closer to following through on that threat every day. And there's Jamison to consider. When Hank and I were at college, he told me that he wanted kids someday. As soon as Lyle got his hooks back into Hank, that changed. We were already on shaky ground when I got pregnant. Hank was *so pissed*."

She closed her eyes, remembering. In retrospect, Savannah believed Hank's anger had stemmed from fear. Fear of being trapped in Hazard. Fear of living under his father's thumb. But mostly, fear of being too weak to do anything about it.

"Hank's always seen Jamison as a pawn," Savannah said. "To gain his father's approval, to control me. He has no desire to be a father to him, and as long as I'm around, he doesn't have to be."

A long moment of silence followed while they both got lost in their own thoughts. Savannah basked in the moment of having someone who cared about her ready to do battle on her behalf. Really do battle. Misty was supportive, but she didn't have any more power in Hazard than Savannah did. Part of her even hoped that Misty's hunch about Ian being part of a military special forces group was true, because then his claims of having friends in important places would also be true. And Savannah knew it would take people outside Hazard and Lyle's influence to free her.

"So, what do you think?" she asked, glancing at his notes. "Ready to run screaming from the room yet?"

"More like ready to take Hank and Lyle into a dark alley." He gestured to his notes on a spiral notepad Savannah had given him. "This is all good stuff, but we need to find something that will lift you outside the Hazard justice system so these threats will be heard." He reached out and picked up the papers she'd sorted. "Tell me about these."

"Hank had a joint bank account with Lyle that I didn't know about. Lyle deposited money into it every month. The amounts varied, and at first, I thought Lyle was helping with our bills. But the numbers didn't add up. It wasn't long before I realized Lyle wouldn't do anything for us out of the goodness of his heart. I suspected Hank was doing something for Lyle on the side, but I never could figure out what." She met his gaze. "After I found those passports..."

Ian nodded. "Lyle is paying Hank to pick them up and deliver them to him."

She shrugged and gestured to the bank statements. "Seems like a lot of money for such a small errand."

"It wasn't small." Ian picked up the pile and skimmed the top statement. "By having Hank handle the passports, Lyle kept his hands clean. If anyone ever discovered the deal, Hank would be the only person physically connected with the passports. Lyle must believe he has sufficient control over Hank to keep him from implicating Lyle in the deal."

"He does." Savannah made a face. "It's a skeezy kind of control. One that combines fear and power and money. Lyle has always known how to dig into all Hank's fears."

Ian's finger slid down the page, his gaze searching line items. "That's because Lyle planted and cultivated every one of them while Hank was growing up."

"So true." Savannah was in a daily battle to keep Hank and Lyle from planting and cultivating the same bad seeds in Jamison.

While Ian looked through the papers, Savannah distracted herself by focusing on Ian. On the way his hair felt sliding through her fingers. The way her fingers could smooth away the fine lines radiating from the corner of his eyes. The texture of his skin. The fullness of his bottom lip.

"Baby." He curled his fingers around hers and brought her hand to his lips for a kiss without looking away from the papers. "You're distracting me."

"I'm trying," she said, pressing a kiss to his temple, then his cheekbone, then his jaw, while Ian turned pages. "Really hard." She let her hand skim across the soft cotton covering his hard abdomen, then fall to the waistband of his jeans, where she worked the button open. "Really, *really* hard."

His lips curved in a smile. "It's working really, *really* well."

She hummed against the skin just below his ear. He would be such an easy man to love. He was warm and kind and strong. Determined and tenacious and intelligent. And he cared. Yes, he'd also lied. But she didn't know the circumstances of that lie. Nor did she know if he'd been part of the team Misty had discovered. She wasn't going to make assumptions until she had all the information. And she'd get it. Just not right now. Right now, she wanted to bask in his compassionate attention. They had plenty of time to sort out the potentially sketchy details of their pasts.

Savannah slipped her hand beneath his shirt and stroked his ripped abs as Ian turned another page.

His body tensed. "What's this?"

Savannah lifted her head from his shoulder to see what he was looking at—two sheets of names and dates. "I don't know. I never figured it out. It was from a notebook Hank kept in the safe. One of those accounting journals."

His gaze pivoted to hers. "A ledger?"

"I guess that's what they're called. I recognized the names of guys who worked at the mine at the time, so I took photocopies in case I figured out what it was for. But I never did."

"I might know." Excitement sparked in his eyes, and he sat forward, angling toward her. "It could be a list of people who got passports."

She frowned down at the list, her mind working backward to sift through the names and piece together the backgrounds of the men. "Maybe..." She took the list from Ian. "I don't know about Cutler and Bosniack, but Tandor, Wilson, and Hurt were all from Canada. Everyone Lyle offers into the work-visa program comes from Canada, though they're not all Canadian. Many are immigrants from other places."

A slow smile crossed Ian's face. One that revealed a sharp, cunning intellect. He scanned the papers one more time, then set them aside and half rolled, half twisted toward her, covering her body with his. He expertly worked his hips between her thighs and smiled down at her. "All your hard work is going to pay off."

"It is?"

"It is." He dropped a kiss to the skin exposed in the vee in her T-shirt, then her collarbone, her throat, the side of her neck... Just like that, Savannah was on fire.

Ian's mouth found its way to hers, and she fisted the back of his shirt, pulling it over his head. Then stroked all his warm skin and thick muscle.

He pulled his mouth from hers, breaking the spell. "Sure Jamison's asleep?"

"He's asleep, and he hasn't woken in the night for months."

Ian vaulted off the bed, then paused. "Can I close the door? Just to give myself an extra few seconds' stopping power in case he does wake? I can't grind to a halt on a dime with you."

Savannah was touched he'd even think about it, let alone ask her for permission. She also liked the insinuation that she tested his control. "You can close it."

He rolled back in bed with her in seconds. She was laughing when he cupped her face and kissed her silent. Savannah opened to him, and he took the invitation as if he'd been holding back for days.

By the time he broke the kiss, Savannah was completely intoxicated. With his knees flanking her hips, he sat back and dragged her shirt up and off. Then his hands slid over her shoulders, down her arms, across her stomach.

"If that ledger contains the names of the three passports we have pictures of"—he popped the button on her jeans—"with Hank's fingerprints all over the ledger"—he tugged them down her thighs and off her legs, then planted his hands on either side of her head and grinned—"it will be the end of him."

He leaned in and kissed her. Savannah struggled to comprehend what he was telling her. "Wait, what?"

Ian eased his body against hers, kissing her neck.

"Ian?" she pushed at his shoulder. "Explain, please."

"Crimes involving passport fraud are investigated by the Diplomatic Security Service, which is the federal law enforcement arm of the State Department. Federal crimes require federal prosecution. And federal prosecutors won't give a shit who Hank and Lyle are or who they know."

Smiling, he tapped her chin with a finger, then let it drop to her chest, sliding it between her breasts and clicking the clasp of her bra open. "His crimes just spilled over the borders of Hazard County and beyond his sphere of influence, beautiful."

He dropped a kiss to her lips, her jaw, her neck.

Savannah's eyes slid closed. "I can't think when you're doing that."

"I can't think when you're naked and touching me."

She wanted nothing more in the moment than to let Ian have her any way he wanted her for the rest of the night. But even though her brain wasn't working at full throttle, she was pretty sure this was a huge development.

"Ian." She rolled to her side and pushed him to his back.

He slipped his arms around her waist and pulled her on top of him. "Okay, I like this too. I'll take you any way I can get you."

She started laughing. "*Ian.*"

He dropped his head back with a dramatic sigh. "Are you listening? Because I'm not going to say this again until you've thoroughly worn me out." He didn't wait to continue. "If we can get our hands on the ledger and do some research on the names, we can connect Hank to multiple federal crimes, and poof, he's got bigger problems to worry about than whether you're getting lucky with the hottest new guy in town."

"And...what if we can't get our hands on the ledger?"

Ian stared at the ceiling for a long, quiet second. "Let's think positively." In a flash, he sat up and flipped her to her back. He kissed her, then pulled back and looked down at her with a fresh sobriety. "Did Hank know you got into his safe and took these copies?"

"No."

"Then he wouldn't have felt the need to change the code."

"True."

"In the event he did change the code, there's always safe-cracking."

"Um..." A sense of unease snuck in.

"Do you remember it?" he asked. "The code?"

"Maybe," she lied for a reason she couldn't clearly pinpoint, but which probably circled around the threat of Ian breaking into not only Hank's house but his safe. If Hank caught Ian, he'd kill him. Even if Ian got in and out without Hank knowing, just Hank's suspicion would create trouble for Savannah and Jamison. "It's been a long time."

"Don't worry about that now." He lowered his head and rubbed the tip of his nose against hers, then he kissed her. Kissed her again. And again.

Savannah was thinking how easily she could get used to being loved like this when Ian abruptly pulled back. He tightened his hands in her hair and met her gaze with a fierce, serious expression. "I'm crazy about you." He searched her eyes a moment with a look she couldn't quite read. "I want you to remember that."

Nerves fluttered in her belly. "What's wrong?"

"Nothing." He smiled, and the Ian she knew returned in a flash. "Not a damn thing."

He leaned into one arm and used the other to stroke his hand down her belly before slipping his fingertips under the waistband of her panties and deep between her legs.

Excitement burned a path through her body and flipped Savannah's mind to standby. She arched and moan, letting her worries fade into the background.

EVERLY CHEWED the inside of her cheek as she watched the front of the brothel. "Think she'll come through?"

Roman lowered his night-vision binoculars. "I do."

"Optimist," she accused.

"Spoken like a true pessimist." He lifted his binoculars again. "By the time I got done explaining her reality, it was all I could do to keep her from latching on to my leg on the way out. She'll come through."

Movement stirred on the porch.

"He's on his way out," Liam said from his car parked a few hundred yards down the street.

"So he is," Roman murmured. He lowered his binoculars and glanced at Everly. "Ready to do this?"

She patted the left side of her bra, where she'd tucked the wireless USB reader. "All set."

Bishop descended the stairs and got into his SUV. When his

taillights disappeared down the street, Roman got out of the car. When Everly didn't move, he cut a look her way.

"I'm going to let you open my door." She batted her lashes at him. "Like the gentleman bringing his girl to a brothel for a three-way naturally would."

"Naturally."

He rounded the car to open Everly's door. She slipped her arm through his and leaned into him as they crossed the street. "We're going in."

"Roger that," Sam responded from his warm, cushy office in Whitefish. "Fingers warm and ready."

Everly and Roman cut a look at each other, grinned, and shook their heads.

"Oblivious," she said, earning a wider smile from Roman.

"Truly," he agreed.

"What are you talking about?" Sam asked.

At the front steps, they greeted the guards, who nodded a welcome to Roman. He opened his arms while one guard patted him down. Another guard instructed Everly to do the same.

"Well"—she gave her guard a sassy grin—"this is unexpected foreplay."

He didn't find her amusing and did a half-assed search before ushering them in the front door.

"I was hoping you'd come back." The woman who stood from the lounge was incredibly young and even more beautiful. She approached them a little too quickly, drawing the disapproving gazes of two other women in the foyer. She slid her hands down Roman's chest and glanced at Everly. "How nice, you brought a friend." She returned her gaze to Roman. "That'll cost extra."

"Of course it will," Roman said.

One of the other women sauntered up to Everly and took her hand, but her glare was narrowed in on Brandy. "It's not your turn, sister."

A spark of desperation flared in Brandy's dark eyes.

"Sorry, sugar," Everly said, drawing the woman's gaze. "My man has a thing for Brandy." She grinned and cupped the woman's cheek. "But you can bet I'll be angling for you next time."

Mollified, the woman stepped back and let Brandy lead them upstairs. But the girl was acting nervous and squirrely, showing all the signs of panic. When they reached the landing between stairs, Roman grabbed Brandy's arm and stopped her.

"Slow. Down," he told her. "Remember what we talked about."

The girl's dark eyes darted between Roman and Everly.

"Take a breath," Everly told her. "And focus."

Brandy nodded and continued up the stairs at a slower pace. At the top of the stairs, another guard eyed them before Brandy led them into her bedroom. When she closed the door, she leaned back against it and whispered, "I don't know if I can do this."

Everly reached around her and locked the door.

"You can do this," Roman encouraged her. "It's almost done."

"We're in," Everly told Sam and pulled the USB reader from her bra. Then she looked at Brandy. "Where's the bracelet?"

She darted a look at Roman.

Everly turned to the dresser and started searching. This was why she didn't do kids. They were so damned tedious, always needing reassurance and coddling. Making such stupid, impulsive decisions, all based on emotion. She simply didn't have the patience for it.

"What's she doing?" Brandy whined. That was another thing Everly hated—whining. "She's messing things up."

While Roman was trying to charm and cajole the bracelet's location out of her, Everly pulled open the bottom drawer of the jewelry box on the dresser and pulled the USB bracelet from the velvet. "Got it."

Brandy drew a breath to argue, but Roman covered her mouth with his hand.

Everly was happy to leave the teen to Roman. She pushed the male end of the USB into the reader. "It's in."

"I see it." The frenzied clack of computer keys streamed across the earbud. "There's a password. Hacking in."

"Heads-up, lovebirds." Liam's voice came across the line. "He's back. Just screeched to the curb."

"Sam?" Everly nudged.

"Just another few seconds. There's some weird encryption..."

Voices rose in the foyer.

"Don't have a few seconds," Everly said.

She pressed her ear to the door. The other women tried to coax Lyle into their beds while he was trying to tell them he wasn't there for sex.

"I'm in," Sam said.

"She's with another client," a man's voice rang in the foyer. "I can check her room as soon as she's free. I promise to call you the minute—"

"I can't wait," he said, his voice coming closer. "This is important."

"Sam," Everly said. "We've got about thirty seconds."

"I'm aware," he said with that I'm-going-as-fast-as-I-can clip in his voice.

A heavy knock came at the door. "Brandy," Lyle called. "I need to see you."

Brandy spun toward Roman, frantic. "Now what? If they find out, they'll kill me."

Roman opened his mouth to answer her, but Lyle knocked and bellowed again.

Everly gripped Brandy by the arms and gave her a little shake. "Do you want to live?" she whispered. When she nodded, Everly said, "Then tell him just a minute, you're coming." When the girl just kept staring at her with those big deer-in-the-headlights eyes, Everly said, "*Now.*"

On cue, Lyle knocked again, but this time, he pounded with the side of his fist and rattled the doorknob.

Brandy jumped. "J-just a minute, Lyle." She looked at Everly, who nodded encouragement. "I'll be right there."

"Done." Sam's voice came over the line.

Everly tilted her head toward the door leading to the bathroom, and Roman headed that direction, unbuttoning his shirt. She stuffed the bracelet back into the bottom drawer of the jewelry box just as Lyle hammered the door again.

Everly gripped Brandy's shoulders. "If you want out, make this good."

She stepped behind the door and motioned for Brandy to open it.

Brandy was shaking as she turned the lock and opened the door, hiding Everly. "Hey, baby." Her voice sounded smooth enough. This couldn't have been the first time the girl had to pretend in a dicey situation. "Did you come back for seconds?"

"Where is it?" His voice vibrated with tension as he pushed into the room.

"Lyle, I have another client right now—"

"My bracelet," he demanded. "Where is it?"

From Everly's position, she saw Roman open the bathroom door and come into the room, shirtless with that terror-inducing steel gaze drilling into Lyle. "What's going on here?"

"I—I—apologize," Lyle told Roman. "I left something of mine behind—"

"Here it is, lover." Brandy pulled open the drawer to the jewelry box. "I had it in safekeeping."

Lyle's tension drained. "Thank you." He looked at Roman. "Again, I apologize for interrupting. Tonight's on me. I'll take care of it at the desk."

"Good night," Brandy called sweetly, closing the door behind Lyle.

Then she promptly sank to her knees with a hand on her stomach.

Okay, Everly had to give the girl props. Even Everly's nerves were singed. She crouched next to Brandy and put a hand on her shoulder. "You'd better get some clothes on if you're coming with us."

The girl twisted and locked Everly in a hug so hard, Brandy almost took her to the ground. Roman grinned and started tearing the sheets from the bed and knotting them together to form the rope Brandy would use to climb to freedom.

While the teen nearly strangled her, Everly said, "Liam, are you in position?"

"Affirmative."

Everly pried Brandy away from her and drew open a dresser drawer, searching for warm clothes and asking the teenager, "Did you ever play in a tree house as a kid?"

"Tree house?" she asked, sniffling through tears of relief. "What's this tree house?"

"Never mind. Just trust me, this will be fun."

13

The pleasure Ian infused into her the night before continued to pulse in her blood as the café's breakfast rush slowed. But Misty didn't say anything about her glowing this morning. She seemed distracted and a little moody, which wasn't like Misty at all. But the café had been too busy for Savannah to slow down to ask Misty if everything was okay.

When they were both behind the counter with only a handful of retirees lingering in the restaurant, Savannah said, "You seem a little off today."

She shrugged. "Just didn't sleep very well last night."

Before Savannah could dig deeper, Misty grabbed a wet rag and moved into the dining room to wipe down tables. Her friend's unhappiness took the edge off Savannah's pleasure. Misty could be jealous of Savannah's newfound happiness. God knew it was difficult to watch other people find happiness when you were struggling. Or she might be frustrated with Savannah for not taking her worries about Ian's background to heart.

Savannah brought a tray of dishes into the back. She turned toward Karen, who was rolling out dough, prepared to ask if she'd noticed Misty's mood change. Before she could get the words out, the bell on the front door signaled someone coming or leaving. Then Hank's voice filled the restaurant.

"Where is she?" he bellowed, making Savannah cringe. "Savannah!"

Karen's expression tightened into frustration. "He's got to stop coming in here to harass you."

"Savannah," he yelled again. "Get out here."

"I'm working on it." Savannah forced her feet into action and entered the dining room with her shoulders squared for whatever he was going to throw at her next.

She found Misty already chastising Hank. "You've got the manners of a spoiled brat."

"I'm right here," Savannah said, drawing Hank's gaze. She gripped his arm and turned him toward the hallway leading to the restrooms.

He jerked from her grip, but Savannah kept walking. "If you want to talk to me, you'll do it away from customers."

Hank followed long enough to grab her. He whirled her around and slammed her back against the wall. Pain clawed through her spine, stealing her air. Hank bent, getting right in her face. "I'll talk to you when and where and how I choose."

She forced her throat to unlock and pulled in a raspy breath. "What do you want?"

He lifted a hand filled with folded papers and waved them in her face. "Judge Burns had an opening in his schedule. Our custody hearing has been moved to Friday."

"*This* Friday?" Ice spread through her veins. She jerked the papers from his hand and unfolded the court documents. "You can't just move it like that. Audrey needs to schedule—"

"I can and I did. Too bad for you."

"It's Sunday. How did you get this done on a Sunday?"

"I saw Judge Burns coming out of church. We had a nice little talk. Since his wife is his assistant, they didn't mind making the change right away."

"Why are you doing this?" She glared at Hank. "I've been Jamison's rock from day one. You know it would traumatize him to be taken away from me."

"What's going to traumatize him is watching his mother whore it up with the easiest man around. Your next-door neighbor, Savannah? You couldn't look any farther than your front yard?"

Maybe that blocker hadn't worked the way Ian thought it would. "If you really cared about him, you'd stick with the agreement we worked out in the divorce."

"And if you really cared about him, you'd dump the grease monkey and focus on our son."

"You started this long before Ian got to town."

"But you fucking him cemented my decision."

"Whoa, whoa, whoa." The female voice startled Savannah. She straightened and fought to focus on the woman in the hallway with them. Someone new in town, working for the mine. Savannah remembered she'd been surprised that Lyle had hired a woman for a managerial position. The woman's gaze cut to Hank, clearly disgusted. "Even the guys in the mine treat me better."

"Mind your own business," Hank bit back. "Get the fuck out of here."

"You're blocking my path," she told Hank while putting a comforting hand on Savannah's arm. "That makes it my business. And if you touch her again, I'll go way above your head to make sure you never do it again."

Hank's furious gaze swung back to Savannah. "Friday. Say your goodbyes before we go to court, because it's the last time you'll ever see him."

He turned and stalked out of the diner. Mortification burned in her gut. Panic rippled up her spine.

"Are you okay?" the woman asked. She was young and pretty with jet black hair and bright blue eyes.

"I'm so sorry you had to see that." The words came out choppy as Savannah tried to catch her breath and calm her nerves. "I don't remember your name."

"Everly," she said. "What an ass."

Savannah huffed. "Understatement."

"Did he hurt you?" she asked, her eyes scanning Savannah.

She straightened, wincing when her back pinched with pain. "I'll be all right. Even better when he's out of my life for good."

The woman dragged something from her back pocket and offered it to Savannah. "This is my number. If you ever need anything, just give me a call."

Savannah took the card, even though she knew she'd never call the woman. "Thank you."

Everly leaned in and gave her a hug. "I used to have a guy like him in my life. Things get so much better when they're gone."

Tears burned Savannah's eyes out of nowhere. "That's what I keep telling myself."

Everly pulled back with a smile.

"Thanks again," Savannah said.

When Everly returned to her table in the dining room, Savannah pulled out her phone. Her hands shook when she tried to dial Audrey's number.

Karen stepped into the hallway, a look of pity filling her round face. "Take the rest of the day, honey. I'll cover."

"I'm sorry," Savannah told her. "Once this is straightened out, he won't bother me so much."

"If you think this will *ever* get straightened out, you're delusional. That man will never stop fighting. He lives for conflict." Karen pulled off her food-stained apron while turning back toward the kitchen. "Tell Misty I'll be right out."

Savannah squeezed her eyes shut and tried to catch her breath, but her body shook from the fight-or-flight rush. Her mind was jumbled with problems and fears. She wasn't prepared to run with Jamison. She didn't have new identities, and they'd never make it out of the state without them.

"Hey." Misty put a hand on Savannah's shoulder, breaking her out of the whirlwind of worries. "What can I do?"

Savannah shook her head. "I...I don't know. I need to talk to Audrey. I need to think."

The bell chimed as the local bridge group of eight older women pushed in.

Misty glanced out front. "If you get out of here before your shift's over, you'll miss Corwin. Get your feet back under you. I'll come over when I'm done here. We'll figure something out."

Savannah pulled off her apron. "Thanks."

She grabbed her car keys and her jacket and called Audrey on her way to the car. Her attorney didn't answer, so Savannah left her a frantic message with the news as she slid into her car.

Savannah disconnected and stared out her snowy windshield. Hank's power pressed in all around her. She felt helpless. All her possible moves, futile. Her troubled mind turned to Ian. But he was at work, and she didn't want to get him in trouble with Mo. He hadn't even had the job for a month yet.

Still, she started the car and headed toward the garage. Maybe she could just get in a quick talk with him. She needed an objective, rational sounding board before her brain short-circuited.

It only took her minutes to slide past Mo's Garage at the other end of Main Street. The garage only had one bay door open and only three cars lining the drive instead of a dozen. Since Ian had started working there, Mo stayed open seven days a week to clear the backlog of repairs he'd been putting off. Mo was out front talking to customers as they picked up or dropped off their vehicles, and Ian was elbows deep in an old truck.

She sat there a moment, gnawing on her thumbnail with indecision. "What would you tell me to do?"

Her mind drifted back to their night together. To his passion, his affection, his sincerity. He'd be livid at the way Hank had treated her. He'd tell her they needed to get that ledger. Then he'd insist on being the person who stole it.

No. It had to be her. She could dig up an excuse to be in the house if Hank caught her. Ian couldn't.

Savannah picked up her phone and dialed the police station. She expected the receptionist to answer, but Officer Rosen picked up.

"Hi, Joe, it's Savannah."

"Hi there. What can I do for you?"

"Is Hank there?"

"No, ma'am, I'm sorry."

"That's okay. Do you know when he'll be back?"

"Not until this afternoon sometime, ma'am. He's at the county board meeting."

Yes. Those meetings lasted for hours.

"Can I leave him a message or help you with anything?" Rosen asked.

"No, thanks, Joe. I'll catch him later."

Savannah disconnected, her gut tight with the realization that she had to take control of this situation on her own.

IAN'S PHONE pulled him out of the engine of an ancient Ford F150. He saw Everly's name and answered, "What's up?"

"Hank just ripped Savannah a new one," Everly said. "She just left the café, and she's pretty shaken up."

Ian straightened and wiped his hands on a rag. "You're at the diner?"

"I get lunch too, slave driver."

"What happened?" he asked.

"Hank got the custody hearing moved up to Friday."

"Shit." Ian wandered a few feet from the truck and looked

outside. Vehicles lined the drive, and Mo talked with more customers leaving their cars. "I'm getting slammed here. After taking off yesterday for the meeting, Mo would be royally pissed if I left again."

"I gave Savannah my number. Told her to call if she needed anything."

Ian caught sight of Savannah's car stopped across the street. "Hold on."

He wandered that direction, but Savannah took off before he reached her. Ian watched her head straight up Third Street. When she reached Pine Street, where she should have turned left to head home, she turned right instead.

"Oh hell," he said. "I think she's headed to Bishop's house. She's going to break into the safe to get the ledger."

"Did Sam figure out if Bishop has another security system in place yet?"

"Not that I've heard. Can you find out? Locate her? Call me if she's at Bishop's?"

"On it."

Everly disconnected, and Ian got back under his customer's hood to tie up the job so he'd be free to leave.

His mind darted to Savannah, to Hank, to the safe. Ian was almost certain Hank would have a security system. Criminals loved keeping their crimes safe and sound.

By the time he shut the truck's hood, his skin was crawling with unease.

His phone rang.

"What's happening?" he answered.

"Her car's parked outside Bishop's house, and Sam found one of those remote security systems registered to that address. No alarm reported yet."

"Shit. I'm on my way." He jogged toward his own truck, parked on a side street, calling to Mo, "I'm grabbing lunch. Back soon."

Ian was there in three minutes flat, but he lost at least a day of his life in those three minutes. He also reflected on how unreasonable it was to be so concerned about a woman he'd known for less than three weeks. But that didn't do anything to calm him.

He already knew the layout of the house from the team's expeditions in bug placement. He pulled to the curb across the street and spotted Everly when she popped her head out from behind a juniper on the side of the house.

Ian's heart pounded as he surveyed the street. When everything looked quiet, he set a leisurely pace toward the house, only breaking into a sprint once he was mostly hidden behind a picket fence.

He dropped to a crouch beside Everly and pulled the weapon from his ankle holster. "Where is she?"

"Office," Everly said. "She's pretty freaked out."

"How'd she get in?"

"Pulled a hide-a-key from the back porch. Went in the back door."

He needed to grab her and go before the neighbors noticed activity at a normally quiet house. "Cover me."

Everly moved to the front corner of the house to watch the street while Ian trotted up the back steps and turned the knob on the back door. It opened smoothly, and Ian hurried through the kitchen to a room on the far side of the house.

He kept his weapon at his thigh as he peered around the doorjamb into the office. Savannah was alone in the room, standing behind the desk facing an open safe that had been hidden behind a large landscape painting.

"Savannah." His tone was hushed, but she still jumped and swiveled. Her eyes were wide and terrified, her arms laden with books and papers.

"Oh my God," she said, breathless, her eyes darting behind him. "What are you doing here?"

"Why didn't you call me?" He moved toward her, sliding his

weapon into the waistband of his jeans. "I told you I should come."

"If you get caught, my life falls apart. Please leave. I'm almost—"

A sound cut her off. Ian swiveled, pulling his weapon as he put himself between Savannah and the office door.

"It's me." Everly's voice touched his ear before she peeked around the doorjamb. "Don't shoot my head off."

Ian lowered his weapon and exhaled. "Girl, don't do that. I told you to cover—"

Everly stepped into the room with someone behind her. Ian registered the person as male and wearing a uniform, and Ian's gun was already up and aiming at his forehead before his face came into focus. It was Rosen.

"What are they doing here?" Savannah asked, her voice tight and terrified.

"Hank called me," Rosen told Ian. "His cell pinged with a warning that his home alarm had been tripped. Asked me to check it out."

"Oh my God."

"It's okay." Ian put his weapon away and turned toward her. "Is that everything?"

She kept backing up, arms tight around her treasure, eyes darting between everyone. "What are they doing here?" she asked again, confused and frightened. "How did you know I was here? *What's happening?*"

"I'm going to call Hank, tell him everything's fine." Rosen pulled his phone from his pocket. "You all need to finish up and get out of here."

He turned and exited through the back door.

"Come on," Ian said. "We need to go."

Everly moved to the safe and rummaged through the remaining contents. "She's got all the important stuff. We need to shut off her phones so he doesn't track them."

Savannah's confusion deepened, increasing her fear. "Would someone tell me what the hell is going on?"

"Later," Everly said, her tone brisk and businesslike. She closed the safe and replaced the picture. "Unless you'd like us to explain everything in front of Hank or Lyle, whoever shows up first." She held her hand out. "I need your phones. Both of them."

"What? No. I need them."

"I have fresh disposables in my car. I'll give you one of those."

Ian wrapped a restrictive arm around her shoulders and guided her toward the door. "I'll explain once we're out of here."

"Don't." She shook his arm off and sidestepped out of reach while moving toward the door. "Just...don't."

Ian's heart took a hard hit. He'd known it was coming. Knew it was absolutely reasonable for her to respond this way, but that didn't take the sting out of her rejection.

Outside, Rosen confirmed that Hank was still at the board meeting.

"Go pick up Jamison, would you?" Ian asked him.

"What? Why?" Savannah said. "Stop giving everyone orders involving *my life*."

Ian patted her down, then dug her cell from the pocket of her jacket and tossed it to Everly. "The other one must be at the house."

"Hey...stop...*Ian*."

Everly darted a this-ought-to-be-fun smirk at Ian before she hustled to her Jeep parked nearby.

"I'm sorry." Ian wrenched the contents of the safe out of Savannah's arms, then muscled her into her car. "We need to hurry."

Her eyes flashed with fury as he stood over her, one hand on the roof over the driver's door.

"Go home, Savannah. Do you hear me? Straight home. When Corwin finds out you're not at work, he'll go to your house and report that you're there. Rosen's cleared the break-in with Hank, and Corwin will report you're home alone, as usual. Hank won't check the safe until he gets home, which gives us time to pick up Jamison from Bailey's and make a plan."

When she opened her mouth to yell at him—he could see it in her eyes—Ian slipped his hand around the back of her neck and lowered his forehead to hers. "Stop fighting me. I know you're confused and angry, but you have to trust me here. This is all going to work out. You're going to get what you want in the end, but you really have to do it our way."

"*Trust you?*" she snapped, pulling away. "Are you serious right now? Who's *us*? For that matter, who the hell are *you*?"

"I'll answer all your questions when we're safely out of this town." He pulled away, gave her one more "Home, Savannah" warning and slammed her door.

Ian jogged to his truck, turned over the engine, and followed on Savannah's bumper as she made the short drive home. Having to expose himself and their mission that way made him sick. He'd envisioned something far more congenial. Something actually planned for the appropriate place and time, when he had his explanation all figured out.

Now, he was fucked.

He broke the tail by turning down a side street and entering the alley behind the duplex to avoid Corwin's watchful gaze.

Everly parked behind him but stayed in the car. "I'm calling Roman," she told him through the window. With a better-you-than-me look, she tossed out, "Good luck with her."

14

Savannah stood frozen in the middle of her bedroom and pressed her hands to either side of her head. She couldn't stop her mind from pinging in every direction. She didn't know what to do—or not do. How could she trust Ian when he was involved in something she didn't understand? Something he'd kept from her.

"Grab a few things for Jamison." Ian's voice made her jump. She hadn't heard him come in. He tapped the face of his phone and dropped it on her bed with the blocking app filling the screen. "There's no telling how much time we have."

She stabbed her finger at the phone. "That doesn't work. He knows we were together last night."

"It works," Ian told her. "If it didn't, that safe would have been empty and he would have been waiting for you."

He turned for the door, crossed the hallway in three strides, and opened Jamison's dresser. "You don't need much. Make sure you bring medications and identification."

Savannah crossed the hallway. "What would you do if I said no? Shoot me?"

He gave her a that's-a-stupid-thing-to-say look. "I'd have to force you. Please don't make me do that."

"I'm not going anywhere until you tell me what is going on, how you know Everly, how you pulled Rosen in on this, and how you know you can even trust him."

"We don't have time—"

"Then talk fast."

He glanced around the room. "Does Jamison have anything he can't live without? Like a stuffed animal?"

Furious and frantic, she ripped Jamison's clothes out of his hands and threw them on the floor. "Stop it. Just stop. I don't *understand*."

He gripped her arms and gave her a little shake. "Do you want to get away from him or not?"

"You know I do."

"I know it feels like your world is imploding," he said, voice steady and deliberate, "but if you'll trust me just a little longer, I'll get you and Jamison through this."

"You aren't exactly giving me a choice, are you?"

He bent, swept the clothes off the floor, then grabbed a throw blanket from Jamison's bed. He pushed past her, crossing the living room and disappearing into the kitchen.

Fear twined around her lungs and made it hard to breathe. Every muscle in her body was coiled tight, her fingernails digging into her palms. She took shallow sips of air and closed her eyes, fighting to find level ground.

"Savannah." The woman's voice pierced her bubble of terror. Savannah opened her eyes and had to fight to remember the woman's name. Everly, that was it.

"Are you with him?" She had no idea why this felt like a pressing question considering the circumstances, but she had to know. "Are you two together?"

A look of dismay flashed across Everly's face. "Romantically?" She scoffed. "He's like my brother. They all are."

"All of who?" A new layer of confusion piled on. "There are more people involved?"

"We'll have to explain on the road." She started toward Savannah's room. "Jamison will be here soon."

Everly pulled open her dresser drawers and created a small pile of underwear, T-shirts, and jeans. When she turned toward her again, she gave Savannah's arm a reassuring squeeze.

"I'll tell you now that Ian has been a champion for you and Jamison from the beginning. He's a genuine man and one of the best human beings I've ever met. Whatever you're feeling or thinking right now, set it aside until we can give you the whole story, okay?"

"Champion to *who*? And *why*?"

The back door closed, and Jamison's voice floated through the kitchen. Savannah's focus took a one-hundred-eighty-degree turn —to her boy. He was her soul. Her true north.

"Come on," Everly said. "We've got to move."

Savannah grabbed Everly's arm. When the other woman's blue eyes met Savannah's, she said, "Promise me, no matter what happens, you'll keep Jamison safe. Keep him away from Hank and Lyle. If something happens to me, I want him with Misty."

Everly covered Savannah's hand and squeezed. "I'll do you one better. I'll promise he'll stay with you. Let's go."

Jamison passed Everly in the hall with a quick "Hi" as if having strangers in the house was no big deal.

"Hey, buddy," Everly said as she passed. "Grab your mom and let's hit the road."

Everly turned out of sight just as Jamison launched himself at Savannah. She crouched and caught him. She pressed her face to his hair and held him tight.

"Officer Rosen says we're going on an adventure with Mr. Ian."

Savannah ground her teeth but curbed her anger and hurt before she pulled back and looked at her adorable son. She pushed his hair out of his eyes, thinking she needed to get his hair cut. Those mundane things felt so solid and safe in the moment.

"I just heard about it," she told him. Jamison was clearly thrilled by the idea, and she played along. There would be plenty of time for reality later. "Ian has your blanket and clothes." She kissed Jamison's forehead, closing her eyes to absorb his little-boy scent. Savannah pulled back. "I just need to grab a few things from my room."

Jamison pulled from Savannah's arms and sprinted back through the living room, calling Ian's name with glee. That grated over Savannah's nerves and stoked her anger. She moved into her room and opened the closet, where she pulled up the floorboards and dragged out her box of cash. She stuffed all the money into a backpack and tossed the bag over her shoulder just as Ian appeared in the doorway.

"Ready?" he asked.

"That's a rhetorical question, right?" She pushed past him on her way to the kitchen. The back door was open, and the cold swept through the space. She took hold of Jamison's hand and looked at Everly. "Where are we going?"

"To meet the rest of the team."

Great, more strangers. She cut a look at Ian. "Why are there so many people involved in this? If we needed to get out of town, we could have planned it between the two of us."

"I'll tell you once we're on the move," was his answer.

She looked at Everly, who was giving her more answers than Ian. "What's going to happen with our car? With all our things?"

Everly's gaze darted to Ian standing behind her, then moved back to Savannah. "We aren't sure yet."

"When will you be sure?"

"We don't know. A couple of days, maybe."

Savannah's stomach dropped lower. "Perfect."

Jamison tugged on her hand, smiling up at her with complete and utter trust. "Let's go, Mom."

Savannah let him pull her forward even as fear swamped her. Outside, she was faced with two vehicles. "We'll go with Everly."

"No, Mom. I want to go with Mr. Ian. He said I could watch movies on a DVD player."

She cut a look at Ian. He stood nearby, hands on hips. He didn't exactly look contrite or apologetic, but he didn't look the least bit happy either.

"How long is the drive?" she asked Everly.

"We'll stop just inside the county line to regroup."

"This is insane," she murmured. She thought she was desperate to escape Hank, Lyle, and Hazard, but now, given the opportunity with a group of strangers with some clandestine agenda, she realized she feared the unknown more than she feared Hank.

And that shook her resistance.

"Fine." She turned toward Ian's truck and passed him without a word.

She opened the door and flipped the passenger's seat forward, then remembered Jamison's car seat. Just as she opened her mouth to say she had to get it, Savannah spotted one of his two seats already belted into the center of the bench, a DVD player attached to the back of the passenger's seat.

Ian slid behind the wheel, and she shot him a glare across the cab. "Just think of everything, don't you?"

He jammed the keys into the ignition and turned the engine over while Jamison climbed in, oblivious to the tension between them.

Everly slid into her Jeep with her phone pressed to her ear.

Savannah climbed into the truck, and Ian pulled out of the alley as she buckled her seat belt.

While Ian explained the DVD player to Jamison, Savannah closed her eyes and rested her head back against the seat, trying to prepare herself for the immediate future. It would be a long, bumpy ride until she found stability again. Her feelings for Ian only complicated the challenge. She could only hope for distraction to keep her from falling apart.

How could she have let another man do this to her? Dupe her into trusting him. Into believing he was someone he wasn't. At this point, Ian could be as bad or even worse than Hank. A sense of self-loathing flooded her. She had to stop trusting people.

Misty popped to mind. Savannah opened her eyes. Staring straight out the windshield, she told Ian, "I need to tell Misty." When he didn't respond, she added an emphatic "She'll worry."

Ian glanced in the rearview mirror at Jamison. Savannah checked on him over her shoulder and found him with headphones on, absorbed in a movie, dancing in his seat.

"I'm sorry," Ian said. "This isn't the way I'd hoped things would go down."

"That means nothing to me. What things? Go down with who? What, exactly, are you sorry for? Lying to me? Sleeping with me? Uprooting us? Running roughshod over my life?"

He exhaled and rubbed his forehead. "Very little of what I have to tell you will make you happy or make things right."

"I've already figured that out. Can I *please* call Misty?" The thought of her worrying made Savannah sick. "She's going to think Hank chopped us up into pieces and threw us down a mine shaft."

"I'm sorry, baby," he said, shaking his head. "You can't call Misty."

"Don't call me that, and why not?"

"Because, unfortunately, Misty is at the center of the reason we're here. God, I hate having to be the one to tell you this, but she's involved in Hank and Lyle's manipulation."

More confusion tightened her already tangled thoughts. "That's ridiculous. No, it's insane. Misty hates Hank and Lyle. She loathes them. And she's a good, honest, hardworking person. She would never do anything for them. You have *no idea* what you're talking about."

He heaved a sigh, shifting in his seat. "Yesterday, before I came into the café, I heard Hank threaten her in the parking lot while she was taking out the trash."

"Misty's never let Hank intimidate her, and he has nothing to threaten her with."

"I know this is going to be hard to grasp, but Misty has been counterfeiting those passports you found in Hank's patrol car."

"Are you pulling this stuff out of your ass?" she yelled. "That's *crazy*. That's *laughable*."

"I heard him tell her that if she didn't get you to dump me, he was going to send the FBI to raid her barn. So my team and I went to the barn while she was at work and found a basement hidden under all the junk."

Savannah's mouth hung open. She was beginning to think he might actually be insane. Or on drugs. Or delusional. Or maybe this was all a nightmare, and she'd wake and have a wild tale to tell Misty and Ian in the morning.

Only she was still stuck in this car. With a very probable lunatic. A lunatic she'd slept with and thought she knew intimately up until half an hour ago.

"You're either full of shit, certifiable, a con artist or your eyes and your brain were playing tricks on you. Her father was a hoarder. That place is rotting from the baseboards up. She works double shifts at the diner just to pay the bills. She doesn't know anything about counterfeiting, and if she'd found that kind of equipment, she'd have sold it long ago to pay off the property's back taxes so she didn't have to work so hard."

"I know that's what she's told you," he said, his voice maddeningly compassionate. "And what you believe."

"It's not blind loyalty. I've *seen* that barn." She had to fight to keep her voice down. "I've spent days helping her rummage through the place to find things to auction on eBay for extra cash.

She certainly wouldn't be doing that if she was making money counterfeiting passports."

She wanted to drop all this nonsense and just stop talking, but she was so angry, so confused. Her whole world was upside down. Everything she thought she knew was being challenged.

"This whole thing is insane. I'm beginning to think *you're* insane," she told him. "You and Everly and this supposed team we're going to meet. When we roll through Rockport in about ten minutes, just stop and let us out of this truck. I'm about to have a nuclear melt—"

Something connected in her brain. Something vague and just out of her mind's reach. But the whisper cut off her words and made her stomach drop to her feet.

She cut a look at Ian. At his strong profile, the jump of his jaw beneath a day's worth of stubble. "The reason you're here?" She thought for a moment, forced the wheels of her brain to turn, and repeated words he'd just said. "'At the center of the reason we're here'?"

He repositioned his hand on the steering wheel and kept his gaze out the window while he scraped his lower lip between his teeth. He looked decidedly uncomfortable. Cold seeped into her gut, chilling the burn of anger.

"Are you saying you're not here, fresh out of the military, looking for a new start? That you didn't call in friends when these crazy notions about Misty popped into your warped mind?"

"I never said—"

"Because that would mean this was all *planned*."

"Like I said, things didn't go as expected."

All the dots connected at once, and the flash of information burned like the stab of a knife. "A security team? The Manhunters?"

He cut a look at her, surprised. "Where did you hear that?"

"Misty. I told her about your tattoo, and she found it on the internet, connected it to the Manhunters." The depths of her gullibility stunned her. Shame washed over her, heating her face, burning her neck. "Oh my God. You're after Hank and Lyle. This was all planned. Everything between us was...nothing. Less than nothing. I was a tool. A means to an end. Just part of the plot or the mission or operation or whatever the hell you call it."

"Savannah—"

"No." She held up her hands. "I get it now." She crossed her arms and looked out the passenger's window, unable to look him in the face. Her gut throbbed with a fresh ache, a mess of fury, self-loathing, disgust. "Talk about pathetic. I let you into my life. I let you close to my boy. Jesus, I must have been your easiest lay ever."

"Don't do that."

She laughed at herself, the sound dark and ugly, exactly how she felt right now. "How could I not have seen it? How could I have put Jamison at risk like this? Maybe he would be better off with Hank."

Hearing those words out of her mouth told her exactly how badly she'd screwed up. Screwed up because she'd trusted Ian.

Everything inside her cooled and hardened. She stuffed all her emotions behind a solid concrete wall inside her—at least something she'd learned from Hank had proved useful.

"I know this doesn't look good from where you're sitting," he told her, "but I—"

"Just tell me this." She didn't want to hear any more lies. Didn't need him rubbing salt in her fresh wounds—wounds she'd thought she'd insulated herself from. "Will Jamison and I be free of Hank? Forever?"

"Yes." His answer was immediate and unequivocal.

Something unraveled inside her, a little relief, a little insanity, a lot of pain. "Fine. As long as that happens, I'll do what you say for now. Beyond that, there's nothing left for us to talk about."

She closed her eyes and fought to keep the burning tears from spilling out. She meant nothing to him. Showing the hurt he'd caused her would only make her even more pitiful. She was stronger than that. Better than that. And she wouldn't let another deceitful man ruin the woman she'd been fighting to recover for years.

But the tension wafting off Ian was palpable, and he didn't listen to her any better now than fifteen minutes ago. "I was going to tell you when we had all the concrete information."

"When you got evidence against me," she corrected. "Everly told me."

"No," he said. "When we had evidence against everyone else and had cleared you."

"Same thing."

"No," he repeated, his voice tense with frustration. "One assumes guilt, the other assumes innocence. I knew you weren't part of it. Savannah, I'm the same man that was with you last night."

Her frustration rose. Her sense of control plummeted. "It's obvious I have *no idea* who I was with last night."

How had this happened? Since she'd walked away from Hank, she'd developed personal barriers that had strengthened over time. How had this man slipped through a crack she hadn't even realized was there and invaded the security she'd created for herself and Jamison so damn quickly?

"God," she whispered, rubbing her forehead. "I'm *so* stupid."

"You're not stupid," he insisted.

She huffed a laugh, disgusted with herself. "What do you call dropping all my defenses for a smile from one hot guy?"

"I call that attraction."

She cut a look at him. "It's not attraction when you were ordered to act like you care."

"I wasn't." He met her gaze with equal frustration. "I *do* care."

"This conversation is pointless." She turned her gaze out the windshield, focusing on the taillights of Everly's Jeep.

When would she learn? She'd been taught the same lesson

over and over throughout her life, yet she kept making the same mistake. Every time she thought she'd found someone genuine and committed, they morphed and changed into something completely different.

Her father had taught her that men don't stay. Her mother had taught her that she didn't matter, she wasn't worth fighting for, wasn't worth loving. Hank had combined both of her parents' lessons into one ugly mess of a marriage.

And now Ian had confirmed all of it. That people say one thing and do another. That they make empty promises, then twist them to fit their own agenda.

The only thing that kept Savannah sane was Jamison. So pure, so innocent, so open and loving. The one person in the world who gave Savannah hope she could break this cycle in her life.

To do that now, Savannah needed to understand what was happening, who she was with, and how to secure her son's safety.

"What branch of the military is this Manhunters team part of?" Her question came out flat and emotionless, signaling her internal barriers shoring up.

"I'm not in the military," he said. "I'm on a nonmilitary security team. What I told you about my mom and retiring was true. All the important stuff you know about me is true."

"Your truth, maybe. If it's not military, what is this security team? Who are you working for?"

"The government." He paused and added, "Indirectly."

"Indirectly." She laughed at his attempt to warp reality. "You either work for the government or you don't."

"I work for an agency that works for the government." Frustration colored his tone.

"That's convoluted at best." Her voice rose with anger, despite knowing the emotion was futile and draining. "How can you expect me to believe anything you say at this point?"

"Why do you keep asking questions if you're not going to believe anything I say?"

"*Insanity*, obviously," she shot back.

"Mommy?" Jamison drew off his headphones with an irritated frown. "Could you talk quieter, please? I can't hear my movie."

Regret instantly pulled the plug on her anger. "Sure, honey." She reached back and squeezed his hand. "I'm sorry."

He slid his headphones back on with a sweet "Thank you."

A smile flickered over her mouth. Softness filled her heart. Ian glanced back at Jamison, then at Savannah. The instant his eyes met hers, his mouth lifted with the same smile and in that instant, their affection for Jamison shone through the turmoil. Her heart screamed *He's a good man*. But she forced logic to override her ignorant emotions.

Everly's SUV turned onto another side road plowed into a single lane and pulled up behind an idling black Suburban. Three men exited the Suburban. They looked like they belonged here, wearing cargo pants and jeans, parkas, hats, snow boots. Everly parked and slid out of her Jeep to approach the men.

Savannah unbuckled her seat belt and looked at Jamison. When he pulled one of the earphones away from his head, Savannah said, "You stay in the truck where it's warm. I'm just going to talk to some people and come right back."

Then she opened the door as Ian slowed, prepared to slide out on the move.

"Savannah." He hit the brakes and reached for her. "Wait."

She dropped to the snow before he could grab her arm. She had a son to secure. A life to salvage. Strangers to assess.

"Who's that?" Jamison asked, his voice drifting to her from the truck.

"They're friends of mine," Ian told Jamison. "Everything's fine, buddy."

The men turned toward her, and Everly followed their gazes.

She glanced behind Savannah toward the truck, then introduced her to the men.

"Savannah, this is Roman, our CO, Sam our tech genius, and Liam, who evidently tagged along whether we liked it or not."

Savannah didn't know what a CO was, but she didn't care. "I need to see some credentials."

They all stared at her a long second, as if she hadn't spoken English.

"I have no idea who you all are," she clarified her position. "I've discovered Ian—if that's even his real name—has been lying to me for over a week, the ex-husband, who's trying to steal our child, has been dealing in counterfeit passports, and you all believe my best friend is in on it, which you're wrong about, by the way. Before I listen to what you have to say, before my son and I go anywhere with you, I want to know who you are and whether or not you truly have the ability to do something more for me than I can do for myself, because I can screw up my own life just fine. I don't need anyone's help to make things worse."

As anticipated, they didn't look pleased, but Savannah had stopped giving a damn what people thought of her a long time ago. She was angry and hurt and scared, and there would be no holding it back in this insane situation.

Two of the men reached into their pockets and pulled out wallets. She took them both. Roman's ID claimed he was with the Department of Defense. Liam's ID was from the FBI. Neither impressed her. Law enforcement hadn't exactly earned her respect. Besides, she had no way of knowing whether the IDs were authentic.

She handed their IDs back and tilted her head toward Ian, still standing at the truck's front bumper. "Which one of you is his boss?"

"I am," Roman said.

She crossed her arms against the cold and met his gaze steadily. "Are you the one who told him to sleep with me?"

The gaze Roman turned on Ian could have burned the hair off his head. "*No.*"

The you-fucking-idiot tone in Roman's voice confirmed that sleeping with Savannah had been Ian's idea. She didn't know if that was good or bad, but it was immaterial.

"You're so in the doghouse," Everly said, grinning at Ian like a bratty little sister.

"You're so not one to talk," he shot back.

The man named Sam burst out laughing. But Everly cut it short with a smack to Sam's gut. "Neither are you."

"Come on," Roman said, clearly the disapproving father of the group. "We need to get going."

"You're wrong about Misty," she told him. "I've known her for five years. If she was involved in something as odd and illegal as counterfeiting passports, I'd know."

Roman cut another frown at Ian. "What?" he asked with sarcasm. "You didn't show her pictures too?"

"I'll do it," Sam said with too much enthusiasm. He stepped toward her and handed her his phone. The camera app was open, and Sam angled behind her to point out all the areas in a sterile, concrete room.

Sam went on and on, sliding picture after picture of unidentifiable images past her.

"I've never seen any of this. That room is not on Misty's property and certainly not in her barn." She frowned at Roman, her confidence in this group dropping. "Are you sure you had the right address?"

"Oh, wait," Sam scrolled ahead. "Here I'm coming up from the basement."

He tapped a video, and Savannah watched Roman, Liam, and Ian scout the space, which was, as Ian had claimed, decked out with some seriously high-tech computers and printers. They were wearing fatigues, helmets with cameras or binoculars or something attached to the top, and seriously scary-looking rifles.

Savannah had no experience with the military, had no way of reliably determining whether this was even real. She could only say the way they moved and handled the equipment held a casual mastery learned from years and years of doing what they were doing in the video.

"What have you got there?" Sam's voice came over the cell as he approached Ian, who picked up bottles off a shelf.

"Thermochromic and optically variable security ink." His voice was familiar, but his tone was direct and businesslike.

"I've seen my share of counterfeit material," this came from Liam. "But never anything this sophisticated."

They discussed counterfeiting terms Savannah had never heard.

"I thought she might have picked up some passports on the darknet," Ian said, "doctored them, and passed them on to Bishop, but this..." He shook his head. "I never imagined she was capable of *this*."

Savannah's stomach dropped. He'd known? He'd known and hadn't told her?

She couldn't listen anymore. She shoved the phone back at Sam. "You still haven't proved to me this has anything to do with—"

"Keep watching," Everly said.

Sam sped up the tape, and Savannah refocused on the screen. She found the camera following the group up some stairs. When they reached the top, the image went dark but for the light glowing from the basement. Savannah couldn't make much out. Then someone turned off a light, and everything went black a moment before the camera adjusted for the new setting.

By the open rafters, tin roof, and wooden walls, it was clear they were in a barn, but...

"Here." Sam pointed at the screen to direct her attention as if she wasn't already riveted to it. "The work desk."

A desk lamp clicked on, illuminating an old desk piled high

with junk and paper. Savannah squinted, searching for that unmistakable association to Misty. "There's so much junk, how could you ever link any of that to—"

"Right there," Sam said.

The camera's lens focused on a pile of mail. Old mail, judging by the yellow stain across the envelopes. One of the guys grabbed a stack and went through it piece by piece while Sam held the camera. Mail for David Klein—Misty's father.

Shock jolted Savannah's brain.

"Sam," Roman's voice sounded in the distance, "get your ass out before we lock you in."

Her vision blurred as her mind worked.

"You need to prep Savannah for what's coming," she heard Roman say. "We're going to need her cooperation."

And in the next instant, she heard Ian's voice, sober, serious, and determined, claiming, "We'll have it."

15

Ian launched himself toward Sam but grabbed the phone only after Savannah had heard him claim he'd make sure she cooperated.

His fear was realized the moment he saw the look on her face, anger covering hurt even as he watched the transformation.

"Sam, you piece of—"

"Dude." Sam grabbed his phone. "What's wrong with you?"

"Me? I swear sometimes for all your brains, you don't have an ounce of common sense."

Everly's phone rang. "Shut up," she told the guys. "It's Rosen."

She turned away, answering the phone with one hand, the other blocking noise in her opposite ear. When Ian turned toward Savannah, he found her walking toward his truck.

"Jesus Christ," Ian said. "You sure know how to make problems, Slaughter."

"You're the one making problems with her, dude. I don't have anything to do with that."

"I'd have to agree with him," Roman told Ian, clearly unhappy.

Not only had Ian stepped over the line with Savannah, he hadn't prepared her for all this.

Everly ended her call and waited for Savannah to return with Jamison.

"We want to go home," she told the group, primarily holding Roman's gaze. Then she glanced at Everly. "Everly can take us."

Fuck. Ian felt like he'd swallowed a boulder.

Everly glanced at Jamison and said, "Sam, why don't you show Jamison how you make your special snowballs."

"My what?" Sam said.

"Stop with the absentminded-professor routine," she told him. "Your. Special. Snowballs."

Roman nudged Sam's shoulder. "Go play with the kid, would you?"

When Sam and Jamison were out of earshot, Everly gave Savannah an apologetic look. "Sorry, girl, you can't go home." She turned her gaze on the guys. "Someone called in a Savannah sighting at Bishop's house. He left the board meeting and discovered everything missing from the safe. Then found Savannah and Jamison MIA."

"Shit," Ian bit out.

"He's geared up his cavalry of half-wits and sent them out on the hunt with an order to use any force necessary to capture Savannah on sight and to bring Jamison and the contents of the safe back."

"Oh my God," Savannah murmured, stricken. Her gaze instantly locked on Ian, her expression scared and searching. But then dropped away a split second later, as if she realized he wasn't her ally anymore.

"Every cop in the county is looking for them. He said to take the back roads to get out of Hazard. Join up with the highway once we're fifty miles clear."

"After all the recent snow?" Ian said. "That's going to take hours. Do we even know which roads are plowed?"

"Sam will be able to tell us," Roman told them. "He can hack into the state transportation database. Let's get moving. The bigger our head start, the better. Liam and I will switch cars with Ian and take the lead. Everly, you and Sam take Jamison and the middle position. Ian, you and Savannah are the chaser."

"I don't know what a chaser is," Savannah said, "but Jamison is *not* going in a different car. He stays with me."

"He can't," Ian told her.

"Don't tell me—" Savannah immediately attacked.

"We aren't trying to keep him from you," Everly cut in, her voice soft but deliberate. "It's safer to have you in different cars."

Liam stepped away from the conversation to pull the seat and the DVD player from the truck.

"Why?" Savannah demanded. "Safer *how*?"

"His chances of getting both of you are significantly diminished," Ian told her.

"If he captures you," Roman told her in his signature all-business commander tone, "he won't kill you if he thinks you have Jamison's location."

"And we'd get you back before he realizes you can't help him," Ian added, hoping to calm the hysteria brewing in her eyes. "If he captures Jamison, you stay alive, and then we'll find Jamison."

"This isn't a fucking video game." Terror pulled the color from her cheeks. Shock darkened her eyes. Ian ached to reach out to her, reassure her. But he sank deeper into enemy territory with every new complication that slashed at her life. "This is my *life*."

"Which we're trying to save," Roman told her. "Sam, get the kid. Let's go."

In a snowbank to the left, Jamison hit Sam with a snowball and giggled. But terror broke across Savannah's face. "Oh my God. I can't believe this is happening."

Everly stepped up to Savannah and gave her arm a reassuring squeeze. "I'll keep him in his seat and run the DVD player nonstop. Sam's just a five-year-old genius in an adult's body. He'll be Jamison's new best friend in twenty minutes."

She finally looked at Ian. "What do you think? Where will Jamison be safest?"

Hope buoyed her heart. Until he had to tell her, "With Everly and Sam in the middle car."

Tears welled in her eyes. But she pressed her lips together and turned back to Everly. "You promised…"

Her voice broke, and Everly pulled her into a quick hug. "And I keep my promises."

Everly called to Sam and started toward the Jeep. Savannah followed. She settled Jamison into the back and did a decent job of making the situation seem like an adventure rather than a tenuous life-saving escape.

"We're burnin' daylight here, people," Roman called out the truck's window.

Ian had to stuff his feelings and pull Savannah from the Jeep. She jerked her arm away and walked ahead of him to the Suburban. Inside, Savannah dropped her head into her hands and choked down sobs. Regret swamped Ian. But with time as their enemy, he couldn't wallow. At least not outwardly.

He followed the others' lead and backed onto the road they'd come in on, then followed Everly's Jeep. Savannah stopped crying almost immediately, curled into her seat, and stared out the passenger's window.

She stayed silent so long, Ian was convinced she'd never talk to him again. In his ear, the team relayed travel information and Bishop updates as Rosen phoned them into Everly. So far, Bishop and the deputies were weaving a futile pattern around Hazard County, but Lyle had enlisted the help of locals to cover the town so the deputies could cross county lines and patrol the highway farther south. Ian had no doubt Sam was tracking every Hazard sheriff's vehicle on a map that showed open and plowed roads.

With no immediate threat and Savannah giving him a well-deserved cold shoulder, Ian was trapped in his own head. The scenery might have been breathtaking, but he couldn't do more than glance at the occasional vacation home off the road while he fought to figure out how he was going to get back into Savannah's good graces.

Twenty minutes into the drive, she broke the silence with "Why did we switch cars?"

Internally, he winced. While he'd been craving connection and the sound of her voice, he also dreaded the questions he'd have to answer in ways she wouldn't understand or like.

"So the lead car has a shooter," he answered.

"I shoot." Her voice was flat and tired. "But not like you guys, I guess."

That made a smile tip his lips. "You shoot?"

"Everyone in Montana shoots."

Silence filled the car again but lasted only five minutes this time.

"Where are we going?" she asked.

"We have a temporary headquarters in Whitefish. We'll regroup there."

Another long silence.

In the Jeep, Jamison and Sam started singing *If You're Happy and You Know It.*

"Oh my God," Everly groaned over the mic. "Kill me now. Roman, you owe me."

Ian took his earpiece out and offered it to Savannah. "This will put a smile on your face."

When she didn't reject him, Ian positioned it in her ear and Savannah held it there with one hand. He watched as joy lifted her features and her mouth curved in a smile. She laughed and closed her eyes with a look of happiness he hadn't seen in what seemed like far too long. In fact, it had been less than twenty-four hours ago, when they'd been lying in bed together.

In the next instant, her smile fell. Fear tightened her features, and she cut a look at Ian.

"What?" He took the earbud and replaced it in his ear.

"—two vehicles a quarter of a mile ahead of us," Sam was saying.

"Cops?" he asked.

"Weren't you listening?" Sam shot back.

"Plan?" he asked.

"Take a left at the next plowed road," Sam said, "then your first right onto forest service land. We'll cut across the pass and hook up with Highway Thirty-two just south of Kalispell."

"Roger that." Ian picked up speed to stay on the tail of the other vehicles.

"We're driving too fast," Savannah said. "It isn't safe."

"It's less safe to let the cops catch up," he told her.

They turned onto the forest service road, and the four-wheel drives lumbered up the rough terrain. Private homes disappeared, replaced by scattered government admin outposts, campgrounds, and tourist information booths. All closed until summer returned.

Savannah pressed her hand to the dash to steady herself. She stared out at the mountains looming on either side of them as they approached a narrow pass. "This area is a bad avalanche zone. With the heavy snow we've had this last week—"

"Sam," Ian said into the mic. "Can you pull up avalanche risk information?"

"On it."

The trio of vehicles rumbled over a particularly rough stretch of road.

"Oh my God," Savannah said, her voice humming with fear and tension. "We could get stuck. Are you sure this is plowed all the way through? I've never been this way in the winter."

"It's plowed," he assured her, "just not as often as the main roads. We'll be fine. Try not to worry. Sam will keep us on the right roads."

"Bumpy, right?" Sam said to Jamison as he climbed into the back seat. "Think of it as a roller coaster." He put his arm around the kid and snugged him against his body. "There. Better?"

"What's he doing?" Savannah said. "What's wrong?"

"He's just making the ride more comfortable for Jamison."

"Ian..." The tension in Savannah's voice drew his gaze from the road. She was looking out the back window. "There's someone behind us."

His gaze cut to the rearview, where a white SUV thundered up behind them. "What the... Sam. Unidentified behind us. Did you miss a cop?"

"*Dude,*" he said, his tone offended. "I'll let that pass, what with you being all hung up on a chick and all. There's no cop behind you."

"Then who the fuck is crawling up my ass?" A distinct *plunk-plunk* sounded against the tailgate.

Savannah chirped a squeal.

A surge of adrenaline heated Ian's veins. "They're shooting. Long gun. Probably a hunting rifle."

"Must be from Lyle's band of dimwits," Sam said. "And they must have radios, because two cops just changed directions, heading toward us."

Taking hold of the steering wheel with a steel grip, Ian reached behind the seat and grappled in the equipment there. He dragged out the first Kevlar vest he felt and tossed it into Savannah's lap. She wouldn't need it inside the car, but at these speeds, there was no telling what could happen.

"Put it on," he told her. "*Now.*"

She dropped the vest over her head without argument and tightened the Velcro side straps.

"We've got a short straightaway up ahead," Sam said, "a small meadow area between mountains."

Ian split his attention between the road ahead and the car behind. When the other SUV bounced, veering right, he caught sight of another truck behind him. "There are *two* assholes on our bumper. Repeat, two vehicles."

"Copy," Roman came back. "When we reach the straightaway, Ian and I will spin and open fire. Shaw and Slaughter, you keep going."

That wouldn't go over well with Savannah, but it was the right thing to do. "Copy."

Plunk-plunk, pink-pink. Another couple of double taps hit the SUV.

"Did that hit the back window?" Savannah asked, confused and shocked.

"You *do* know a thing or two about shooting."

"Why didn't it shatter?"

"Bulletproof," he said, prepping for the firefight that would erupt in about sixty seconds.

"It's why we traded vehicles?" she wanted to know. "Is Jamison's bulletproof too?"

"As soon as we hit the straightaway, we're going to turn on the guys behind us and open fire. Everly and Sam will keep going. Jamison will be—"

"No," she said, instantly terrified. "I don't want to split up. I want to stay with him."

"We'll catch up to him. I swear on my life, that boy is as safe as he can be right now." The opening to the meadow loomed. "Stay down, and hold on."

She obediently gripped the handle and sank lower in the seat. "I'm so killing you if we make it out of this alive."

Roman's car cleared the mountain pass, and Ian started the countdown. "Three."

Everly's car cleared the pass. "Two."

His car cleared the pass. He lowered his window halfway. The icy wind burned his lungs.

"One."

Ian turned the wheel and hit the brake. While Roman's vehicle spun to clear the road for Everly to pass, Ian made an abrupt about-face in the middle of the road. His weapon was already pointed out the window when he came to a stop. Roman skidded up behind Ian at an angle, using his vehicle as a shield.

The drivers of the two pursuing SUVs scrambled to avoid a collision. Both came to a stop just inside the mouth of the canyon.

Ian's mind quieted with intense focus.

More bullets pinged off the SUV. Savannah muffled a squeal.

Ian rested the barrel of the Glock on the edge of his window. The passengers of the SUVs swung their doors wide, using the metal as shields.

A distant rumble saved the shooter of the white SUV from a double tap to the brain. Ian eased back on the trigger, searching for the source of the thunder.

"Hear that?" he asked Roman.

"Affirmative."

"Cops twenty miles behind you," Sam cautioned. "More changing direction and headed toward you. Eight miles ahead."

The rumble grew louder. Ian looked up and found the very top of the mountain shattering at the seams.

"Avalanche!" Savannah yelled. "Ian!"

"*Roman, bail,*" he yelled into the mic. "*Bail.*"

"Affirmative."

Ian and Roman peeled out of the frozen field. With Roman leading the way, Ian floored the gas. The tires spun, then grabbed, and the SUV shot forward.

Savannah turned in her seat, and Ian watched in the rearview as snow pummeled the mountainside, crashed across the road, and swallowed their assailants.

The sight stole Ian's breath.

"Ho-ly shit," he muttered, watching in awe as the wrath of

nature buried them under more and more snow. "Didn't see that comin'."

"Oh my God." Savannah's murmur was laced with equal parts shock and terror.

"Mother nature saved us a few bullets," Roman said.

"You're going to need them," Sam cut in. "Because the cops just passed our hideout on the only side road for miles, which means you're trapped between that avalanche and the cops."

Jesus Christ. Ian was glad Savannah couldn't hear this.

His mind darted from the cops to another potential avalanche. They'd already passed from the meadow into another valley flanked by skyscraping mountains.

"Roman?" Ian said. "How do you want to handle this?"

"Handle what?" Savannah asked, still trying to catch her breath.

"I don't know that we have a lot of choices," Roman said.

He cut a look at Savannah. "The cops know better than to shoot at us under these conditions, right?"

She shook her head with a simultaneous shrug. "Some do, but..."

"Sam," Ian said, evaluating options. "Where is the next meadow?"

"Three-point-four miles. It flattens out on the right, near the base of the next campground. But you won't reach it before the cops reach you. Right about...now."

A sheriff's SUV barreled around a bend, headed straight for them.

"Ready for some chicken?" Roman pulled to the right of the road, leaving room for Ian to move up next to him, effectively blocking the entire road.

Savannah was going to have a coronary, but Ian moved into position.

"What are you doing?" she asked, her voice shrill.

"You know how the flight attendants tell you to brace for

impact?" He pushed on her back. "Curl up in a ball. Head between your knees. Arms covering your head."

"Ian—"

"I know, baby. I know. Just do it."

He met Roman's gaze over Savannah's head. His boss gave Ian one approving nod, and they both focused on the cruisers headed toward them, one in front of the other, lights and sirens blazing.

The sting of fear buzzed over Ian's breastbone. He repositioned his grip on the steering wheel, settled deeper into his seat, and matched Roman's speed.

The next ten seconds passed like minutes while Ian absorbed every detail in sharp relief. And in that second when someone had to decide to bail on this challenge or risk the very real possibility of death, Ian prayed they came out of this alive so he could tell Savannah he loved her.

Ian pushed out one quick breath a millisecond before the first cop veered right. In the next second, the other cop veered left.

He cut a look at Roman at the same time Roman met his gaze. They were both grinning like idiots. Roman saluted Ian and accelerated. Ian fell in behind him, and he ran his hand over Savannah's hair. "We're good. You can sit up."

But when he looked in the rearview, he found the cops pulling out of the snowdrifts and turning to follow.

Savannah sat up and turned to look out the back.

"Sam," Ian prodded.

"Yeah, yeah, I'm trying to learn to breathe again here. Okay, let's see. You've got six more coming at you from the south. No telling how many civilian members of the posse are with them. There are more side roads coming up. Okay, take the third one on the right. It turns into a public road about two miles down and eventually winds you down into a town called Bleak. Jesus, Hazard and Bleak? What's next? Grim? Harsh? Clusterfuck?"

Punk, punk-punk-punk. Shots dented the body of the SUV.

"Seriously?" Ian said, yelling at the rearview. "Didn't you learn anything from those other idiots?"

Punk-punk, pink-pink-pink-pink.

Ian swore. Savannah pulled her knees into her chest and wrapped her arms around her legs, her terrified blue gaze tilted toward the sky. Watching the snow on the mountains, he knew. If he didn't have to concentrate so hard on his driving, he'd be doing the same thing.

"Hang in there, baby," he told her. "I'll get your feet on solid ground soon."

"Sam," Roman said. "When we pass you, drop in behind them. And when we reach a clearing, pin them in. We're going to end this."

"Roger and ready," Sam sent back.

Savannah turned her gaze on Ian. "Is Jamison okay?"

"How's our recruit doing?" Ian asked.

"I think he's addicted. Having a grand old time. Big eyes, taking it all in. He especially likes it when the car spins around."

Ian smiled for Savannah. "I think you've got a daredevil on your hands."

She closed her eyes on a groan.

Punk-punk-punk, pink-pink, punk, punk, punk.

"Jesus," Ian bit out. He knew the car was solid, but those mountains...

Punk-punk-punk. Zing. Pink-pink. Punk, punk, punk.

The deputies had taken a play from the Manhunters' play-book and now drove side-by-side, shooting at the SUV from both directions.

"Ian." Savannah's thin, terrified voice pulled his gaze from the men behind him and followed her finger, pointed at the mountains on their left. "The snow's shifting. If they don't stop shooting—"

She pulled in a sharp breath.

Ian saw it. "Avalanche," he confirmed to the team. "Left side."

"Shit," Roman bit out.

"You either have to run it," Sam said, "or deal with the two behind you and the reinforcements coming in, which will outnumber all of us."

A millisecond passed while Ian watched the mountain crumble and played out those very real scenarios in his head.

He and Roman seemed to come to the same conclusion at the same time and echoed each other with their solution: "Run it."

Roman sped up, and Ian followed, foot to the floor, hands working to find the finesse required to control a vehicle on snow at this speed. He felt like they were racing a train, hoping to get ahead of it just enough to cross the tracks without being flattened.

Savannah mewled and pressed her forehead to her knees, then yelled, "*Everly, you promised.*"

"She keeps her promises, baby," Ian told her. "But you're not going to need it."

As if to mock him, bowling-ball-size chunks of ice smashed the windshield. The sheer force of it pushed the car sideways. Coupled with their speed, the car spun out.

The steering wheel was wrenched from his hands. They went up on two wheels. Ian grabbed for the wheel and wrestled it back under control. The SUV dropped back to all four wheels, and Ian floored the gas.

"Punch it, Heller," Roman yelled. "*Punch it.*"

In the rearview, a wave of snow swept through the valley. The cops behind Ian vanished, swallowed by the white monster.

"Come on, come on, *come on—*"

The edge of the avalanche clipped the rear bumper, spinning the car like a top. Savannah screamed. Then the momentum of the snow picked them up like a shell in the surf and toppled them over and over and over.

S avannah blinked her eyes open but immediately focused inside, on the pain thrumming through her body. Her head throbbed. Her back ached. Her left shoulder burned. In fact, just about every inch of her body hurt.

A nagging sense of fear forced her to focus, but her equilibrium was off. She felt like she was sitting at an angle. And her eyes weren't working right. All she saw was white. White filling every window of the car. Yet the interior seemed dim.

Reality flooded in, swamping her brain with white-hot terror. Hank. Cops. Gunshots. *Avalanche.*

She turned her head, searching for Ian. But she moved too quickly, and pain shot down her neck, making her wince. "Shit."

The sound of her own voice pried her mind open, and everything spilled in at once. Her heart rate jumped, and adrenaline gushed through her veins. She forced her eyes to open and her brain to turn.

Her surroundings were intensely silent. She had no idea how long they'd been unconscious. Had no idea how far the avalanche had taken them. Had *absolutely* no idea how to get out of this.

She found Ian still in the driver's seat. The blood registered first. Bright red, matting his hair, painting his face. A sob bubbled out of her. "Ian. *Ian*, wake up."

The car had come to rest at an angle with Ian's side of the car up. Or maybe Savannah's side was up. She was so disoriented, she didn't know. The roof over Ian's side of the car jutted into the space. In the back, the roof had been smashed in, crowding the interior. Several windows had shattered but remained intact, the bulletproof glass spiderwebbed.

Fear clawed at her gut. She reached for Ian, but her seat belt had cinched down on her like a vise. "*Ian*."

His head lolled toward her. Blood dripped onto the console from his forehead. That was good, right? He couldn't bleed if he wasn't alive, right?

Her mind darted to Jamison, and fear burned her heart. "He was miles away from the avalanche," she told herself. "He was hidden away on a back road with Everly and Sam. He's okay."

Those realizations helped her drag her panic back into line with the present. The thought of getting back to her boy gave her the motivation to fight.

She pushed against the seat belt until her fingers touched his forehead and found his skin still warm. She tapped his head. "Ian. *Ian*."

When he didn't stir, the barriers on her fear broke, and panic rushed in. Her quick breaths billowed in the car. "You can't die. *You can't*."

She searched his skin for any kind of heartbeat. When she couldn't detect one, she slid her fingers through the blood, pausing on his neck.

She closed her eyes and focused on the connection, murmuring, "Please be alive. *Please* be alive."

A gentle thump rolled beneath her fingers. Her heart surged. Her eyes opened, and she repositioned her fingers to make sure what she felt was real.

"Come on, you big military stud," she murmured. "Stay with me."

Another thump tapped her fingers. Then another. And another.

Relief washed through her, the wave so powerful, she slumped into her seat. "Thank you, God."

Savannah attacked her seat belt buckle again, but her numb, weak fingers gave out. "Ian," she yelled in frustration, "wake up, dammit."

His lashes never fluttered. Every second that ticked by felt intensely precious. His head wound looked severe. His brain could be hemorrhaging. He could be bleeding internally.

Savannah tried to wiggle out from the constriction of her seat belt and for the first time realized she was still wearing the bullet-proof vest. She ripped at the Velcro and lifted the vest over her head, growling through the pain cutting across her torso.

With the vest off, she had an extra inch or two to work with. But she was already exhausted. She sobbed in frustration. "Ian, *please* wake up."

She leaned forward, reaching for the glove box. Her fingers barely brushed the metal. She grimaced against the pain. Pushed against the locked belt crossing her torso. Jabbed at the button. The glove box door fell open. With urgency driving her, she wiggled and shifted for another half inch and grabbed at anything she could reach.

She pulled at papers and let them fall to the floor. Grabbed the string of a tiny flashlight and dropped the device into her jacket pocket. Tugged at something leather.

Falling back in her seat, she stared at the hunting knife. "Yes."

A burst of excitement had her hands fumbling to pull the leather from the blade. She was shaking with fear, shivering with cold. But she pulled the knife free and sawed at the nylon belt across her chest. Something so simple had never felt so difficult. It was like cutting stone with a butter knife. Her numb fingers struggled to hold on to the handle tight enough to cut. Her other hand fought to hold the belt still.

Finally, she sliced through the last tendril of nylon. The belt fell loose. Savannah pulled her feet under her, knelt on the seat, and leaned over Ian. "Okay, I've got you now."

She cradled his face, holding his head still in case he had a spinal injury. If she cut off his seat belt, he'd fall to her side of the car. She couldn't begin to fathom how they'd get out of here. Or what they'd face even if they did.

Savannah snuffed out her defeatist thoughts and supported Ian's head with one hand, tapping his cheek with the other. "Hey, Ian, wake up. I need you."

She tentatively checked the wound on his head. His scalp had a good slash in it. She was less worried about that than she was the knot swelling nearby.

"Come on, Ian. You've got to wake up. I can't do this on my own." She tapped his cheek harder. "I still have all kinds of things to yell at you for, and you're damn well going to wake up to hear them."

Still nothing.

"Dammit." She climbed into the back to see what she could find.

Every move seemed to make her hurt somewhere. Just as she slung one leg over the second seat to investigate a box in the very back, the Suburban teetered. And her equilibrium teetered with it. She froze, struggling to get her bearings. The SUV's movement made it seem like gravity was pulling the car toward the driver's side. But her brain told her that the ground should be on the passenger's side.

Trying to figure it out made her head ache. She closed her eyes and pressed the palm of her hand to the throb in her forehead. She met wet, sticky skin. Her stomach dropped. And when she pulled her hand away, she found what she'd feared—more blood. But she was alert and moving, so she continued her quest, praying the car didn't break through some threshold and plummet.

Holding on to the back seat for stability, Savannah lifted the flap of the box and reached inside. Her hand touched metal. Guns. She recognized the feeling instantly. The small boxes in the corner were probably ammunition. Then she touched something soft and dragged it out.

A blanket. "Thank God." She reached back in. "Water would probably be too much to ask for—" Her hand closed on something cold and plastic. Hope swelled inside her. She pulled out a jug of water and exhaled in relief. "Thank you, thank you, thank you."

Tentatively, she moved back to the front of the car without any more teetering incidents. Once she slipped into her seat, her body settled and her equilibrium was restored—gravity pulled her toward the passenger's side. Ian's side of the car was pointed up; her side, down.

Savannah shook out the blanket and leaned over the console. She passed her hands over his arms, his belly, his thighs, searching for any obvious injuries. When she didn't find any, she slid the blanket across Ian's body. Then she eased closer, and ran her hands up and down over his arms, using friction to create warmth.

"Come on, Ian. Enough slacking."

She continued to jostle and talk to him, as much to wake him as it was to keep her mind off the very real, very potentially fatal situation.

"You went to all this trouble to get me out of that town. You need to follow through. Jamison needs me. You know he needs me."

She took a break from warming him and rested her forehead against his jaw. Tears burned her eyes. Tears of fear, of regret. "I'm sorry I got so mad," she whispered. "I just...I was just...so crazy about you. Thought you might be the one." Savannah lifted her head and cupped his face again. Desperation snuck in, and she gave him a little shake. "Come on, Ian. *I need you.*"

His lips moved. Then his lashes fluttered. Hope burned through her heart. She stroked his face. "That's it. Right here. Open your eyes. I'm right here."

His lids lifted, exposing confusion-hazed hazel eyes. Savannah laughed with relief. "There you are. Damn, you had me scared."

He immediately tried to sit up. Savannah put a hand on his shoulder. "No, no." When his gaze jumped to hers, she said, "You've got a couple of head injuries."

He exhaled and relaxed against the seat. "Okay."

His voice was groggy, but Savannah was so relieved and thrilled to hear it, she leaned close and kissed him gently. His lips were cold, but he lifted a hand to stroke her hair. When Savannah pulled back, he said, "You're bleeding."

"Not as much as you."

A smile flickered at the corner of his lips. "I'm competitive like that."

She smiled. "God, I'm glad you're talking."

He tried to look around, but Savannah kept his head in her hands. "I'm afraid for you to move. What about your spine?"

Ian's feet scraped across the floor, then his thighs moved. "I think I'm okay."

"Move slowly," she cautioned before releasing his head.

He grimaced and moaned, but he seemed to move well enough. Once he was sitting upright, he took stock of the SUV. "Did a number on this thing."

"Yeah. Imagine how this would have turned out if we'd stayed in the truck."

He made a dark sound in his throat.

"When Roman sees this, he's going to skin you alive." Their reality sank in again. "If we make it out."

"We're making it out," he said with an intensity and finality that soothed her nerves. He rolled his wrist and pushed up the sleeve, glancing at his watch. The face had been crushed. "My watch has a GPS tracker. Don't know if it's still working, but we need to get it to the surface." He paused, seeming to fight to get his thoughts together. "No telling how deep we are. Doesn't transmit through snow." His words slurred a little, and his gaze went distant again, as if he might pass out. "Need to start digging out."

"We could be under a mile of snow."

He let his eyes close and rested his head against the seat. "We were at the edge of it. Don't think we're that deep." He cast a look toward the back of the SUV. "What kind of equipment do they have in here?"

"The blanket, and I have a jug of water. There are guns and ammunition in the back."

"Can never have enough weapons, right?"

She smiled, and a wave of emotion swept through her again. Gratitude, love, hope. "Ian, I'm so sorry—"

He lifted his hand and pressed his fingers to her lips. "I'm the one who's sorry." He opened his eyes and met hers. "I'm going to make it right, Savannah. I'm going to make it up to you."

More tears pressed at the backs of her eyes. She smiled, nodded, and pressed her cheek to his.

"Water," he said. "Pull out the jug."

She slid back into her seat. Grabbing the jug at her feet, she settled it on the console and opened the top and helped him steady the jug as he drank.

When he finished, he said, "Drink as much as you need. We have to empty it."

"Why?"

Ian picked up the knife she'd left in the console's cup holder. "Because it's going to become a digging tool."

Savannah took a few long swallows and recapped it.

Ian tried the buttons on the driver's door, and Savannah's

window slid down an inch. The snow was packed tight against the car. "Pour the rest out—slow at first."

Savannah tilted the jug and poured the water into the snow, which melted instantly, giving her room to empty the jug. Ian took the empty plastic and cut away the top, leaving the bottom attached to the handle. "Voilá."

She smiled at his less than enthusiastic expression. "What a Boy Scout."

"So my mom said." He straightened up in the seat with another grimace and looked around the car. "We'll work in shifts. One of us in the back seat with the blanket, warming up, while the other shovels. We'll chuck the snow over to the passenger's side."

She closed her eyes. "I can't believe this is happening."

"Don't think about the big picture," he told her. "We're living moment by moment right now."

She nodded. "Okay." Then she swiped the jug from his hand. "I'm taking the first shift. Get your ass back here and rest."

IAN WAS DRIFTING in and out of consciousness when Savannah yelled, "We did it!"

He opened his eyes and looked around the car. No matter how many times he'd done that over the last hour—or two, he wasn't sure anymore—reality jabbed him in the gut again.

"Ian," she said, sliding back to the car through the tunnel to the surface. "We did it. I'm through."

"*You* did it. You're amazing." He must have told her that fifty times by now, but he meant it every damn time. She was bruised, bloodied, and terrified, yet she never stopped fighting, never stopped digging, even when Ian couldn't help because he kept passing out. "What did you see? Any search parties? Any equipment? Anything?"

She leaned over him and, just as she'd done a dozen times before, rubbed his arms until warmth collected beneath the blanket. Her gaze went distant for a second before she smiled. "I don't know. I was so excited to see sky, I slid back down here to tell you."

He chuckled and brushed the hair back from her face. "Guess I'd better get my lazy ass up, then."

"Hold on. Stay put a minute." She knelt on the edge of the seat and leaned into the back. "I want to pull out some of these guns, 'cause, you know"—she faced him again, holding a Glock in one hand and a box of bullets in the other—"you can never have enough."

He started laughing—partly because of what she said, but mostly because of the look on her face. She was bloody and dirty and pale from the cold, but she looked like a kid who'd just stolen a cookie from the cookie jar. Only the pressure of laughing stabbed pain through his head. He put a hand to his head and groaned. "Oh, shit. Don't make me laugh, baby."

She set the gun on his stomach and scanned his face with a frown. "Are you going to be able to climb to the top and walk out? Because don't even think about telling me to go ahead. I'm not leaving you—"

His lips twitched into a smile. "I wouldn't *let* you leave me."

She exhaled and nodded. As soon as her gaze went distant, he knew what was coming next, so he jumped in front of it. "Right now, I'll bet Sam has Jamison dancing in the back seat, singing karaoke.

She laughed at the absurd image.

"I'm only half kidding," he told her. "The kid is probably having the time of his life."

She nodded. "Sorry I keep asking. It's not like you have a direct line into the Jeep or anything. I just..."

He pulled her close and kissed her forehead. "You're worried because you're an incredible mom."

She sighed and looked down at the gun. "Can you help me load this? I've never used this model before, and I'd really rather not shoot myself trying to load it."

"My pleasure." He took the Glock, filled the magazine, and primed the chamber. Now that he was awake, his head throbbed. "There's one in the chamber, and this weapon has a trigger safety, so just squeeze the trigger."

"No safety. Got it."

Ian forced himself to sit up, but he couldn't keep the groan from spilling out. He wasn't sure how much of the pain was the drop in body temp and how much was injury, but he was having a damn difficult time moving. And that would be problematic if the cops were nearby.

"Let me take a trial run at it," he told her. "See how I do."

Savannah climbed into the back to give him room to get up, over the console, and maneuver—painfully—out the window.

When he looked up the length of the tunnel, he swore. They'd ended up far deeper than he'd thought. More like ten or twelve feet than two or three. But that dusky early evening sky was compelling. He could see why she'd gotten so excited. But they still had a lot to worry about.

Ian worked himself up the tunnel, realizing that Savannah had carved out enough room for her small frame, but Ian's was another story. He had to use his shoulders like a snowplow to get through the space. He also realized his left knee had gotten pretty banged up in the accident.

It took what felt like forever to reach the top. Ian had to stop twice to keep from blacking out. The last time he'd done that, he'd fallen back down the tunnel and into the car.

Not fun. Definitely not something he wanted to repeat.

When he finally poked his head above the surface, he was light-headed. His brain and knee battled for the most-messed-up award. He drew a deep lungful of frozen but fresh air. And he thanked God for Savannah. If she wasn't so damn strong, they probably would have succumbed to the cold by now.

The first thing to catch Ian's attention was voices. He peered left, where just a couple of hours ago, there had been a road. The new mound of snow was dotted with a couple of dozen people, methodically sticking metal poles into the snow to search for vehicles and people. Between the dimming light, the distance, and the backdrop of complex mountain terrain, he couldn't see who was working, but he'd bet it was the same band of cops and dimwits Bishop had released with a kill order.

He closed his eyes to improve his hearing and listened. If there were Manhunters in that search party, he didn't hear their voices. Ian couldn't envision anyone but Everly infiltrating a search party. Roman, Liam, and Sam would be strangers and immediately suspect. But no female voices floated on the air.

No matter. They were all nearby; that, Ian knew for a fact. They just needed to find each other. Until that could happen, he and Savannah needed warmth and rest.

He pulled his phone from his pocket and checked for a signal. As expected, he got nothing. He laid both his phone and his watch on the snow, but he didn't hold out a lot of hope for catching a signal. Not in these mountains.

Ian scanned the terrain. It would be dark soon. The search party would be called off any time now. Everyone under the snow would be written off as dead. The rescue would be reclassified as a recovery effort. And that was good. Because as long as Bishop thought he and Savannah were dead, he'd refocus the bulk of his resources on recovering Jamison.

He and Savannah weren't home free by any means. Tomorrow, at some point, this hole in the snow would be found, the SUV would be recovered, and their tracks leading away from the site would be followed.

At least that would give them a good head start. But a head start to where?

A gust of wind blew through the pass, and Ian backed down the tunnel. In the Suburban, Savannah sat in the second row of seats, huddled beneath the blanket. She opened it in invitation, and after Ian shucked all the ice clinging to his pants and jacket, he sat beside her, pulled her into him, and dragged the blanket closed.

"What do you think?" she asked, her voice nervous. "It's starting to get dark."

He shared his thoughts on their next move: getting out of here, finding shelter, and, hopefully, a GPS signal.

Savannah sat back and met his gaze. Her expression was a mix of stark fear and raw fury. She scraped her lips between her teeth and covered her face for a moment.

Just when Ian thought she'd burst into tears, she lifted her head with an expression of renewed strength and asked, "Have we got an AK-47 back there? 'Cause I'm just about ready to mow those assholes down and steal their vehicles."

Ian laughed, then groaned and swore. "Savannah..."

"Sorry," she muttered. "I couldn't help myself. I'm freezing, exhausted, hurt, and terrified. And I'm over it. All of it. Seriously. I'm *done*. I'm not looking forward to sloshing through snow up to my ass. Hypothermia is not my friend."

He pulled her close again. "We don't have to stay in the deep snow for long. Just until we get clear of any searchers and the cops Hank will assign to protect the scene overnight. And if we take the road, he'll only be able to follow our footprints to that point. Plows will clear them overnight."

"What about cars? People might see us on the road, report back to Hank."

"Road's blocked. The avalanches will be in the local news. The only people on this road will be cops and my team. If we're not sure, we'll hightail it into the brush or behind a berm."

She thought about it, frowning as she searched his expression. "I guess it's our best option."

"We really need to catch a signal," he told her.

"Where will we go?"

"I'm trying to remember what we might be close to, but my brain's not working on all cylinders." He closed his eyes and fought the pain and the fatigue to pull up landmarks. "We passed onto forest service land. There were a few campsites... That's all I remember."

"We passed Robinson Camp, McGuire Camp, Calx Camp..." Her voice trailed off, then she turned her head to look at Ian. "Did we pass Koocanusa?"

He shook his head. "I'm not sure. The others sound familiar. That one doesn't. I could have missed the sign in the chase, but how would a campground help us?"

"Because they have cabins. You can rent a campsite and pitch a tent, or you can pay more and get a little cabin. But I could never get Hank to go with me, so I have no idea where the cabins are on the property."

"A secluded cabin in the mountains with you? And he didn't go?" Ian said with sincere dismay. "Damn, that man is a loser in too many ways to count."

"Maybe once I'm outside, I'll be able to figure out if we're close. There's a unique mountain just before you turn into the campground."

"Unique mountain," he echoed. "That's a little hard to believe around here."

She grinned. "It's a phallic symbol. The guys at the mine have a couple dozen jokes about it."

He matched her smile. "Well, if you're ready to go hunting for a giant penis and a remote cabin, let's do this."

17

The trek through thigh-high powder had not been fun. Even with her knee-high, waterproof North Face boots that were rated to withstand temperatures down to minus twenty degrees, Savannah had lost feeling in her feet.

They'd been walking for about an hour. Twenty minutes through powder and forty minutes on this road with only two vehicle sightings—both cops. The rescue search had continued past sunset, hampering Ian and Savannah's escape.

The trek raised her body temperature and her feet had regained some feeling, but Ian's limp had worsened and his pace had slowed. He claimed to be fine and remained determined to keep going, but Savannah was worried.

"How far have we walked?" she asked. "And don't say 'ten minutes farther than the last time you asked,' smart-ass."

"I love how you retain your sense of humor under the worst conditions."

"I'm trying to figure out if we passed the campground," she told him. "I thought there was a caretaker that lived there year-round to keep up the property, but if they shut the place down, the road leading to the property would be snowed over. Did you have a plan B in mind?"

He stopped walking, and Savannah came up beside him. "We don't need one, baby." He angled his flashlight across the road. "Look."

A wooden sign had been carved with: Welcome to Koocanusa Camp.

Her knees went weak with relief, and she grabbed a handful of his jacket to stay upright. "And the road's plowed."

"Things are looking up."

She pulled her phone from her jacket. "Still no service."

"Maybe up by the cabins."

She nodded and headed up the dark road, praying they could find a place to rest and get warm. Fifteen minutes later, they'd passed a tiny booth at the entrance to the campground and came to a cluster of small, freestanding cabins.

"Oh my God," Savannah breathed. "I was beginning to believe I'd imagined them."

Ian swept the buildings with his flashlight and walked behind one to look down the row. "They're all the same." He pointed to the third in a row on the opposite side of the road. It was set a little farther back against the trees. "This one."

He circled the building, checking the front door, then the windows—all locked. A rustle and a minute later, he appeared at the front door, opening it from the inside.

Relief tingled through her belly "How'd you do that?"

"Jimmied a window."

"What about your bad knee?"

He shrugged. "I have another one."

When she stepped into the small space, Ian closed the door behind her. The flashlight illuminated the space. "Not bad for an impromptu visit."

"Not bad for a *planned* visit."

There was one big bed against the back wall, positioned

under the window Ian had come in if the screen on the floor was
any indication. And it was made up with blankets and pillows.
The front of the cabin had been set up like a living room with a
love seat and a lounger. A two-person table sat next to a tiny
kitchen area.

"Do you want the good news or the bad news first?" he
asked her.

"Bad news?" Her shoulders slumped. "I can't take any more
bad news."

"Then let's just get it out of the way," he said. "There's no electricity."

She exhaled in relief and eased to a seat on the sofa. "Hardly
the worst thing I've heard today. What's the good news?"

"It's got an older water heater that doesn't need electricity to
operate." He grinned. "And the propane tank used to heat it
is full."

Excitement burst at the center of her body. "We'll have hot
water? Are you serious?"

"In about twenty minutes."

"That's downright civilized." She pulled out her phone,
checking for a signal. "But...still no service."

"Me either," he said. "I tossed my watch onto the roof. If it's
working, if it can pick up a signal, my team will find us."

"If, if, if..." She sighed. "I guess I'll take them. Better than a
definite no." She patted the sofa. "Come sit. Let me look at your
head and your knee."

He pressed his hand to the arm of the couch, put his weight
on the other leg, and eased onto a seat next to her. Turning the
flashlight upside down, he set it on the floor. The beam hit the
ceiling and dispersed, filling the cabin with soft light.

The relief of having a safe, comfortable place to rest sank
deep into her bones. She cupped his face, tilted his head down,
and fingered away the hair around his injuries. "What do you
think Sam's got Jamison doing now?"

"Hmmm. My guess? Jumping on the bed of the closest motel, face covered in camo grease."

She smiled at the image his words created. "Your team would go to a hotel?"

"No, just Sam. They'd want Jamison to get some sleep."

"Why Sam, not Everly?"

"Sam's naturally better with kids."

"Your lump has gone down, and your cut isn't bleeding anymore, but I think you're going to need stitches."

He winced. "Can't wait."

"I was definitely the luckier one today."

He lifted his head and met her eyes. He slid his knuckles across her cheek. "That's arguable. I've gotten pretty damn lucky with you."

She gave his hand a squeeze, then leaned sideways against the back of the sofa. "I guess we have a lot to talk about." She pushed her boots off and curled her feet beneath her, searching for warmth. "Do you really think Misty was counterfeiting for Hank?"

"I'm sorry, baby. I really do."

Her heart grew heavy with sadness, regret, disillusionment. "Nobody is what they seem, are they?"

"You're the first exception I've ever met."

She shrugged. Savannah's history had forced her to appreciate the simple things. She had simple needs. Simple wants. But even those had proved too complicated to attain.

"Do you have enough evidence to put Hank and Lyle away?" she asked him, watching his expression for deception. "*Really* put them away?"

"They're going down. That is for sure."

She searched his expression and realized she couldn't tell if he was lying or not. But she admittedly sucked as a lie detector. Still, she relished the thought of not fighting them anymore.

"How did this all start, anyway?"

"Mason's death," he told her. "He was undercover for a joint task force run out of the State Department. He'd been assigned here because they tracked counterfeit passports back to Bishop Mining. Some were being used by terrorists."

Disbelief and fear flared. "You're not telling me Misty's selling passports to terrorists, are you? Because there is no way she would be part of that. She has the biggest heart of anyone I know. She'd never want to do anything to deliberately hurt someone else."

"We don't think so. In fact, I think Hank was blackmailing her to create the passports. But they were used in some horrific terrorist attacks."

"Oh my God." When Misty heard this, she'd be heartbroken. "What's going to happen to her?"

"They'll arrest her, try to get information about what she's doing and why. But no matter what deal authorities might be willing to make with her, I imagine she'll go to prison for some length of time. All that will depend on how she cooperates and what they can prove."

Savannah's heart broke for Misty. "This is going to crush Jamison. He *loves* her. She's been like an aunt to him. And a sister to me."

"I know. It's going to be hard on both of you." He picked up her hand and threaded their fingers. The gesture was so simple, yet so sweet. "Are you going to stay in Hazard after Hank and Lyle are gone?"

"Hell no." Her immediate and emphatic answer made Ian smile. And man, what a smile. Even amid the dried blood and dirt, the man was heart melting.

"Where will you go?"

She shrugged, smiled. "I have no idea. Just the thought of taking that next step exhausts me right now."

He leaned forward and took her hands in his. Then he met her eyes. "I didn't sleep with you to trick you. I slept with you because I wanted to. Because you're beautiful and sweet and damned amazing. I admit, from a professional perspective, Roman's right, I shouldn't have. And while I am sorry I lied to you, I'm not sorry I slept with you."

She pulled in a breath. "No more lies?"

He smiled a little. "No more lies."

She nodded and let it go. After everything she'd been through, she wasn't going to hold it against him. "Tell me about your team. About the company."

"Misty told you about the military version of the team?"

Savannah nodded. "Said you were called the American Taliban because you swept in, killed, and bailed."

He shook his head on a long exhale. "The thing is, we didn't do anything different from SEAL Team Six. They get movie deals and accolades. We get labeled Taliban."

"So, you've killed people."

"I have." He answered without hesitation and without apology. "Every kill I've ever made was directly related to the country's safety."

She could respect that. "And Roman's team?"

"Is totally different. We're civilians. We're sent where we're needed for non-military-related issues that need a quick and permanent solution to a problem the government and few security teams will take on. But we are not dispatched to neutralize."

Neutralize. Such bizarre language. Language she was sure felt like second nature to Ian. She had so much to learn about this man. She wondered if she'd get the chance. Or if she even wanted that chance.

"This is my first mission with them. After my mom died, I tried to go back. Everything I told you about that is true."

"Are you going to stay with the team?"

"I don't know. I think it depends on how pissed Roman is about me stepping over the line with you."

She had so many questions. They rose in her mind like

bubbles, but fatigue popped them before she could ask them. She had to focus hard as the exhaustion dragged at her.

"Have you been married?"

"Never."

She nodded, and he waited, focused and determined. But Savannah was too tired to talk. "Pull up your pant leg. Let me see your knee."

"Can't. Too swollen."

She sighed and rested her head against the sofa. "God, what a mess."

Ian wrapped his arms around her and dragged her close. "As long as you come out of this okay, I don't care what else happens."

She put a hand against his chest and looked up at him. "Don't say that. You scared the shit out of me today."

He sighed and stroked her jaw with his knuckles. His gaze was so warm, so loving. When he looked at her like this, Savannah felt showered in affection.

"I know you're worried about Jamison," he said, "and we still have to get out of this, but when this is settled, I want to sit down with you before you make your next big life move. If you'll let me, I want to be part of that move."

She couldn't quite believe he still wanted her after he'd seen all her flaws, all her weaknesses, all her mistakes. And they had some hard talks ahead to hash out his lies. But she agreed those talks were best saved for later.

She eased up and kissed him. "I can agree to that."

She loved the feel of him sinking into the kiss. Loved the low groan in his throat, the pressure of his lips, the slide of his tongue. She kissed him until she couldn't breathe.

She pulled back. "Think the water's warm yet?"

"Shower by flashlight?" he asked with a grin.

"Together. Definitely." Then she remembered his watch. "What if the team finds us?"

He smiled. "They can wait."

She stood and offered her hand to help him up. Ian turned on the shower, and Savannah found towels in a bathroom cabinet. She tossed them onto the shower enclosure. Ian leaned against the sink and pulled her between his legs. "You know this isn't going to feel as good as you think, right? Hot water on open wounds isn't fun."

She nodded, snuggled close, and laid her head against his chest. The ache in her heart over Misty's involvement with Hank and the passports snuck in. Then her worry over Jamison.

Even though she knew she had to be driving Ian crazy asking about Jamison, she couldn't keep herself from saying, "What do you think Sam has Jamison doing now?"

"I think Sam's passed out and Jamison's watching cartoons, eating everything in the mini fridge and calling room service."

She laughed. Fatigue made her punch drunk, and the image she created in her mind of Jamison and Sam kept her giggling. Savannah welcomed the moment of relief.

"He's probably making swans out of towels by now," Ian continued. "Reading the Bible. Ordering movies. Hell, I hope he didn't find the porn."

Savannah laughed so hard, tears burned her eyes. When she caught her breath, she exhaled, "I love you."

As soon as she heard the words, she froze. *Shit.* She hadn't meant to say that. Had she? A quick check of her emotions and, yes, she loved him. But...

She lifted her head and looked at him. "I'm sorry, I didn't mean to—"

He pressed his fingers against her lips. "I love you too. I kept hoping we survived long enough for me to tell you. You can trust me with your heart, Savannah. I'm going to prove it to you."

She searched his eyes and found honesty and affection. He lifted his fingers and pressed his lips to hers. The kiss was tender, emotional, but quickly turned hungry.

When Ian finally lifted his head, Savannah was dizzy with lust and the bathroom was filled with steam.

Ian smiled. "I think the water's hot."

He reached into the shower and adjusted the temperature. The warmth in the room felt so good, Savannah moaned. "Can we leave the water running and sleep in here? It's *so warm.*"

"We can do anything you want," Ian told her. "But first, shower."

Undressing proved more painful and problematic than either of them had realized. With every piece of clothing finally stripped away, more bruises and injuries appeared, and Ian's knee was worse than he ever let on.

Savannah winced. "Ouch."

"I've been worse," he told her. "Are you ready to brave the shower?"

"Definitely. I want warmth like you don't know."

"Oh, I know."

He slipped his arm around her waist and held her steady as she stepped over the side of the tub, then joined her.

With more extensive injuries, Ian suffered the most in the first few minutes. As the water ran over the cut on his head, he growled and swore. Once their injuries had become desensitized and their bodies adjusted to the heat, the shower became luxurious. They lingered under the hot water, skin on skin, lips against lips.

Water slicked his hair off his handsome face and clumped his long lashes. The sight of rivulets coursing down his muscled body sparked her desire. The pressure of his erection low against her belly primed her bloodstream with lust. He was so strong, so primitively male, yet so tender with her. The contrast turned her inside out with want.

She slid her hand between their bodies and over his erection. Ian groaned and kissed her harder, deeper. The same way she wanted to feel him inside her.

He broke the kiss, pushed the shower curtain aside, and leaned out to search his wallet. With the condom's foil packet between his teeth, he ripped it open. Savannah took the condom and rolled it on, quickly, efficiently. Her hands worked much better when they weren't frozen.

Ian wrapped a strong arm around her waist and lifted her.

She grabbed his shoulders for balance. "Ian, no, your knee."

He pressed her back against the wall and pulled her thigh to his hip. "I've got another one."

Her laughter melted in another searing kiss. He gripped her ass with both hands, lifting and supporting her. She wrapped both legs around his waist, and Ian expertly guided himself inside her.

"Oh God..." She drew out the words in a groan of pleasure. She'd never felt anything as good as this man filling her. Then he moved, proving her wrong. Driving pleasure through her with every thrust. He swallowed her sounds of ecstasy with his kiss and methodically, rhythmically urged her toward bliss.

Ian dropped his forehead to her shoulder. "Baby, you feel...so good."

Emotions swamped her. Too many and too mixed to sort anything out. She held him tight and rode his every thrust, pushing off the shower wall to meet him.

Her orgasm rose in a sharp wave of pleasure and crashed with a fury that tensed every exhausted muscle in her body. Ian's growl of approval shivered through her, followed by his own climax, so intense, it stole Savannah's breath.

His body relaxed, leaning into hers and pressing her against the shower wall while their breathing returned to normal. He lifted his head from her shoulder, his eyes heavy-lidded with satisfaction, and Savannah kissed him with all the affection and gratitude and love spiraling through her chest. He returned her kiss with a tenderness and reverence and sweetness that filled every hole in her heart.

He eased from her body and set her on her feet. When she turned toward the spray, rinsing one more time, Ian wrapped his arms around her from behind and kissed her neck. "We'll have to sleep in shifts."

"Why?"

"We may both have concussions. One of us needs to stay awake to prod the other every half hour or so."

"I'll take the first shift." She turned off the water and pulled a towel from the shower enclosure, handing it to Ian before she pulled her own down. "I won't be able to sleep worrying about Jamison anyway."

EVERLY SET a deliberate path through the snow with Roman on one side of her, Liam on the other. Flakes continued to fall, erasing any sign of footsteps Ian and Savannah might have left.

Snowshoes kept them on top of the powder as they picked up the search the rescue team had abandoned after dark. But unlike the search party, instead of looking for signs of death, they were looking for signs of life. Signs that Ian and Savannah had escaped the avalanche or were still alive beneath the snow.

With half the area already scoured by the search effort, they only needed to cover the other half. Everly was sick over this. And the more ground they covered without any sign of Ian and Savannah, the heavier the rock in the pit of her stomach became.

Because cops had been stationed around the avalanche site, the team couldn't use flashlights to search the snow's surface. They'd donned their night vision to get an enhanced look at the snow surface to spot irregularities. But for the last hour, all they saw were miles of pristine snow cover.

Everly's phone vibrated in her pocket, shocking her to a stop.

"What?" Roman asked, looking back at her over his shoulder.

"My phone." She pulled it out and looked at the screen. "It's Sam. We have signal."

Roman ripped his phone from his pocket, and Everly answered Sam's FaceTime video while she looked over Roman's shoulder at the GPS app. "Hold on," she told Sam.

When Ian's signal didn't light up the screen, Everly's hope extinguished. "Useless. You should get your money back on that app."

"That app found you when you wandered off course in Mogadishu," Roman told her.

"I didn't wander off course. It's called wind. Wind catches parachutes. It's not like the damn things have handlebars."

Sam piped up. "How come that wind didn't catch everyone else's parachutes?"

She glared at him over FaceTime. "Because you're all twice my size, so I'm easier to blow around. It's called physics."

On the screen behind Sam, Jamison climbed onto a bed and started jumping, singing another nonsensical kid's song.

"Oh my God," Sam looked over his shoulder. "Not again."

"What the *hell*, Sam?" She would have yelled if sound didn't travel so far in the open.

"Help," he said. "How do I get him to sleep?"

"Try not feeding him sugar," Liam offered.

"Too late," Sam replied.

"I figured," Liam said with a smirk.

"Dammit, Sam, handle it. I promised Savannah I'd keep him safe."

His brows shot up, and a truly shocked, confused look broke out over his face. "*You?*"

"Shut up. I may be the least parental of this group, but I know enough not to let a five-year-old jump on the bed. I swear to God, if you break him, you buy him."

"Any sign of Ian and Savannah?" Sam asked.

"No," Everly said, "which makes keeping that kid safe all the more important. I will pluck your short hairs out by the root if he hurts himself."

"Harsh," Sam said. "You're so bitchy when you're worried."

Everly growled and hung up on him. "For all his brilliance, I swear…"

"He's right," Roman said. "You do get bitchy when you're stressed."

"The fact that we have cell service but no GPS location is something to be stressed about." Everly started walking again, headed toward some ruffled snow that would most likely turn out to be an animal's dinner spot. "I should never have brought Ian on board. Should have told him to take that bodyguard job so his brain could turn to mush."

"He's a big boy," Roman said. "He can make his own decisions. And he's been in situations way worse than this and survived."

"You'd better not ream him for sleeping with Savannah if we find them alive," she told Roman. "You live in a glass house, buddy."

"Excuse me?"

His irritated tone only added fuel to Everly's frustration. She stopped hiking, flipped her night vision up, and pinned Roman with a look. "Gianna?"

He hesitated a split second too long, and Everly knew the rumor was true.

He lifted his own night vision. "What about Gianna?"

"Like I said, glass houses."

"You don't know what you're talking about," he said. "And you'd better not spread rumors—"

She laughed. "No need. Everyone already knows."

Everly looked at Liam, and Roman cut a glance at the other man.

Liam shrugged. "I didn't hear any rumor, but I figured…"

"Why?" Roman demanded. "Why would anyone *figure* something like that?"

"Because the attraction between you two is palpable." Everly flipped her night vision down and continued toward the disturbed snow. "Don't punish Ian for doing something you're too chicken to go for."

"You're fired." Roman pulled his night vision into place and continued searching the snow with an irritated "As soon as we find them."

"Right. Like the last twenty times you've fired me." Everly neared the uneven patch of snow that turned out to be more of a depression. Her intuition pulsed, shooting tingles down her neck. She picked up her pace. "Got something here."

It was a hole in the snow. A big hole. Way too big for any of the small animals in the area to make. She tipped the night vision out of the way and shone a flashlight down the hole. The sight of black metal made her heart skip. Her spirits soared.

"This is it. They dug out." Everly was breathless with relief. If Ian had gotten Savannah out of this, he surely would have found shelter, even if he had to build a damn igloo.

She turned off the light and unsnapped her snowshoes, then she shuffled down the hole. Scanning the interior, she could see signs of what had occurred. "They're hurt—there's blood on the seats and windows. They found supplies in the back. They took blankets, flashlights, and weapons."

Though there was no sign of where they might have headed.

By the time Everly made her way to the surface again, Roman had already pinpointed the closest campground, one that also had cabins. "Let's go."

18

I an pressed another kiss to Savannah's soft hair. Before Savannah, it had been forever since he'd shared a bed with a woman—at least once the sex was over. And he had to be honest, it felt amazing to have Savannah sleeping in his arms, even if it was fully clothed. It was way too cold to sleep naked with no auxiliary heat source.

He had no way of telling time, but he'd guess it was around two a.m. They still had a lot of night left, and it was obvious the GPS on his watch was shot. As soon as dawn hinted through the window, they'd have to get on the move again. It had been snowing nonstop through the evening and into the night. He doubted there had been any trace of what direction they'd gone by the time the team had found their location. Which meant Ian was going to have to get Savannah out of this on his own.

Savannah had said there was a tiny town about twenty miles up the road. The thought of dodging cops for another twenty miles in this weather, with this knee, was bad enough. The thought of dragging Savannah along, risking her health and safety, made his gut knot. If he knew she'd be safe in the cabin, he'd leave her there, but once the cops found their escape tunnel, every location with any kind of shelter would be raided.

He tossed around more ideas, but none had a positive risk ratio. There should be at least one forest service building between here and the town. It would have landlines. Maybe they wouldn't have to go the whole twenty miles. But could he risk it? She didn't have the muscle mass he did to generate warmth—

Light flashed through a window, and every cell in Ian's body came alert. His fingers curled around the grip of his Glock where it lay on his stomach. He eased away from Savannah, sat up, and pushed his feet into his boots. The cold stole his breath.

He moved to the window that looked toward the road leading to the cabins. Headlights came at them. An SUV. Jeep by the look of it. The problem was that both Everly's SUV and the deputies' cruisers were Jeeps.

"What wrong?" Savannah's sleepy voice tightened the knot in his gut.

"Someone's coming. Get into your jacket and boots."

She was beside him in a moment, bundled for the weather. "Who is it?"

"Can't tell yet." He had a couple of loose plans if the car turned out to be the cops and not his team, but again, none were great.

As soon as he saw an identical set of headlights behind the first, he knew. "Cops."

She pulled in a sharp breath. "Wh-what do we do?"

Options snapped through his mind in seconds. Run in five-degree weather and waist-deep snow got the axe first. Which meant he had to prepare for close-quarters combat.

Savannah moved to another window and peeked out. "It's Hank," she whispered just as he stood from the lead vehicle. "How did he find us?"

"The same way we found this place. Who's with him?"

"Lyle for sure, in the passenger's seat. I can't see the car behind them."

Urgency pushed him into action. He grabbed the Glock from the nightstand on Savannah's side of the bed and pushed the grip into her hand, then looked out the window again. The two other cops joined Hank beside the first car, their faces illuminated in the headlights' glow: Corwin and Rosen.

Lyle stood from the passenger's side, his hand clutching a rifle.

"Stay in the car, Dad," Hank told Lyle with some force.

But Lyle didn't listen. He rounded the front of the cruiser. "This is as much my fight as it is yours."

"Rosen, you stay put. No one gets past you, got it?" Hank pointed at Lyle and added, "Including him."

"Corwin, you're with me." They moved to the first cabin on the left and kicked in the door, clearing it with a by-the-book procedure. Rosen acted like a blockade to Lyle, who didn't like being told to stand down.

"Rosen helped us before," she said. "Wouldn't he do it again?"

"As much as he can when there are three others who'd put a bullet in his head for looking at them wrong. He doesn't even know we're here."

Ian turned Savannah to face him. He squeezed her arms and looked her in the eye. "You need to do exactly what I tell you, okay?" He opened the closet just around the corner from the front door and backed her into the tiny space, easing her to the floor. "Stay here and stay quiet. If someone opens this door, be prepared to shoot. Just don't shoot *me*."

Terror filled her eyes. "What are you—?"

Footsteps neared their cabin. Ian lifted a finger to his lips and closed the closet door. He pressed his back to the wall just around the corner from the entry. If they maintained their current method, Corwin would kick the door in and enter first, followed by Hank. *Fucking lazy coward.*

Their boots crunched on the snow outside the door.

Hank said, "Go," and Corwin put a boot to the door. The lock snapped, and the door flung open.

THE FRONT DOOR hit the wall between the closet and the entry. The *boom-rattle* shocked Savannah's heart, and she clamped a hand over her mouth to keep the fear inside.

"Police!" Corwin yelled.

Silence followed. Savannah held her breath. The quiet stretched and thickened until Savannah thought she'd be sick with stress. She couldn't do this. Couldn't just sit in the corner and do nothing. It wasn't who she was.

She rose to her feet, careful to remain silent, and eased the door open just enough to slip through. Ian had his back to her, his weapon down by his thigh. In the light drifting in through the windows, Savannah saw someone easing into the space, weapon first.

Ian remained intensely still for several long heartbeats. Then he pushed his gun into his waistband and went still again. Once Corwin's elbow cleared the corner of the wall, Ian twisted Corwin's wrist with brutal efficiency. His moves were swift, sharp, and violent. The snap of bone shivered down Savannah's spine and flipped her stomach. Corwin's cry blended with the *thunk* of his gun hitting the floor. Ian hauled Corwin forward and right into a hard chop to the throat.

Corwin garbled a scream and crumpled to the floor.

Savannah grimaced and looked away. Her stomach pitched.

Ian pressed his back to the wall again and looked at her, not at all surprised to see her. "I told you to stay in there."

"Corwin!" Hank yelled. "Corwin!"

"I'm going to let that attitude slide," Savannah told him, "because you're clearly under a lot of stress.

"*Corwin,*" Hank yelled.

"He can't talk right now," Ian told Hank. "He's drowning in his own blood. How about it, Hank? Want to give it a try?"

"Rosen," Hank called. "Get over here."

Corwin gasped for air, gurgling in an attempt to speak. Savannah tried to think about all he'd done, day in and day out to make her life utterly miserable for no other reason than that he could. But her gut still rolled as she watched Corwin writhe in pain, effectively dying before her eyes.

This was what Ian was capable of, up close and personal.

"No one can help you now," he told Hank. "Your own father is the one who pulled you into this mess."

"Shut up, you piece of trash," Lyle yelled from a distance.

"More cops are on the way, Heller," Hank said. "You're not getting out of this."

"Says you."

"Rosen," Hank yelled. "Get the fuck over here." To Ian, he said, "This isn't your fight. Send Savannah out, and I'll let you go."

"Come on in," Ian said, his voice eerily congenial, as if this situation didn't stress him in the least. "Let's talk about it."

"Lyle," Rosen yelled. "Put that down, or I'll shoot you."

Savannah's gut cranked tighter. A gleam pulled her eyes toward the window on her left.

Rosen's next command started with "I won't tell you again—"

Savannah focused on the movement and found Lyle's rifle aimed right at them through the window. She didn't think, just reacted, raising the Glock and pulling the trigger. The dirty glass shattered, but she didn't hear it. She felt her finger squeezing the trigger, again and again, but only the rush of blood in her ears registered.

Lyle went down, and Ian put a hand over hers on the grip of the weapon. She turned her head, saw the fear in his eyes, saw his lips moving with words, but couldn't hear anything.

She was cold. So cold. From the inside out, she felt like ice.

More yelling echoed in her head, like voices in a canyon. Hank charged the cabin, and Ian pivoted away from her, returning fire.

In slow motion, Savannah saw Hank fall off-balance, saw red burst from somewhere in the area of his head or neck. The sheetrock to her right exploded. Savannah cringed and turned away. She opened her eyes just as Hank fell into a heap on top of Corwin and go still.

Her gaze jumped back to Ian, scanned his body, terrified he'd been hit. He turned toward her, his eyes sharp and free of pain. But he was splattered in blood. Not the kind from a bullet wound, but the speckling of blowback, across his face, his shirt. Hank's blood.

Ian came toward her. He was speaking, but she couldn't understand anything. Her face turned icy. Her limbs went cold. And she started to shake. A bone-deep tremor of terror and sickness and relief. With her back pressed against the wall, she slid away from him, pushing herself into the corner. Ian pulled back, worry etching his features, and crouched to her level. He continued talking to her, but Savannah couldn't process anything. She curled into a terrified, sickened ball, dropped her head to her knees.

She focused on her breathing. One in, one out. One in, one out. One in, one out.

Her hearing returned slowly but still sounded as if she were inside a tin can. Rosen asking if Savannah was okay. Ian asking Rosen to call Roman. Then quiet.

"I'm just going to take the gun." Ian's voice was quiet and steady, morphing from tinny to a normal tone. His hand closed over hers, and she released the weapon. Then he sat on the floor next to her and wrapped her in his arms. Savannah curled into him, burying her face against his neck. "It's over, baby." He held her tight. "It's over now."

She couldn't move. Her muscles were rigid. Her mind frozen. Three people were dead all around her.

The sound of tires on snow raked down her spine like a claw. She sat up and reached for the gun Ian had just taken. "Someone's coming."

Ian held tight to the weapon and covered her hand with his. "Savannah, look at me."

She had to fight to get her gaze to cooperate.

When she focused on his eyes, he said, "It's my team, not cops. It's Everly and Roman and Liam."

She couldn't seem to catch her breath. Her heart galloped in her chest. Savanna focused on the woman who entered the cabin. Everly. It was Everly. His team was here. Lyle and Hank were dead.

Everly glanced down at Hank and Corwin, then turned a frown on Ian. "You left a mess. As usual."

She stepped over the bodies and pushed him away from Savannah, replacing his arm with hers, easing her to her feet. "Let's get you warm. The car is toasty."

Everly put a hand against Savannah's cheek and turned her head into her shoulder. "Eyes closed," Everly said, her voice soothing and comforting. "Keep breathing."

She guided Savannah to the passenger's seat of the Jeep, then took the driver's spot and redirected all the vents toward Savannah. "How's that?"

Her question barely registered. Her fragmented mind darted in every direction. "Jamison? Where's Jamison?"

"At a hotel with Sam. He's perfectly fine. He'll probably be cranky tomorrow because Sam is more of a playmate than a parent, but he's had a great night."

Savannah exhaled heavily. "*Thank you.*"

"Of course."

She looked at Everly. "I shot Lyle," she told her in a hushed voice. The realization shook her. "I *shot* him. Oh my God. He was going to shoot us, so I shot him. I can't go to prison. Jamison—"

Everly's hand closed over hers again. "You're not going to prison. It was self-defense. I promise, everything's going to work out fine. And remember—"

"You keep your promises."

Everly smiled.

A rush of emotion overwhelmed Savannah. She leaned across the console and hugged Everly hard. "Thank you."

"You're okay," she said, hugging Savannah back. "Everything's okay now." She pulled away and smiled. "You've got your whole life ahead of you."

That was too much to think about now, so Savannah focused on her breathing.

Everly stayed with her as more cops arrived. As Rosen explained the situation to others in the department, the mayor, the state police. Finally, Everly was called away, and Savannah was left with her own thoughts.

An hour passed before Ian broke away from everyone to come to the car. Savannah got out before he reached her, then jumped into his arms. He hugged her tight. "How are you doing?"

"Better now." She pulled back. "When can we leave?"

"Soon." He ran his gloved hand over her hair and searched her expression. "I am so damn impressed at the way you've handled all this."

She didn't respond. It would take a long time to get her mind around what had happened here tonight. "What happens now?"

"The State Police will take over the department until the county can staff it up with good cops. Rosen is going to be the lead deputy until everything is settled. He'll testify against the dirty cops and be resettled in the state of his choice with his family and a new job."

That shocked Savannah. "Really?"

He nodded. "And if you're also willing to testify, you'll get the same. The government will pay for your relocation, first three months of rent, and give you employment training in a new vocation. I believe that would extend to going back to school if that's what you wanted to do."

She was speechless, trying to take it all in. "I...I can't testify against Misty. I love her. She's my family. Besides, I don't know anything about what she was doing."

He shook his head. "You won't have to. That's going to be a whole different issue, handled by the FBI and the State Department. You'd be testifying about local deputies."

"What's going to happen with Misty? Can I talk to her before you arrest her? To, I don't know, explain things or something? She's always been there for me."

"You can't be there for the arrest, but you can see her after she's been interviewed."

"Can you or Everly be there for the arrest? I don't want her to think she's all alone."

Someone called his name, and Ian acknowledged them with a raised hand.

"One of us will be there." He pressed a kiss to her forehead. "You should get back in the car, keep warm. I'll be done here in another fifteen minutes." He lowered cold lips to hers for a gentle kiss. "When I'm done, let's get a hotel room where Sam and Jamison are staying. We can bring Jamison to our room. He can sleep with us."

She sobbed a laugh and nodded. "But only after you've been to the ER for your knee."

He smiled. "Deal."

Gratitude and love and relief pushed tears to her eyes. She stretched up and kissed him again. "I love you so much."

He returned the kiss. "I love you too, baby."

ix months later.

Ian pulled up to the curb at Ocean Beach in San Diego, where he knew he'd find Savannah and Jamison. It was Friday. After Savannah finished her Friday classes at University of California at San Diego, she always picked up Jamison from school and took him to the beach.

Ian climbed from the car, slipped on his sunglasses, and took a deep breath of the sea air. Every time he returned from a mission, he silently thanked Savannah for choosing such a gorgeous place to relocate. And he added a thank-you to his buddy, Hawk, a Navy SEAL, for letting them live in his town house while he was overseas. It was the only way Savannah could afford to live six blocks from one of the most beautiful beaches in California.

Ian pushed out of his shoes and pulled off his socks, then started down the beach. The sun was warm, the breeze gentle. He'd never lived in California, and he hated the taxes, but after a month here, he decided you got what you paid for. In this case, he saw the extra taxes as payment for blessed weather every damned day.

The beach was crowded today, and Ian wove among the sunbathers as he searched for the telltale polka-dot umbrella Savannah had picked up the very day they'd arrived in town.

When he found it, his heart kicked. He'd only been gone seven days on a security job for a diplomat in Haiti, but whenever he was away from her and Jamison, every day felt a week long.

Savannah and Jamison weren't under the umbrella. He tossed his shoes on the sand beside their towels. One scan of the beach, and he spotted them at the water's edge, where Jamison slid into the surf on the skin board Ian had bought him a couple of months ago for his birthday. Savannah stood by, watching him run, jump, slide, and swim. And she was wearing his favorite bikini.

He pulled off his shirt, cleared the pockets of his cargo shorts, and jogged to the water line. Coming up behind Savannah, he wrapped his arms around her, pulling her off her feet.

She squealed. "Ian, what are you doing home?"

When he set her down, she turned in his arms, locked her arms around his neck, and pressed her body to his. He kissed her, then looked over her shoulder and spotted Jamison.

"You weren't supposed to be back for three more days. Everything okay on the job?"

"Fine," he told her. "The ambassador got called back to the States because of something happening in DC. When I hear I'm getting back to you sooner than I thought, my only answer is always 'yes, sir.'"

"Welcome home." She kissed him again, a lingering kiss that made him think of rolling her around the sheets.

"Ian! Watch me."

He smiled past her shoulder. "Hey, buddy. Lookin' good out there."

As soon as Jamison headed toward the surf, Ian kissed his mother again. He slid his hands down her back over the curve of her waist and squeezed her with a growl. "If I wear him out, you think he'll take a nap when we get home? I'm dying to get you alone."

"He hasn't taken a nap in years, but go ahead and give it your best shot."

He kissed her one more time, then jogged into the surf and scooped Jamison up for a hug. "I missed you, kid. How's school?"

"Good."

"Can I give the skin board a try?"

He laughed. "Yeah."

Ian played in the surf with Jamison another half hour before dragging him up the beach to their towels. Savannah was already under the umbrella, pulling food from a picnic basket.

"Bet my boys are hungry." She put plastic plates in front of them, then stacked them with peanut butter and jelly sandwiches and potato chips. "I was going to call you tonight," she told Ian. "I talked to Misty today."

"Yeah? How's she doing?"

"Great, considering. She complains about the heat and humidity of DC, but she's really enjoying the work. I think she secretly loves knowing more about counterfeiting than even the best guys in the Bureau."

"It's a wild way to start a new life, that's for sure."

"Aunt Misty's going to move here to be with us," Jamison told him, his eyes bright with excitement.

Ian lifted his brows at Savannah. "Is that right?"

"She says they're going to let her transfer after another six months," Savannah said. "She thinks she might be able to get in at the San Diego offices. Wouldn't that be amazing?"

Right now, everything seemed amazing—this amazing woman's love, this perfect family, enjoying a job he'd started out hating. But, yes, the offer of redemption Misty had received from the FBI was truly remarkable.

Gianna had played a pivotal role in that plan, but Ian also knew it was the best alternative, because once they'd processed all the evidence, it turned out that Misty had done an excellent job of erasing all direct connections between herself and the passports. And while everyone knew Misty was the counterfeiter, none of her prints were found on the equipment. Authorities hadn't been able to link the bank account where Lyle had sent payments to Misty either. And the other circumstantial evidence wouldn't have put her behind bars.

Now, Misty worked at the Pentagon, tracing and uncovering counterfeiters by dissecting their fake documents, then training federal agents how to do the same. She was out of debt, out of Hazard, and making a real difference. She often said the only thing that would make her life better was living close to Savannah and Jamison.

"Turns out her father left her with something more valuable than anyone would have guessed—a skill only a handful of people around the world possess," he told Savannah. "And having her in San Diego sounds downright perfect."

"Sure does," Savannah said, smiling at him. "All the people I love in one place. I couldn't ask for anything more."

"Well, I hope all your wishes haven't come true, quite yet, because I have a surprise for you." He looked at Jamison. "Want to help me out here?"

He turned those big blue eyes on Ian with a grin that melted his heart, the same way his mother's did. "Yeah."

Ian pulled his wallet from his shoe, then the black box, hiding it in his palm. He planted one knee in the sand and pulled Jamison to his side.

"What are you two up to?" she asked with a suspicious tone.

Jamison rested against Ian's side as he offered the box.

Savannah's smile evaporated. Her gaze darted from the box to Ian to the box again. "What..."

He blew out a hard breath. "Okay, here goes."

Jamison grinned at him. "You got this."

It was something he told Jamison every time he was afraid to do something, and now it made both Savannah and Ian laugh so hard, they had to take a second to catch their breath.

"Let's try this again." Ian cleared his throat and lifted the lid on the box. The solitaire sparkled in the sunlight.

Savannah gasped and tented her hands over her mouth, her eyes wide.

"I love you and Jamison more than anything in the world," he told her. "I want us to be a family. A real family." He took another quick breath and pushed out the words that both terrified and thrilled him. "Savannah, will you marry me?"

She pulled her hands away from her mouth at the same time that she took a sharp breath. She tried to speak, but the words didn't come out. Tears spilled over her lashes, and she fanned her face with her hands.

"Are you okay, Mom?" Jamison's concerned frown turned on Ian. In a secretive tone, he said, "Uh-oh. You made her cry."

Savannah laughed, squeezed Jamison's hand, and choked out, "Happy tears, baby." Then she looked at Ian, and his heart grew wings. "Yes. *Yes.*"

Ian exhaled, and relief gave way to joy. So much joy, he felt like he'd implode. Savannah rolled to her knees and threw her arms around him.

"Family sandwich!" Jamison yelled, jumping in.

Applause broke out around them. Only when they pulled out of the hug did Ian realize they'd drawn quite a crowd. He slid the ring onto her finger to more applause.

While Jamison dug into his peanut butter and jelly, Ian pulled Savannah close and wiped at her tears. "When you're ready," he murmured, the words for her ears only, "I'd like to talk about adopting Jamison."

She laughed and nodded. "How's tomorrow?"

"Perfect." He pulled her close again, holding her tight. "You two mean everything to me."

She choked out "Same, baby. Same."

When he pulled away, Ian dragged his phone from his shoe.

"What are you doing?" Savannah asked.

"Texting Everly. She made me promise I'd let her know when it was official."

"You told Everly already?"

He grinned at her. "Who do you think helped me pick out the ring?"

Savannah kissed him. "Tell her it's perfect."

ABOUT THE AUTHOR

Skye's New York Times bestselling novels are all about enjoying that little wild streak we all have, but probably don't let out often enough. About those fantasies we usually don't get the opportunity to indulge. About stretching limits, checking out the dark side, playing naughty and maybe even acting a little wicked. They're about escape and fun and pleasure and romance. And, yes, even love, because Skye is ultimately a happily ever after kinda gal.

Skye is a California native recently transplanted to the East Coast and living in Alexandria, Virginia, just outside Washington DC with her husband and rescue pup. She has two grown daughters in California and Oregon.

When Skye's not writing or plotting (to take over the world), she travels to teach ultrasound to doctors in third wold countries or taking courses in her favorite hobbies and rowing on the Potomac.

Make sure you sign up for her newsletter to get the first news of her upcoming releases, giveaways, freebies and more! http://bit.ly/2bGqJhG

You can find Skye online here
Website
Facebook
Twitter
Email

You can join Skye's reader's group here:
Skye's Starlets
And Skye's self-improvement group here:
Your Best You

ALSO BY SKYE JORDAN

MANHUNTERS SERIES:

GRAVE SECRETS

NO REMORSE

DEADLY TRUTHS

RENEGADES SERIES:

RECKLESS

REBEL

RICOCHET

RUMOR

RELENTLESS

RENDEZVOUS

RIPTIDE

QUICK & DIRTY COLLECTION:

DIRTIEST LITTLE SECRET

WILDWOOD SERIES:

FORBIDDEN FLING

WILD KISSES

ROUGH RIDERS HOCKEY SERIES:

QUICK TRICK

HOT PUCK

DIRTY SCORE

WILD ZONE

COVERT AFFAIRS SERIES:

INTIMATE ENEMIES

FIRST TEMPTATION

SINFUL DECEPTION

Get a FREE copy of THE RISK, A Stand Alone Sports Romance, by signing up for my newsletter here:

http://bit.ly/2bGqJhG